# You Cannot Grasp the River

Frank,
Thanks for the years of
blessing my family.
May you and yours
be blessed :)

Frank Brantley

# ENDORSEMENTS

*You Cannot Grasp the River* tells an engrossing and relatable story. I found myself caring about the characters from the first "It must be a ghost!" declaration to the tender and love-filled conclusion. I thoroughly enjoyed sharing the journey with Benjad, Clay, and Alice. Brent Brantley expertly weaves their experiences together, creating a tapestry of faith and hope. He gives us authentic people with genuine imperfections. Most importantly, Brantley injects God's strength and provision, deftly demonstrating how faith supports and emboldens God's followers.

The story is told in an image-filled and beautiful style. As I read, I visualized the jungles, rivers, and villages of Indonesia. I could taste the food and feel the heat. I experienced the hand-to-mouth existence of those living away from civilization and appreciated the dedication of those living as missionaries.

I loved this book!

**—Steven Rogers**, author of *Into the Room*

Brent Brantley's debut novel is a fast-paced, skillfully written account of a child's physical and spiritual growth and his struggle to turn from the vengeful tribal customs and beliefs of his childhood to embrace a God of love. Brantley's both beautiful and dark, haunting scenes take the reader from a small Papuan village to the home of

Christian missionaries, always in the shadow of an evil shaman. Riveting, informative story that leaves the reader wanting more.

**—Rosemarie Fitzsimmons**, author of Selah award winner, *Caged Sparrow*, and *From the Remnants*.

Whenever good triumphs over evil, we have cause to celebrate. Despite differences in culture and heritage, whether this broken world is viewed through the eyes of an orphaned Indonesian native or a western missionary pilot, both of whom have known the ravages of conflict, loss, and death, one yet hopes for the good in this world to prevail in the end. In his debut novel, *You Cannot Grasp The River*, Brent Brantley provides his readers with such a cause. Simply and guilelessly told, this tale of ultimate good that comes from intended evil is welcome refreshment in this age of the anti-hero, like stumbling upon a clear spring in a wasteland.

**—Alton Fletcher**, author of *Find the Wind's Eye*.

Brantley weaves a beautiful tale of love & faith in this wonderful novel. You will find yourself completely captivated as you journey from childhood to early adulthood with Benjad. From the intense opening to the heartwarming end, you won't want to put this one down for a second!

**—Erica Marie Hogan**, author of the A League of Extraordinary Women Series.

# You Cannot Grasp the River

# Brent Brantley

ELK LAKE PUBLISHING INC

PUBLISHING THE POSITIVE
Plymouth, Massachusetts

# Copyright Notice

*You Cannot Grasp the River*

Cover and Interior Design: Derinda Babcock

Editor(s): Peggy Ellis, Deb Haggerty

Author Represented By: WordWise Media Services

PUBLISHED BY: Elk Lake Publishing, Inc., 35 Dogwood Drive, Plymouth, MA 02360, 2021

Library Cataloging Data

Names: Brantley, Brent (Brent Brantley)

You Cannot Grasp the River / Brent Brantley

374 p. 23cm × 15cm (9in × 6 in.)

Identifiers: ISBN-13: 978-1-64949-152-7 (paperback) | 978-1-64949-153-4 (trade paperback)

| 978-1-64949-154-1 (e-book)

Key Words: West Papua, worldview, missionaries, indigenous people groups, revenge, salvation, forgiveness

Library of Congress Control Number: 2021934577 Fiction

# DEDICATION

To my wife, Jeanette, who has been editor and cheerleader.

# ACKNOWLEDGMENTS

In appreciation of my editors who made this book possible: Jeanette, Becky, Sally, Rose, Brenda, Mel, and Deb. And to Derinda, who created the beautiful cover.

# CHAPTER 1

*It must be a ghost!*

Benjad lay motionless in the vegetation alongside the slow-flowing Mamberamo River, transfixed by the unrecognizable figure approaching in a dugout canoe. He fought the urge to swat at the insects buzzing about his head and shoulders. Any movement might draw the man-like creature's attention.

With one hand, Benjad rubbed the two-inch crocodile tooth that hung from his woven necklace, his fingertips tracing an engraved figure of a man bending a bow.

Father would want him to be brave.

His other hand clutched the stone he had picked up earlier when a rat crossed his path.

He stole a glance downward. His loincloth seemed to blend with the mud and reeds along his riverbank hideaway. Still, he pressed himself further against the damp ground before returning his attention to the approaching craft. What is this thing? Why is it here? Perhaps it's a scout sent by other creatures to attack the Koto clan. Why hadn't he listened to Mother and stayed away from the river?

YOU CANNOT GRASP THE RIVER

It was the rat's fault for racing down here. A plump rat would have made a tasty addition to the dinner that evening. But instead of carrying home a prize, he was now trapped in the bushes, wondering if he'd ever eat another meal. A wave of sickness washed over him. The dugout drew closer, and beads of sweat dripped down Benjad's face and stung his eyes, forcing him to squint. Something seemed odd about the way the canoe moved. It was faster than the canoes of his clan. Smoother. No rhythm of dipping paddles—

No paddles. Yet it moved upstream with ease.

Benjad strained his senses to process the peculiar buzzing that seemed to come from the dugout and identify the unusual creature at its helm who made it fly across the water. His heart pounded like a lizard-skin drum. Could the canoe be powered by a swarm of hornets?

Perhaps he had the fever sickness.

He pressed his eyes closed, but when he reopened them, the apparition still loomed. Peering through the reeds, he could now make out the creature's light-colored skin, certainly paler than any man he had ever seen. Its hair and beard were longer than the Koto men wore theirs and must have been dyed with the juice of red beetle nut. His well-muscled arms reminded Benjad of Father's—except they were the color of old bamboo.

With such lightened skin, he must be a ghost.

Ghost? Demon? Man?

Benjad wished only it would go away.

He thought about stories told around the fire of strange beings with magical possessions like this flying dugout. Could this man-like creature be from that outside world or maybe from across the great waters?

4

And those coverings, draped over his skin like bark on a tree. He'd seen clansmen enter the village proudly wearing material made from neither animal skins nor plants. Perhaps this was similar.

The buzz of angry hornets grew louder. They must be chasing the canoe. The dugout turned, giving Benjad a glimpse of its stern. A pot fastened to the back of the dugout glistened in the sunlight.

The hornets were trapped in that pot! The ghost captured them and trained them to use their wings to move the canoe. The hornets in the container started sputtering, raised their voices a short time again, and then apparently died. The boatman jerked his head to the prison and turned to kneel before it as the canoe slowed, then stopped. He flipped the pot on its side and appeared to twist something on the pot.

Benjad continued to rub Father's crocodile tooth as he waited for the hornets to attack, but they must have all died. The creature seemed unafraid as he lowered the pot and yanked on what appeared to be a vine attached to it, most likely to whip any surviving hornets into action. That would be good because then he could move on up the river and Benjad would be free to run to Mother.

The canoe had drifted close enough that Benjad could see sweat raining from the boatman's forehead.

Whatever he was, he was no ghost. Ghosts didn't perspire. He was a man, but a strange one, for sure.

The man had apparently given up on the dead hornets because he took up a paddle from the bottom of the canoe, which had begun to drift downstream with the current. Benjad dared to hope that the current would take him back from where he came.

Instead, he plunged the cracked paddle into the water and drove the now-quiet dugout straight toward Benjad's hiding place.

Benjad trembled as he tightened his grip on the stone, feeling its sharp edges bite into his hand.

Could he kill him with it? No, that man had magical powers. If he could control hornets, a boy with a rock would be no match.

Running wasn't an option either. Someone with powers like that could summon eagles to chase his enemies from above and pluck them up the way they snatched fish from the river.

Panic roiled in his belly. He held his breath, forcing air out in abbreviated whispers lest the man detect his heavy panting. The boatman's deep, powerful strokes drew him closer to the bank.

His eyes were not like men's—they were the color of the sky.

The dugout scraped river gravel as it grounded in a level area almost on top of Benjad's hiding place. The enormous occupant stepped over the side of the canoe into shallow water and seized the boat. Benjad could see only his massive backside and the huge knife sheath strapped across it. The knife inside must be larger than the one Shaka had used to kill Benjad's father. With a loud grunt, he yanked the heavy dugout further onto the gravel bar and then stood erect and examined the craft.

Benjad's stomach lurched. He'd have to make a run for it. He pressed his hands into the ground, pulled his legs beneath his body, then shot up. The giant man turned toward him, unsheathing the knife as he spun. For a fraction of a second, Benjad stared into those sky-blue eyes. Then the glint of sun on metal yanked his gaze up to the raised blade, confirming his worst fears.

This man intended to kill him.

the current could drag him backward. He grabbed his short paddle, intended only for tight maneuverings and emergencies. This was an emergency with no help nearby.

At least there was daylight, and a good-looking landing spot just up ahead.

Clay fixed his eyes on the potentially clear area and thrust the stunted paddle into the unrelenting current, driving the ponderous dugout forward.

He should have convinced Alice he needed to invest in an aluminum boat. Paddling this log around was exhausting.

Reaching the shore took longer than he anticipated. He leapt from the dugout into a few inches of shallow water and waded ashore, lugging the rustic canoe with him. Clay had landed the boat and was surveying his surroundings while catching his breath when the reeds and brush rustled behind him. In one swift movement, he spun around to meet the source of the sound, crouching as he did so, and drawing the machete from the scabbard on his back.

To his consternation, he saw only a small boy of about six or seven staring, open-mouthed, in apparent terror. Clay locked in on the wide brown eyes.

*Stand down, Burris. Stand down. It's not a wild boar.*

He slowly stood, sliding the machete back into its sheath, trying to project peace. However, the boy wheeled around, leapt up the steep bank, and raced toward the safety of the jungle.

As the boy neared the overhanging trees, he tripped over a vine from a strangler fig and fell. He quickly regained his feet and glanced backward as Clay watched him slide into the dark foliage.

The terrified child would undoubtedly run back to his clan or family and report what he had seen. No doubt, curious adults would then come to investigate. If those investigators had had previous encounters with white-skins, they should welcome him, but if not, they might be apprehensive. Did he want to take a chance?

His original plan was already in shambles without the boat. Glen and Norma would be disappointed when he didn't arrive. However, missionaries who worked in these parts learned early on that disappointments were not rare, but the rule.

Clay sighed and turned his attention to wrestling the now-defunct boat motor into the canoe so it wouldn't drag. Then he could use the current and head back downstream at least.

He secured the boat motor inside the craft. He might be able to salvage some parts from it. Standing, he removed the red bandana from his head and used it to wipe the perspiration from his face. He took one last look at the tree-lined river where the boy had disappeared and saw no sign of first responders. Time to launch the craft.

"Aiyyee!"

A high-pitched scream pierced the concert of insects and birds. The plaintive mix of pain and fear in that scream clutched at Clay's heart. It evoked a Vietnam memory he had long ago blocked out of another woman's scream that had filled the air while his team hid on the perimeter of a village. They could only watch as the enemy regulars tortured the village woman. On that day, Clay had strict orders to guide his team covertly to gather information about troop movements and to not engage the enemy.

This time, however, he was not under orders. He swept up the bank to the source of the scream.

# CHAPTER 3

In the jungle, Kalita had been digging roots for the meals she would serve in days to come. A small edible snake lay sunning on a rock. She could not suppress a smile at her good fortune as she scooped the serpent up and stuffed it into a sixteen-inch-long hollow bamboo joint she had brought along for just this purpose. She sealed the opening with a wad of grasses to prevent the delicacy from escaping.

Kalita worked quietly, keeping a watchful eye on her surroundings. Potential enemies were never far away. Wild animals, dangerous plants, hostile clans. She rested her calloused hands on her digging stick but remained on alert. As she peered through the foliage she strained to hear above the insects and birds.

"Benjad should have returned by now," she whispered.

Kalita stopped at her favorite resting spot, a fallen tree where, long ago, she'd come upon Drako and Benjad, heads together in what was now one of her favorite memories.

She could still envision Drako speaking quietly to their son of six windy seasons as his fingers deftly fashioned a new cord for a necklace to fit Benjad's neck. While her husband and son worked, Kalita had listened in on their muted conversation.

"Father, why do the village women throw mud clods at Mother when you are not there to stop them?"

Drako's fingers paused as he studied the boy's upturned face. "It is a very difficult story to tell. You know your Mother is not from the Koto clan?"

The boy nodded, his brown eyes wide and solemn.

"Her clan was attacked by many men from the Koto clan led by the shaman Shaka. The men from your mother's clan were all killed. Shaka's attack was unnecessary and wrong. I found your mother hiding and protected her."

Benjad's wrinkled brow made Drako smile. "But why do the women call Mother names and throw dirt at her?"

Drako stopped working on the necklace. "They are afraid of Shaka. They know Shaka does not like me, so they want to please him by acting that way. You notice they only do it when he is around, and never when I am around?"

Benjad again nodded and sat up straight, pushing out his chest. "One day they won't throw dirt when I'm around either!" He balled a fist and smashed it against his open hand.

Drako closed his hands over the clenched fingers and said, "Live in peace, my son, and let your character keep them away, not your anger. You cannot grasp the river."

At his son's wide-eyed expression, Drako continued, "We cannot hold life tightly. It's always changing, sometimes for the good and sometimes for the bad. We cannot control the way those women treat your mother or Shaka's hatred for me any more than we can hold the river. We must learn to work in and with the river water as it runs through our fingers, because we cannot tell it how to flow."

Benjad lowered his eyes to the log on which they were seated and watched a rhinoceros beetle scamper toward him. He flipped the insect off the log and looked at his father.

"I'm not sure I understand, Father."

Drako finished shortening the cord and smiled at the upturned face of his child.

"Never mind, I'll explain when you get older." He held up the crocodile tooth amulet that had adorned his own neck for many seasons. "For now, though ..." He placed the shortened necklace around Benjad's neck. "Wear this, and it will keep you safe."

Benjad stared up at his father's face as he reached up and fingered the engraved tooth. "I will, Father. I will." His voice cracked.

A cockatoo squawked out a warning, wrenching Kalita back to the present. She looked up at the white bird, calming herself with the thought that her presence had caused his alarm. Kalita sighed, trying unsuccessfully to re-conjure that beautiful scene between father and son on the fallen tree log.

Kalita wiped a tear from her eye with the back of her soil-smudged hand. The words Drako had spoken to Benjad were the same words he'd used to console her during the first weeks of her captivity with the Kotos. She had not only accepted his counsel, "You cannot grasp the river," she had embraced it, as feelings of love for Drako replaced fear and despair. Kalita resumed her efforts to collect roots.

Benjad should have returned by now.

Something in her spirit made her uneasy. She searched her surroundings, seeing nothing but jungle. She straightened and prepared to call to her wandering son. Then came the sound of brush being pushed aside, ever so slightly. The hair raised on the nape of her neck.

Just another bird? A wild pig?

She had seen the results of wild pig attacks before, and her heartbeat quickened. Kalita tried to control her mounting panic. If it were a pig, she did not want to call Benjad into dangerous territory. If only Drako were here. She'd always felt secure with him.

Kalita tightened her grip on her digging stick and panned the nearby trees for one with low-lying branches. A stick snapped behind her.

She spun around and saw the source of the noise.

Not a pig, but something far more dangerous—Shaka! Her heart leaped into her throat.

He wore a strange covering over his barrel chest and a peculiar fabric on his loins and legs, but left his calves exposed. He also had something tied on his feet. They looked like flat pieces of leather with cords crossing the tops of his feet to secure them. She'd seen outsiders who sometimes came into her village dressed similarly. He had been fraternizing with the world of the pale beings.

"Ah, the dog woman works alone, I see." The tribal shaman raked her body with a leering smirk. "I have been gone for a long time, but now I am back. Has no one taken you in for a wife?"

"I thought I had seen the last of you." Kalita suppressed the quaver in her voice, but her insides trembled. "I hoped that the demons would take you far from here and devour you."

Shaka edged closer, and Kalita stood her ground, hoping Benjad would not run into this scene.

"I know you would grieve my loss if that happened. You just pretend you do not want me." Shaka continued his advance. "No one else will have you, but I would show mercy on you and allow you to become my wife."

Despite the fear that gripped her, Kalita's anger surged as she countered, "You are lower than the droppings of the snake. I would die before I would allow you to take me. You killed my uncle, my cousin, and others from my clan. And I am certain that it was you who killed my husband. Only your knife could have made that wound in his back, not a pig tusk."

She lowered her eyes to the steel knife tucked into his belt, a knife that had once belonged to her cousin. Then she raised her head to glare into Shaka's cold eyes.

Shaka shrugged. "Your people were weak. I have magic and power. All are dead who stand in my way. I don't need your permission. You are a captive woman, alone and mine for the taking if I wish."

He seized her arm. Still holding the digging stick in her other hand, Kalita swung the pole, hard. It hit the side of his head with a sharp thwack, and blood gushed from his temple.

Shaka roared. He plucked the stick from her hand as if she were a child and threw it into the bushes. He lifted Kalita and slammed her to the ground. He leaped astride her body. One hand swiped at the blood that trickled into his eye, the other grasped at her flailing hands.

Kalita wanted to scream on the remote chance she could attract someone from her village, but she could barely breathe. Besides, screaming could summon her son into danger.

As he paused to wipe at his bloodied head, Kalita managed to roll onto all fours. She now knew his intentions and realized there was little she could do to prevent his assault, but panic drove her to crawl toward the bushes. Shaka grabbed her and turned her over onto her back, twisting her arm in a torturous position beneath her. His face was so close she could smell the stench of his breath and see the sharpened fangs. She let out a high-pitched wail.

Kalita turned her head to avoid Shaka's enraged face and saw branches move in the trees.

*No, Benjad!*

Before she could warn her son, Shaka seized her throat and pressed down with his massive hands. "Shut up, woman!"

Another scream rang out, not hers, but one she recognized.

Benjad's anguished roar filled the clearing. The mix of rage and terror in his wail sent a sadness through her heart, even as Shaka's choking hands slowly put her to sleep.

But at the commotion from her child, Shaka looked up in surprise.

She heard a thud and a grunt. Shaka let go of her throat, covering his face and reeling backwards as he regained his feet. Through her dimmed vision, Kalita saw Shaka stagger backward like a man who had drunk too much palm wine, attempting to dislodge something from his left eye as the blood flowed down his face. A small stone slipped from his hand and fell to earth. He stared at the object with one eye, a bloody hand covering the other.

Benjad flew to Kalita's side. He grabbed her arm to pull her to her feet. He failed. The shaman roared and over her son's shoulder she saw him lunge toward Benjad. Kalita screamed, her voice, hoarse from the bruising her throat had taken, but still sufficient to alert the boy.

Benjad's upraised arm diminished the power of Shaka's strike, but the force of the blow sent him sprawling into the raised root of an ironwood tree. He landed in a heap, unmoving.

Kalita watched a pool of blood spread from Benjad's head. Shaka pulled the shiny hunting knife from his belt and started toward her child. She knew his intent. He had taken the lives of her cousin and uncle when he attacked her clan. He had murdered her husband.

He would not take her son!

Kalita lunged for Shaka's leg and sank her teeth into his calf. He tripped and fell forward. He rolled over, then into a sitting position, shoving his attacker back on the ground. He raised the knife high, as blood dripped from his rage-infused face onto hers.

Kalita saw the blade plunge downward, but, strangely, felt no pain. She felt pressure and heard the sound of metal against bone as it invaded her chest. On the second stab, Kalita did feel pain begin to radiate outward. But the third time, she felt nothing.

She let out her last word in a strangled plea: "Benjad."

Breathing hard, Shaka leaned back from the lifeless body and sat on the ground He calculated his next move while nursing his eye. How would the villagers react if they discovered he had killed the mother and her son? It did not matter that the woman came from an enemy clan. Over time, most of the villagers had accepted Kalita, even though they had not fully embraced her.

His wound pulsated. He used his knife to slash off a piece of nearby moss to stem the blood flow from the eye. He rose slowly. He had to vacate this location before someone hunting or gathering food found him with the bodies. His senses remained alert, even though his vision had been halved.

Someone approached.

The injured man wheeled to face the river and listened. The hurried footsteps hinted of someone skilled in the art of stealth. With his injured eye, Shaka likely couldn't hold his ground, but years of hunting and stalking prey, both animal and human, had taught him much. He melted silently into the jungle but lingered at the tree line to identify his intruder.

A large white man emerged from the undergrowth. Shaka had visited villages who had visitors from the outside and had become familiar to the strange white-skins. Usually, they were men telling the people about their god or claiming they were interested in cutting the Papuan clans' trees. Shaka saw other light-skinned men who claimed ownership of the tribal lands. They had great power. As much as he hated these visitors, he coveted their power and their goods.

From his hiding place, Shaka watched the man kneel by the prone bodies and then lift piercing blue eyes toward the jungle. The eyes showed no fear, only alertness to any remaining threats.

Shaka knew he could not be seen in the thick camouflage of trees and bushes, especially considering the eyes of strange white-skins. They did not have the hunting skills of a jungle dweller, such as he. Yet, he sensed this man might be an exception. When the man turned his attention toward the boy, Shaka silently slipped further into the jungle.

# CHAPTER 4

Clay's sixth sense, honed over too many seasons of jungle warfare, slowly ebbed from Red to Yellow alert, and the insects and birds resumed their chatter. Clay focused on the still forms lying on the jungle floor. He checked Kalita for vital signs, verifying what he already knew. To be certain, Clay removed a small pair of binoculars from one of the multiple pockets of his vest. He allowed the large end to hover an inch or so from her nostrils trying to detect vapors from faint breathing. There were none.

Unable to help her, he turned his attention to the small boy. Clay started to repeat the process with the binoculars but halted. A subtle rising and falling of the boy's chest confirmed that he had cheated death. The child's cheek had begun swelling. Clay felt over his small head for any other injuries and found a bloody gash on the back, accounting for the pool beneath his upper body. An angular root, moist with blood, lay near the boy's head.

Clay reconstructed the crime scene in his mind and determined that this had been neither an accident nor an animal attack. The defensive wounds on the woman's arms and hands, and the three punctures to her chest and abdomen indicated a brutal homicide.

The boy's injuries were consistent with being struck and catapulted with such force to sustain a head wound on the rock-like root. When Clay had last seen him, the boy had likely been retreating to find his mother, or sister perhaps, and interrupted the attack in progress. He may have even tried to intervene.

Clay's untimely arrival had probably alerted the assailant or assailants and they were likely long gone. The question was, what should he do now? He did not know the victims, nor could he identify their clan. He could not leave the woman's body alone to be ravaged by carrion feeders, and the boy obviously needed medical aid he could not provide.

The disabled motor on his canoe compounded the situation. His original plan to ride the current downriver remained the only option. If their home village lay downriver, he could search for it along the way so they could claim the body for burial. Then he would have to convince the villagers that the boy needed professional medical help if he were to survive.

As Clay studied the still forms on the ground, an alarm went off in his mind.

*Perhaps the attacker is from their village. Or worse, they might blame me for the assault. They may want restitution for the injured boy and dead woman.*

Clay thought about a fellow missionary who had stopped at a crossroad waiting for traffic to clear, when an inattentive Papuan on a speeding motorcycle slammed into his car from behind. The Papuan suffered a broken leg and extensive damage to his bike, but the community demanded the missionary replace the motorcycle and pay all medical bills. The cultural view was that if an incident involved a foreigner, he or she was responsible—because if the foreigner had not been in the country, the incident would not have happened. Besides, foreigners were rich and the rich were obligated to pay the poor.

Still, he couldn't leave them there.

"Lord, guide me," he whispered.

Clay picked up the unconscious boy and gingerly carried him to his dugout, laying him in the bow of the craft. He trudged through the sago palms at the water's edge and hacked off three frond branches with his sharp machete. Returning to the canoe, he arranged the fronds on the side rails of the canoe to provide shade and cushioned the boy's head with a lifejacket.

By the time Clay made his way back to the woman, insects were exploring her body. He waved them off, then from the pack he had retrieved from the dugout, he spread an emergency blanket on the ground next to her. He laid her onto the waiting blanket, which he folded tenderly until it enshrouded her body. Clay lifted her nearly weightless form and made his way back down to his watercraft, glancing about to make certain the perpetrators of this crime had not returned.

After placing the woman in the canoe, the missionary shoved the dugout into the current and hopped in the back. He picked up the weathered paddle he'd left on the shore and stroked a few times on either side until the grating sound of gravel on the bottom of the dugout stopped. The current took over, and Clay used the paddle to steer them into the middle of the river.

Clay had time to contemplate various scenarios that might occur when he met with the villagers. He knew the suspicious nature that ruled the lives of many clans—ghosts and departed ancestors. Then there was the revenge factor, not to mention the common belief that killing someone from outside the clan would appease wandering spirits. Clay tried to develop some contingency plans, but none came to mind.

He would just have to trust God and deal with events as they unfolded.

Despite the twists and turns in the river, the current carried the canoe swiftly to an unexpected opening on the bank where a tributary forked from the main river like a finger. Tugged by the smell of wood fires coming from the tributary, he drew even with the finger and turned into it, where he saw twenty-five to thirty thatched huts supported by posts lining the stream. A line of canoes rested upon the bank. Children frolicked along the water's edge, while several women washed some sweet potatoes gleaned from their gardens.

At the village, the children sighted the approaching canoe first. They stood naked and dripping in the water, watching the strange man draw near. Their eyes widened and they shouted an alert to the village. The twenty or so women washing the vegetables stopped their conversations to examine the spectacle and shouted, urging the children to run. Everyone on the bank then sprinted for the village, shouting an alarm. The children quickly caught up to the women and passed them.

Sitting around the fire in the center of the village, the men had been engaged in typical afternoon activities—

sharpening and fire-hardening arrow tips, eating, chewing betel nut, or dozing in woven hammocks.

Chief Ebo's son, Sawsi, had been trying to stay awake while his father pontificated about his time among outside visitors when he had acquired his steel pot. Two other villagers also seemed to be fighting off sleep as they squatted around the fire with Sawsi. The respected chief droned on.

At first, the women's shouts did not seem real, but through heavy eyelids he saw his father stand, his mouth dropping open as he looked at something beyond Sawsi. Sawsi spun around, still squatting, and almost toppled over. He took in the scene of panicked retreat from the river.

Chief Ebo raised his voice above the din and called for calm among his people. Sawsi admired the slow, measured steps his father took, demonstrating a fearless posture as he led his people toward the river. None of the women or children had seen an Orang Barat, or for that matter any Indonesians from the outside. However, a few of the men, Sawsi and the chief among them, had become acquainted with outsiders, having worked for them on occasional endeavors.

Ebo stood still at the river's edge until his armed warriors had lined up behind him, then he approached the large man who had stepped from his canoe. Sawsi stood behind his father at a respectful distance.

The man offered a half smile, and with a booming voice greeted the villagers.

"Selamat sore. Nama saya, Clay. Apakah diantara anda semua ada seseorang yang bias berbicara bahasa Indonesia?"

Ebo nodded at his son, giving silent permission to speak. Sawsi responded in his best authoritative voice, which belied his nervousness, and told the man he spoke Indonesian.

"Saya bisa."

The man repeated his name, calling himself Clay, and stated that he had traveled from the coast. With Sawsi's help, the man explained to the chief he'd come to the region to teach the Papuan people how to find clean water and become healthy, and to introduce new vegetables they could grow in their gardens. After a few words had been exchanged, the canoe man took a deep breath and pointed at his dugout. He looked Sawsi in the eyes and told of his trip upriver, and how he heard screams and, upon investigating, found a woman and a boy. He tried to wake them and discovered the woman was mati, but the boy was just asleep from an injury to his head.

Everyone had been focused on the big fair-skinned stranger encased in fabric. But now their eyes turned to the boat. As they watched Clay remove the fronds to expose the youth, their fears seemed to be overcome by their curiosity and they slowly approached the boat.

"Benjad, Benjad." Their murmurs rose.

Still, no one approached the boat to render aid to the unconscious boy or showed any emotional outpouring indicating a relationship.

Clay asked Sawsi, "Who is this child?"

"He is Benjad, the son of Kalita." Sawsi almost whispered.

Ebo spoke quietly to Sawsi, who translated to Indonesian. "What is wrong with him?" Rather than explain, Clay slowly unwrapped the blanket engulfing Kalita's head. Amid further murmurings and gasps, the crowd pushed forward.

Sawsi stared at the woman's still face and whispered, "Mati." Villagers drew back and began talking among themselves. No one seemed interested in claiming the body.

A tall figure emerged from the trees that surrounded the village and strode into the group, which parted for him as if in fear. The man's left eye had been bandaged with plant fiber and moss, and freshly dried blood stained his cheek. No one questioned him about his wound. Sawsi stood his ground by his father's side. He would not be bullied by the disdainful sneer of the one-eyed man. Still, he swore inwardly. He had thought they'd seen the last of Shaka after he left many suns ago.

Clay watched with interest as the large Papuan commanded the center of attention, giving the chief an animated soliloquy in their language for several minutes. The chief must have said something inflammatory after he finished. Shaka strode toward him, towering over the chief and staring down at him. The chief trembled but stood his ground.

The situation seemed to be spiraling out of control, and Clay did not know why. He said a silent prayer and attempted to sooth things by directing his conversation to Sawsi, raising a question about the woman's burial ceremony.

Whirling about, Shaka hissed in fairly good Indonesian, "This woman is a witch! She is from our enemy clan and has caused problems since we allowed her to live here. She has no family, and she has no one to plan for her funeral or her little demon's funeral."

Shaka, clearly accustomed to making men cower, might have thought he could intimidate Clay.

"The boy is not dead." Clay spoke with an even calm.

Shaka widened his one eye, and he strode toward the canoe. Clay moved quickly to step between the boy and the threatening figure. Shaka, apparently not used to being challenged, stopped short. The two men locked eyes.

Who would make the next move?

Clay shifted his left leg slightly behind his right leg in an old Army fighting stance, and then moved his left hand just above his right elbow. The nonthreatening position would allow for quick deflection of blows or kicks. The last thing he wanted was to engage the man in combat. Fighting belonged to his former life. But he would if he had to.

"Shaka." Ebo's voice quivered behind them. "Shaka!"

The men continued to lock eyes as Ebo gave a command. Swasi translated.

"The chief says we will bury Kalita outside the village, where she will not bring the ghosts of her ancestors down upon us. The boy, we cannot keep. He belongs to no one and will bring a curse upon us."

Clay turned his gaze toward Swasi but remained alert to Shaka's presence—on guard against any potential movement.

"Maybe Shaka could heal the boy before you take him someplace else." Sawsi's eyes widened as soon as the words left his mouth.

"I will not raise the boy to life! That is the same as raising a demon!"

"It is settled!" Ebo announced. "We will free the spirit of the woman here, but the boy, we cannot help."

Sawsi paused, then turned to Clay. In a subdued tone he translated the chief's decision. Sawsi did not look Clay in the eye.

Clay's heart sank. The boy had already been unconscious for an hour or more. He sighed and nodded to Sawsi. "Take her body."

The chief waved to the women, and they stepped forward. They lifted Kalita's lifeless form out of the boat, carrying it a few steps and laying it on dry ground.

Clay pointed to the boy, "What's his name again?"

Sawsi responded, "Benjad."

"Benjad." The chief repeated the name.

"Benjad." The name echoed from the lips of the adults and children in the background.

Clay lowered his eyes to the sad faces of three or four children about Benjad's age. Tears flowed down the cheeks of a small girl. Clay shook his head.

Why was the boy not welcome here?

Clay stepped into the shallow water and pushed the canoe into the deeper channel, hopping into the craft and seizing the paddle. As he rowed away, he prayed silently for a decent burial for the woman, and he prayed for the life of Benjad, alone now in the bottom of the dugout, asking the Lord to forgive the people's rejection of the child. Before he rounded the tributary's juncture with the main river, he looked back in the approaching twilight. From amid the crowd of people still gathered at the river, one tall, shadowy figure took several steps along the bank to watch the departing canoe.

*Shaka. I hope that's the last I see of that character.*

## You Cannot Grasp the River

Back on the bank, in the gathering darkness, the shaman watched the retreating dugout with his good eye. *The boy will certainly die. I will make sure of it by summoning the spirits to choke the life out of him. But that white devil ... he and I will meet again.*

# CHAPTER 5

Time remained Clay's biggest concern. The missionary had to get medical attention for the boy soon. He knew of a government clinic two days away, but he was not certain that it was manned. Home lay two additional day's journey away, but from there, he might be able to call upon Lester Marble, the mission doctor—assuming no obstacles hampered his travel.

He silently thanked the Lord for providing a full moon to help him avoid rocks and swirling eddies. Without that lunar gift, he would have been forced to forgo travel until daylight. Nighttime in Papua's remote jungles without stars and moon created a clinging stygian darkness. Clay had always marveled at how, even miles from towns and cities, one could still receive the benefit of reflected city lights, but not here in this remote wilderness.

He looked down at the child, searching for that subtle rising and falling of his chest.

So far, so good.

Although tired from the long day, he took no time to rest. The sight of the helpless child in the bow of his dugout served as a catalyst for renewed strength.

Clay leaned forward and dug his paddle deep into the river, pulling the waters swiftly behind him with alternating strokes on each side of the craft. Tiny, iridescent bubbles trailed from the dugout and his paddle marking his path. Despite the relative coolness of the night, perspiration collected on his face and arms and trickled down his body as he worked in concert with the current. The river seemed to want to help him reach his objective.

Benjad could not get his head to focus. His brain spiraled from image to image, as though he were flying through a mist. He saw his mother picking fruit from a tree ... he could not discern the type of fruit. She paused and smiled at Benjad, and then she seemed to hear something. She half-turned, and her smile widened. Benjad saw why she smiled. His father, Drako. The tall, handsome warrior matched her smile, stretching his arms out to her. They met and turned to look at him. They continued smiling as they reached out to him, but he could not get to them.

He tried to shout, "Mother! Father! I am coming, wait for me!" But no sound came out of his mouth.

Try as he might, he couldn't get his feet to climb the mountainside of slippery clay between them. He knew to use his toes, but they did not seem to be working. His parents shrank further away as he struggled to join in their embrace. Frustration turned to panic as they grew smaller, until he could no longer distinguish their forms.

Then pain exploded all over his body. He tried to move and felt the sides of a boat.

*Where am I? Why does my head hurt so badly?*

Through half-open lids, he saw a big man glistening from the moonlight, rhythmically paddling. Then he felt the movement of the canoe. Slowly, he made out the features of the man. The ghost from the canoe! He remembered running from this creature. It must have caught him and was taking him to his friends to eat him. Benjad's chest began pounding violently, and he fought the urge to defecate. He would not reveal his fear. If his captor learned he'd awakened, the punishment would be severe.

Benjad's head and jaw throbbed. He tried hard to remember his capture, but mists kept rolling over his thoughts. Through half-closed eyes, he watched the ghost-man lean toward him and place a warm but heavy hand on his chest. The man's face, illuminated by the moon, did not seem so scary. In the pale light, its expression almost seemed to be one of concern. Maybe the creature worried his meat would spoil before he reached his village?

Perhaps he should have soiled himself and fooled the giant into thinking the meat had spoiled, and then he might have tossed him out of the boat so he could escape.

The mist was winning. His senses began to harden again. The terror that had enveloped him dissipated and sleep reasserted control. The last thing he heard before he surrendered was the sound of lapping water and, in the distance, the call of a night bird of prey. He tried to find his mother and father again in his dreams.

Clay paused his paddling to massage his neck, but he knew he couldn't stop. Soon the setting moon would plunge him into darkness. Although the river had widened, making navigation easier, the thought of continuing without the aid of the lunar light gave him concern. He'd thought the boy might be coming to for an instant. He saw movement and heard a slight whimper, glimpsed open eyes for a moment, but then the boy stilled. Placing his hand on the boy's chest, he felt the little heart beat strongly. This did not mean the child was out of the woods, but Clay breathed easier and dared to hope.

The boatman paddled another hour, doubling his speed with the current as the moon slipped into hiding. A warm fog settled onto the water's surface, cloaking the canoe in darkness. He ceased paddling as his eyes strained against the blackness. The canoe drifted with the current as the fog amplified the sound of the dripping paddle.

Clay spoke into the darkness. "Lord, guide me! I don't know what to do."

Almost immediately he recalled a lumber camp he'd passed in his earlier travels. How could he have forgotten about that? They might have a doctor, or at least a medic on staff. Injuries were common in that line of work. At the very least, they would have radio contact with the outside.

Had he passed the camp in the dark? No, impossible. He would have heard sounds from the shore.

Somewhere up ahead lay a series of rapids that could upset the canoe and dump the sleeping boy into angry river. Should he continue or take the safe route and beach the canoe until daylight, hoping the lad would not worsen? He glanced at the boy, now thrashing in some wild dream.

No, he couldn't stop. Not even to rest. But the boy must be made safe in case the canoe hit rough water.

He retrieved a pen light from one of his many vest pockets, which he turned on and gripped between his teeth.

Then he wrenched a flotation device from the bow of the canoe and gently slid it under the sleeping boy, buckling it securely around him. He paused. Surely the child's eyelids had flickered in the dim glow of the penlight.

Just a trick of his imagination?

Back at the stern, he took a deep breath and strained his eyes and ears for any harbingers of dangerous waters as he steered the dugout to what appeared to be the mainstream. Then the river fog lifted, revealing a star-lit sky that made possible seeing, however dimly, any threatening rocks and swirling eddies.

"Thank you, Lord!" Clay whispered. He paddled with renewed but cautious vigor. For the next hour, he rhythmically stroked his way downstream. He caught his first glimpse of the lumber camp as dawn crested over the river. Soon, lights flickered and voices rose out of the receding gloom.

He aimed his canoe toward the floating dock, which bobbed lightly in the current. Three men were staring from the dock, one with a lit cigarette hanging from his open mouth.

Clay smiled at what they must be thinking. No one comes down the river at night, particularly without power and lights. He could now make out the features of the motionless men on the dock. One man was apparently Korean. The other two looked like Indonesian nationals. As Clay watched, the Korean seemed to snap out of his trance to issue orders to the others in Indonesian.

"Is there a doctor in the camp?" Clay spoke before the men could even secure his dugout.

The Korean looked into the canoe and raised his eyebrows at the sight of the small, sleeping figure in the bow.

"Yes, Dr. Park arrived last night on his rounds of the camps." He motioned to his crew for help. "He went to bed late, but he will be up to the job."

The man seemed to grasp the need for a doctor without knowing the situation. Clay offered no explanation but extricated the boy from the life vest and lifted him to the waiting hands of a man who appeared to be Papuan. The Papuan man held Benjad while Clay clambered onto the dock. With the Korean in the lead, Clay followed the Papuan up the steep hill to the group of freshly built wooden buildings roofed with aluminum. The third man trailed behind them.

Clay did not try to reclaim the boy, as exhaustion had set in, along with relief the man had taken responsibility for him. If the movement caused the boy to wake, at least he would be gazing into a more familiar Papuan face. Besides, Clay's balance had been impaired by long hours crouched in the canoe. He sized up the muddy hillside and nodded. Clay envied the way the man used his toes for traction and made the steep, slippery climb look easy.

The doctor's hut was mercifully close. The Korean, who had introduced himself as Jung, started up the steps and slipped, barking his shin on the edge of the stairs and emitting a sudden Korean exclamation. Jung grimaced and apologized to Clay for his curse. "Sorry!"

"De nada," Clay employed what little Spanish he knew. Both men's eyes met for a moment. Clay's lips curled into a faint smile, and Jung chuckled.

Jung tapped lightly on the doctor's door, then a little harder. The Papuan holding the child lowered his head to gaze into the window, shielded only by screen. He made no effort to disguise his attempt to see inside. Windows for

Papuans were an invitation to look out of and look into. Jung uttered a single command: "Don't!" However, the Papuan did not seem to understand the connection and continued his surveillance as he weaved around, holding the boy.

Jung sighed and knocked a little louder. "Dr. Park. Dr. Park, we have an emergency."

The door creaked open to reveal a sleepy-eyed Korean man in his forties, clad in knee-length shorts, a well-worn T-shirt advertising Disneyland, and flip flops. A pair of small reading glasses hung on the neckline of his shirt.

The bleary-eyed doctor addressed Jung.

Jung responded in rapid Korean describing the situation with a slight nod to Clay and then to Benjad. Eyeing the American, Dr. Park quickly switched to English and assured Clay he would take care of the boy. The doctor addressed the Papuan. "Eli, bring him inside."

Eli turned sideways, protecting the child's head as he entered the doorway.

The doctor stepped aside. "Put him on the table."

Eli complied and gently moved away from the still body.

The doctor rummaged through contents on the counters and desk, giving the men a sheepish look when he discovered his glasses hanging from his T-shirt. He lifted a cord from around the boy's neck, a crocodile amulet, which he removed and handed to Eli.

Eli started to place it on a counter when something about it seemed to catch his eye, as if a memory had flickered to life. He peered at the engraving.

"Drako!"

Clay inquired in Indonesian, "What is it?"

"I know the owner of this." Eli stared at the amulet as if it were a ghost.

Before Clay could question him further, Park directed everyone to wait outside while he completed his examination.

The men left the clinic, and Jung nodded toward a long building.

"How about some coffee and breakfast?"

"That sounds great!" Clay had not eaten in twenty-four hours.

Jung led him to the dining hall, and Eli followed. Most of the workers had finished eating and were heading out to start their day's work. The sun had burned off the mist, and Clay drank in the soothing warmth on his back and sore shoulder muscles.

They climbed the stairs, pushed the screen door, and entered the relative coolness of the structure. The scent of rice, coffee, and fried Spam teased Clay's nostrils. They paused as their eyes adjusted to the darker interior of the hall. Jung led Clay and Eli to one of several long wooden tables and gave a sweeping gesture toward an equally long bench. The Korean remained standing, as did Eli, until Clay had seated himself. Eli sat last.

A thin old Korean cook and a young Papuan boy scurried out from the kitchen with hot tea. Jung requested coffee for the American, and the boy raced back to the kitchen and returned with kopi susu, a strong thick coffee laced with Carnation milk and raw sugar. Although Clay preferred his coffee black, he had surrendered to drinking coffee this way to fit into the traditional social scenes in which he found himself.

Sometime during the conversation, a plate of noodles with fried meat called Maling appeared, along with a side dish of sliced papaya, smoky flavored little bananas and mango, and, of course, the inevitable bowl of white rice. Clay doused his rice with hot Sambal sauce to hopefully discourage any intestinal organisms he might have acquired during his journey. Then he devoured the offerings with relish.

While Clay ate, Eli only stared at his plate.

Jung glanced at his watch and excused himself. "Please, I need to make my rounds. You must be exhausted. Eli will make sure you have lodgings after you finish your meal."

Eli jerked his head upward. "Ya, I will."

Clay thanked the foreman for his accommodations and assistance. Jung bowed slightly and smiled, then turned and hurried out the door.

"Pak Eli," Clay began, using the title of respect. "What did you mean when you looked at the talisman and said, Drako? I'm not familiar with that term."

Eli cleared his throat and began with a formal address. "Tuan ..."

"Clay—my name is Clay."

Eli nodded but added an additional title of respect. "Bapak Clay, I have seen that tooth with the carvings before. It belonged to a friend of mine named Drako." Eli's eyes drifted to an open window with a screen cover. Just outside, colorful butterflies fluttered around a papaya tree. He sighed and then continued.

"Drako and I hunted together many times. We were from different villages, but often met in the jungle." A wistful smile crept across his face.

"We were young when we met. Maybe sixteen or seventeen windy seasons. Drako had great hunting skills. We shared much food, many campfires and many stories."

He paused and then grinned. "Well, maybe I told the most stories, with Drako listening politely."

Frown lines clouded his forehead. "One day we were walking on the trail to a hunt when my bare foot almost came down on the serpent of death. My friend Drako threw his body forward, shoving me out of danger." Eli's voice quivered.

"Our people call the snake the death adder. It is said that shamans assume the adder's form to punish their enemies. His bite delivers a swift, horrible, certain death, starting with shaking and painful swelling and ending with foaming at the mouth. Even after that painful death, there is no peace. Your ghost will wander, lost forever." Eli looked Clay in the eye. "Drako saved me from that end."

"Did Drako survive?" Clay leaned forward in his chair.

"Yes. The snake slid away." Eli took a sip of tea before continuing. "Drako had a family. He rescued a woman from a shaman and eventually married her. Drako had great love for this woman, and she did for him also."

Clay had been listening intently to Eli's story, but a single thought kept nagging at him until he had to interrupt. "What about the amulet? The one on the boy?"

Eli nodded. "Yes, that amulet belonged to my friend Drako. I am certain."

He took another sip of his tea, then continued. "That amulet has great powers. It saved him from the snake, I am sure. Maybe this same magic is working on the boy." Eli seemed to be working out a riddle in his head.

"You say you took the boy to Ebo's village?"

Clay nodded.

"That's where Drako and his wife lived until the evil one, Shaka, killed him. At least, it is whispered that Shaka was responsible."

At the familiar name, Clay stopped stirring his coffee and leaned forward. "You said the name Shaka? Is he the shaman?"

Before Eli responded, Clay added another question. "Where does Shaka live now?"

Eli shrugged. "He lives where he wants to, because everyone fears him. But he usually stays at Ebo's village."

The Papuan paused, then answered Clay's real question. "Yes, this boy could be Drako's son. I know he had one with the woman he rescued from Shaka. But we had not seen each other in a long time. The tooth could also be a gift from Drako before he died."

"It very well could be." Clay yawned. He started to ask about Drako's death but did not need to because the Papuan found his second wind.

"Shaka killed my friend. I did not see it, but I am certain he did." He spoke tersely. "People whispered about his involvement, but he is very clever and could not be caught."

Eli squeezed his mug with both hands and met Clay's eyes. "Shaka is a shaman of great powers. No one crosses him."

A door opened, interrupting the conversation. Dr. Park entered the dining hall, letting a shaft of early morning sunlight flash across the room. He stopped just inside the creaking door and removed his glasses, wiping the lenses with his handkerchief and squinting. His eyes combed the darkened room until he saw the men seated at the long tables. He approached and sat down.

A boy delivered a tea to the doctor and stood at his elbow awaiting a breakfast order. Dr. Park waved him off with a soft thank you. "Terima kasih."

The doctor began speaking in English and directing his conversation at the westerner. "The boy has a concussion and several lacerations, including one on his head that needed stitches. I started an IV to keep him hydrated. At this point, we just need to wait and see the extent of the damage."

Dr. Park gazed in his cup and continued, "His vitals are all good, but I don't have the equipment to evaluate his condition. He may have a hematoma—bleeding in the brain. In short, we need to allow him to wake up on his own, and then he will need some rest."

Clay fired his questions. "Do you think he will have brain damage? Based on your experience, what's your best prognosis?"

Park sighed. "I am not a neurologist or a surgeon. I don't know."

Clay said nothing but pursed his lips and made a popping sound.

Park had some questions of his own. "Where is the boy's family? Why did you bring him here alone? I don't know of any clan that would allow an outsider to take a child far from their village."

Clay retold his story but omitted any mention of Shaka.

"What are you going to do with him? I mean if he survives, and if he does not have severe lasting injuries?" inquired the doctor.

Clay rubbed his forehead, and replied, "I don't know. I will just have to see how this rolls out." Clay gave a wry grin. "One thing is for sure. I always bring my wife back a souvenir. This time I may just bring back a child." He chuckled. "She would never expect a present like this, and I wouldn't even need to wrap it!"

Dr. Park' face briefly registered alarm, but then he rolled his eyes and smiled as well.

"What are you two talking about?" Eli had picked up some English, but not enough to glean all the information. Too tired to engage in any more conversation, Dr. Park nodded as Clay gave Eli a brief replay. When Clay finished his summary, Dr. Park added Clay's joke to the translation, and Eli slapped his leg and laughed.

After Eli's laughter subsided, the men fell quiet for several minutes. Dr. Park asked Eli if he would stay with the boy while he attended to some of his patients around camp.

"Yes, sir. I'll clear it with my boss."

Park turned to Clay. "You must be tired. I will arrange a bunk so you can catch up on your sleep."

Thankful for a clean, comfortable bed, Clay accepted the offer, but asked Eli and the doctor to notify him as soon as the boy woke. They assured him he would be apprised of any changes in the child's condition. Satisfied, Clay followed Eli out of the dining hall to the bunkhouse.

He sat on the bunk, clearly made for someone much shorter, and removed his hiking boots. Weariness overtook him, and he collapsed in his clothes on the clean cotton sheets, falling asleep in quick order to the music of distant chainsaws. He would set worry aside tonight. Worries set aside tended to be seated on the side of the bed when one awoke. Sleep promised a temporary reprieve.

# CHAPTER 6

Benjad dreamed again of his father and mother. This time, Benjad's parents stood arm-in-arm in a distant garden ringed with yellow papaya trees. Their faces radiated love as they beckoned to him. He tried to run to them, but something held him back. He looked down and watched in horror as numerous vines crawled up his legs, his arms, and around his body. The vines grew and twisted, like living shackles. No amount of struggling could break their hold.

One vine around his arm was thicker than those encircling his legs, and more active. Suddenly, the end of the vine disconnected from his body and rose close to his eye level. The leaf on the end of the vine took on the appearance of a face—a grinning, familiar face.

*Shaka!*

As he leaned back to escape the sneering monster, the grin vanished, and a terrifying image emerged in its place. The countenance still belonged to Shaka, but it had become ugly with anger. Its lips curled back to reveal two rows of sinister pointed teeth. Where the left eye should have been, Benjad saw only an empty darkened socket.

Benjad fought valiantly against the vines tightening on his body. His heart pounded. He thrashed wildly, screaming and trying to avoid the menacing maw of Shaka. The vines gripped him tighter, but he did not give up.

Just as all seemed lost, Shaka disappeared, and Benjad transferred to yet another strange place, staring at a new adversary. A man stood over him, grappling with his arms just like the vines had done earlier.

Benjad pulled up a leg and kicked wildly, all the while swinging his arms.

Eli had been sitting by the patient for three days. Dr. Park had moved into his newly readied quarters, and Eli now occupied the cot in the clinic. He enjoyed the work a great deal—more than felling trees. The examination table had been transformed into a bed for Benjad.

The missionary stopped by frequently to check on the child. He seemed genuinely concerned about the boy. Missionaries were like that. They seemed to have a great capacity to care about people, even those not of their own clan. Eli had heard preaching by Papuan pastors talking about rewards in the heavens. Maybe this explained why the missionaries were nice to strangers.

Eli liked this friendly white man. At times, they sat just outside Benjad's room. They talked of things that interested Eli, such as pigs, cassowaries, feasts, and Western conveniences. Eli also liked to hear about radios and motors that powered boats. They had been strange to him once, but now he found them fascinating and enjoyed working on them.

Eli stood outside the clinic door preparing a betel nut chew. Darkness had fallen and the stimulant would keep him awake. He retrieved an empty film container filled with lime and some mustard greens from his string bag, which hung from his shoulder. He tucked a betel nut into a comfortable place in the corner of his mouth.

Before he could slip the lime-dipped mustard green in his mouth to stimulate a chemical reaction, the boy stirred, and then started screaming. Eli flew into the room, where the thrashing boy had become entangled in the IV tube. The blood pressure cuff that had been left loose on his arm had tightened in his struggle. By the time Eli reached the bed, Benjad's limbs had become totally entangled in the medical attachments.

Eli seized Benjad's arms, surprised by the strength of the wounded lad. He tried to speak to him in soothing words of his language, but the determined boy fought so hard that Eli had to concentrate on blocking the flailing appendages. Benjad's terror-filled eyes fluttered open and he shouted.

"Go away!"

"I won't hurt you," Eli spoke in the boy's own tongue. "You are safe. I will let you go, but be still."

The boy's convulsions ebbed, so Eli slowly relinquished his grasp.

"Oof!"

The child shot a foot into Eli's solar plexus, knocking the wind out of him.

In a split-second, Eli recovered and seized his arms again. "No! I said you are safe. No one here will harm you, but if I have to, I will tie you up."

Benjad seemed to wake and focus on Eli.

"Will you stop fighting?" Eli gasped, still trying to recover his wind.

Benjad nodded weakly. "Yes. Who are you?"

Eli, half-smiled and released his grip again, but watched the boy's legs warily.

"You kick like a tree kangaroo! My name is Eli of the Amu clan. I have known your clan from the old days." He had a rusty knowledge of the Koto language, but it seemed sufficient for Benjad to understand. He could see recognition in Benjad's eyes.

Benjad looked at the IV tube running down to his arm and at the tangled blue blood pressure cuff. His small body tensed.

"Why have you tried to tie me? If you mean no harm, why do you do this?"

Eli sat on the bed and began to untangle the lines. "It's for your own good, little one. You have been badly injured, and a skilled man is making you well with these tools."

The boy tried to sit up, but his head pounded. He reached up and fingered the welt on the back of his head and the stitches that had been used to close the wound. His eyes widened.

"Mother. Have you seen my mother?"

"A westerner found you hurt and brought you here for care." Eli spoke softly.

Benjad's puzzlement showed on his face, and the clansman continued. "A man, a man from beyond the big waters, found you and brought you here so your wounds could be treated."

A dim light seemed to creep across Benjad's face, but as Eli started to question the boy, a presence darkened the doorway, and Benjad again started to thrash.

50

"The ghost!"

Benjad flailed his arms and legs trying to get off the makeshift bed, kicking Eli once again in the side.

"Oomph! Stop that!" Eli again constrained the boy. "This is the man who saved your life."

"Ghost, ghost!" Benjad squealed, his eyes darting about the room, searching for an escape route.

Eli held him firmly. "No one is going to hurt you. I am from your people, remember! He is not a ghost. Be calm. I am your friend, and so is he."

Still firmly grasping the boy, Eli turned to grin at Clay. "He thinks you are a ghost."

Clay shook his head. "I have been called a lot of names in my life, but never a ghost."

"You are the first white man he has seen."

Clay waited. When the boy seemed calm, or at least not actively resisting, he smiled and spoke Indonesian to the child in soothing tones. "I will not hurt you. What is your name?"

Eli spoke for him, "He does not speak Indonesian, Pak. He is from the Koto clan. But I speak his tongue some.

Then, turning toward the youngster, Eli asked, "What is your name?"

The boy's expression had changed from fear to one of mere distrust. He spoke softly. "Benjad."

"Benjad, I assure you, we are your friends." Eli gestured at the westerner. "This is Bapak Clay."

Clay slowly approached Benjad with open hands. "How are you feeling?"

Clay lightly laid his hand on Benjad's hand. The boy dropped his eyes and made a small gasp.

Wide-eyed, Benjad touched the back of Clay's enormous hand with a forefinger. He lightly rubbed the skin, and then increased the pressure. Benjad's brows knitted and he withdrew his finger only to return it to continue the rubbing action after he moistened it with his tongue.

Eli grinned. "He is trying to see if your whiteness will rub off."

They both chuckled, which startled the boy, and a faint smile of relief lit his face.

Progress.

"Ask him if he is hungry," Clay said.

Eli complied, but the boy responded, "I want to go home."

Eli translated and shrugged. "What should I say?"

The missionary pulled his captive hand back. "Tell him that first he needs to eat for strength, and then we will talk about those things."

Eli repeated Clay's instructions. Benjad's belly growled as if on cue. With a sheepish grin, he nodded.

Dr. Park entered the room, and for a second Benjad seemed as if he would go through another shock. Eli tensed, ready for a spasmodic reaction, but Clay nodded and smiled, patting the boy's hand.

The boy permitted the doctor to examine him, and after a thorough check, Dr. Park smiled and removed the IV needle. "The boy has been through enough excitement," he said. "Let's get some food for him and see how he does."

Eli remained with the child while Dr. Park and Clay returned to the dining hall.

Clay returned holding a tray, which he set on the bed.

"I've procured noodles and chicken broth, water, and saltine crackers." He pulled a spoon from his pocket and offered it to Benjad with a bow and smile. "Food you've never seen, described in words you don't understand."

Benjad looked at the spoon suspiciously, then set it on the tray. He picked up the soup bowl with both hands, sipping gingerly at first, but then with relish. He finished the soup, then gazed at the crackers on the tray.

Clay pushed one cracker toward him and gently commanded in Indonesian, "Eat!"

Eli echoed the command in Koto.

Looking from man to man, Benjad picked up the cracker, turned it over a few times in examination, then bit a small bite from the corner.

"This is probably a new experience for his taste buds," said Eli. "The Koto don't have salt."

Benjad smiled and took a second, larger bite, then started devouring one cracker while reaching for another one.

"Slowly, slowly." Eli cautioned as he placed his hands on his stomach and pantomimed vomiting. Benjad slowed down, but after eating all four crackers, he looked longingly at the tray.

Clay lifted a napkin, revealing a dish of banana pudding. Benjad's eyes searched Clay's, and Clay smiled and nodded. Benjad paused to rub the napkin through his fingers, his eyes wide. Then he retrieved the dish, ignoring the spoon again.

He sniffed, then freed a slice of banana from the cool depths of the pudding. He sniffed it again and nodded, then popped it into his mouth. That's all it took. The pudding disappeared quickly, leaving only traces around his small mouth.

"Eli?" Benjad patted his full belly and gave a furtive glance outside. "My stomach is singing. I must make mud."

Eli translated the request to Clay, who nodded.

"Keep a close eye on him," Clay cautioned. "If he tries to escape into the jungle, it would mean certain death for him."

The lad wobbled as he stood. The doctor had removed his loin cloth, bathed him, and dressed him in clean boxers supplied by one of the smaller Korean nationals. They swallowed his small body and were cinched by a safety pin in the back. His thin little protruding legs made him an even more spindly sight.

The men waited until he found his balance and then walked with him outside, matching his feeble pace. They avoided the busy camp activities and led him to the rear of the clinic to the edge of the jungle. They released their grip on the boy's arms and signaled him to complete his job. Benjad took a few halting steps into the jungle, watching the men as they watched him.

"He seems reluctant to attend to his toilet," said Eli. "In many Papuan belief systems, a shaman has the power to use fingernails, hair, even mud of a person to conjure up a curse on the previous owner. He may be worried we'll report his 'mud' to a shaman."

Clay nodded and both men turned their backs, allowing Benjad privacy. They listened intently for any sound of the child fleeing. He did not, and quietly rejoined the men while their backs were turned to him.

"Finished?" Eli laid a hand on the boy's back.

Benjad thumped his chest and announced, "Food for the insects!"

Eli chuckled and translated for Clay, who also laughed.

They returned to the clinic, allowing Benjad to walk on his own. He seemed less afraid of his new environment, but still anxious. They helped him back into the bed and gave him more water, per doctor's orders. They left a cup of water close to his bed on the examining tray.

Benjad turned his hauntingly sad eyes toward the men.

"Where is my mother? I want to see her. I want to go home."

Eli, touched by the plaintive request, translated for Clay, who took the boy's shoulders in his hands.

"I have a lot to tell you, but you are still too weak. You need more food, and right now, you need sleep. You see how weak you are—you cannot walk any distance."

Eli repeated the speech in soft tones, until Benjad's head began to nod and his eyelids seemed to pull closed.

The pale giant gave the boy a pat. "Rest now."

Eli didn't translate. His words would have been lost into the air.

Benjad slept for a long time, while Eli stayed on guard.

When Dr. Park arrived the next morning, Clay entered the room with him. After a brief examination, the doctor beamed at the men.

"He's in remarkable health, considering what he's been through. Over the next few days, I will treat him for amoeba infestation, malaria, and other assorted afflictions common with people in the isolated communities."

The doctor handed Eli a bottle of quinine for malaria. "You can disguise the bitter taste by mixing it into the banana pudding. The boy seemed to like that last night."

Eli spent many hours with Benjad, chatting in Koto and gradually introducing Indonesian words, which Benjad picked up with surprising speed.

He would miss the boy when the time came to say goodbye.

On the sixth day at camp, Clay rose early to make certain he had time to complete his devotions and prayer time. He had a full list of errands to accomplish. He'd managed to get a radio call out to a missionary air traffic controller, who relayed the message to his wife, Alice. His message had been brief, letting her know he was okay and getting ready to come home as soon as a replacement motor arrived for his outboard.

Clay mentioned nothing of the boy, who gained strength and became more active each day. With this promise to return to Alice, he now had to decide. What does one do with a six-year-old boy nobody seems to want?

Discussing options with both Dr. Park and Eli brought him no closer to a solution. The boy could not stay in the lumber camp, although the folks here had been kind to both of them. One of the local lumberjacks who had been a tailor in an earlier life had even made a shirt and shorts in his spare time for little Benjad. Still, it was hardly the place for a boy to grow up, particularly since most of the laborers were here temporarily and had families back home. Dr. Park had taken a liking to the child and had tended to him faithfully, but he would soon be heading to the next camp on his rounds. Some of the camps ahead were hostile toward outsiders, and their safety couldn't be guaranteed.

Clay found Eli seated on the porch of the clinic, sharpening a chainsaw.

"Eli, we need to talk."

Eli set his project aside and looked intently at Clay. "Bapak, what is it?"

Clay leaned his frame on the porch, folding his hands as if he were about to pray. "We cannot put off telling Benjad about his mother any longer. I think he has recovered sufficiently, and we need to arrange for his future."

Eli scratched the stubble on his jaw and nodded. "The boy has seen death before. Probably many times. Clan children don't know what the morning will bring. They live to wake up."

Clay studied the Papuan's face for a long time, then said, "So you're saying life for children like Benjad is difficult and they accept it."

Eli nodded, staring down at his feet.

"That doesn't really make it any easier to be the one bearing bad news." Clay sighed. "We'll do it together. Tomorrow evening."

Clay turned and walked off.

Poor kid. Could he even stand up to such a crushing blow?

Clay asked Dr. Park to stand by in case there was a need for medical intervention. Evening seemed best, as it allowed the boy to sleep afterward. Benjad would probably be less inclined to run into a nocturnal jungle in a grief-stricken mode.

When the time arrived, Clay and Eli seated Benjad on the front porch of the clinic, his legs dangling off the edge. They stood in front of him putting the child almost at eye-level.

Clay watched Eli remove his bamboo hair pick from the woven bag he kept over his shoulder and plunge it into the back of his curly hair. Something he did as a nervous habit. Clay cleared his throat and spoke gently, halting periodically for Eli to translate.

"Benjad, I want to tell you where I found you and what occurred while you slept. This is not an easy story to tell, but it is true. You and I have become friends now, yes?" Eli's translation came through as Benjad tightened his lips in a small smile and nodded.

Clay continued, "Friends tell the truth to friends. God wants us to always tell the truth, but I could not tell you everything until you were strong enough." A question flickered across Benjad's deep, serious eyes at the word "God," but he nodded again.

The men, working together, told him how Clay had found his body lying unconscious close to his mother.

After he explained that Benjad's mother had died, Clay paused. The little boy fingered the amulet around his neck, as if trying to summon courage. The amulet failed him, and he burst into tears.

Clay leaned forward and embraced the child and let him cry. After a few minutes, Benjad's sobs subsided and he pulled back, looking deeply into Clay's eyes. Clay's heart did a double-take. Did the boy finally see him as something other than a ghost?

"That's not all, Benjad." Clay's heart sank even further. He hated adding insult to injury, but he thought it best to take care of everything at once.

"We brought her to your village, where the tribe promised to bury her according to the custom of your people, but no one could be found to take care of you."

Best to omit Shaka's pronouncement that Benjad represented a curse in the eyes of the village.

Eli patted Benjad's leg. "Your mother is with your ancestors."

The youth rubbed his eyes, nodding acceptance for the proffered sympathy.

Eli cleared his throat and reached out, touching the boy's amulet with his thumb. His people considered it rude to use the finger to point.

"Where did you get this tooth of the buaya?"

The boy lifted his hand to touch it, rubbing the crocodile etching. "My father gave it to me for protection."

"Was your father Drako?"

A surprised look replaced grief on Benjad's face as he stared at the Papuan. "Yes, yes! Did you know him? How did you know him?"

Eli smiled and rocked back and forth. He glanced at Clay with an apologetic shrug. He'd taken matters into his own hand. Clay, with an expressive sweep of his hand, encouraged them to continue in their mutual language.

Eli dipped his head toward Benjad and smiled. They spoke of how his father had saved Eli's life. Benjad seemed convinced that Eli truly had been a friend to his father. Periodically, the two would pause and Eli would switch to Indonesian to include Clay in the conversation. But for the most part, Clay listened and let them talk.

The evening quickly darkened, but stars perforated the black fabric of the night cosmos. The fabric had been spread over the land by unseen hands, the author of the night—someone well acquainted with the need for humans to sleep, Clay mused. He turned and noticed the boy shiver slightly, exposed to the cool tropical nightfall. It never ceased to amaze him how Papuans who were so heat-hardy could be so sensitive to the cold.

"Oh, I almost forgot." Clay plunged his hand into his cargo pocket on his trousers and came out with a macadamia and chocolate chip cookie wrapped in a napkin. "Here!" He offered the pastry to Benjad, who studied it before he took a tentative bite. "We need to let you rest now. This is enough talk for the day."

Clay lifted the boy to his feet. He followed Benjad into the clinic and retrieved a sheet from a cabinet, which he spread over the boy. He wiped some fresh tears from Benjad's cheek with his thumb.

"You are going to be all right." Clay smiled. Benjad could not have known what he said, but he sniffed and smiled back before nodding off to sleep.

# CHAPTER 7

The fog had finally lifted from Benjad's mind, and his head no longer throbbed. Seven suns had arched over the skies to hide behind the mountains since he had awakened in this strange, interesting world. He sat up in bed, but before he could smile at the day, an ache in his heart reminded him all was not well.

The pain he'd experienced yesterday had been worse than anything his body had ever been through. Memories started coming back to him now. He recalled his mother fighting with Shaka, and himself hurling the stone at the shaman. He also recalled Shaka charging toward him in rage with blood running down his face from his eye. It ended there. He could not remember what happened after that.

An image of his mother fighting for her life in the clearing flashed through his mind, causing a fresh wave of emotion to rise within him.

He'd never see her again until he joined his ancestors.

Benjad fought back the tears. Father would want him to be brave.

Before Benjad could travel further down his path of sadness, Eli entered the clinic.

"Good morning, Benjad. Doctor Park says you need to start exercising. You are strong enough to explore this camp now. Would you like that?"

Benjad slid off his bed, swiping an arm across his eyes. "Yes. I would like to see this strange place."

Eli gave Benjad a sidewise glance as they left the machine shop, the last stop on their tour of the lumber camp. The boy had shown great interest, asking many questions about each new discovery. Eli witnessed an occasional wince from the boy and caught him swiping tears from his eyes, but he seemed to be adjusting to the news of his mother's death like a true stoic Papuan.

"Well, it is time to go back to where you sleep. I know you must be tired of walking. You saw so many new things. Maybe too many for your head."

Benjad looked at Eli. "Yes, I am a little tired, and I will have to think about all I have seen. Will I live in this place for my life?"

"I do not know. I don't think so. However, you will be cared for. Don't worry."

They had reached the clinic and Eli opened the door for Benjad, who opened his mouth in a cavernous yawn.

"You go inside and rest. Pak Clay said he would come here as soon as he finished working on the motor."

Benjad nodded and climbed on his bed. His eyes closed almost immediately.

An hour later, Clay entered Benjad's room with some paper and a pencil in his hand. The door scraped against the wooden floor, and the boy's eyes fluttered open. He motioned for Benjad to come to a little table under the window and patted the wooden chair.

Benjad sat up and stretched, then dropped to the floor. He stood motionless for a second, and Clay patted the chair again.

The boy followed Clay's gesture and hopped up on the chair, but he squatted instead of sitting.

He proudly announced "Duduk!" He grinned at Clay.

Clay laughed. "Yes, duduk. But you still don't have it down perfect." Clay held up an item in each hand.

"Pencil," he said, raising a long, pointed stick. "And paper." He offered a flat sheet to Benjad, who turned it over in his hands, rubbing the sheet between his fingers. Then he set it on an empty plate that had been left on the table.

Clay laughed again. "No, it's not a napkin, but I like the way your mind works." He took the piece of paper off the plate and set it on the table. "Watch this."

Clay pulled the pencil across the paper and strange lines began to form.

Benjad fixed his eyes on the lines, which had begun to form a shape, but when Clay rotated the picture in front of him, he furrowed his brows.

"Apa?"

Clay frowned. "Don't you know a tree kangaroo when you see one?"

Still frowning, Clay rotated the drawing back around and stared down at it.

"Hmmm. Well, I never claimed to be Rembrandt." Clay felt the sides of his mouth stretching into a smile as he reworked his tree kangaroo. Every minute spent with Benjad challenged Clay's communication skills. The boy devoured information about his new environment. Clay hoped this interest would distract Benjad from his grief. Nothing helped Clay overcome sadness as well as distractions. He briskly added some additional lines to the sketch. "There!"

He again placed the drawing in front of the boy. A flicker of recognition flashed across Benjad's face. He looked up into Clay's eyes and nodded vigorously.

"See. I do have talent. When we get back, I want you to tell my wife that."

Clay froze.

What had he said? Was he seriously thinking of bringing this boy home with him?

Clay shook his head. Out of the question. Alice would have his hide.

He stood abruptly and tapped a finger against his watch face. "I have to go to the radio shack and call my wife. You just practice drawing on the paper, and who knows, you may become a famous artist like me."

The boy stared at him blankly. Clay just smiled while he placed the paper drawing side down and handed the child the pencil.

He gestured to the paper for Benjad to continue and then opened the door. As he left, he flipped the light switch, and the overhead bulb glowed instantly in the darkening room.

"There. Now you can see what you are doing." He waved, closed the door, leaving Benjad alone.

Benjad turned his attention to the pencil and paper, holding the pencil the way Clay had. He scribbled some lines and circles.

It reminded him of the stones his people marked with charcoal, only this seemed much easier and the drawings clearer.

The young sketcher filled the one side of the paper with doodles and lines. He turned the paper over to scrutinize Clay's drawing again. Then he drew a more accurate kangaroo illustration beside Clay's.

Benjad held the paper up and uttered the name in his language. "Attuti!"

He lay the paper and pencil upon the desk and leaned back. His legs had begun to cramp, so he hopped down from the chair.

The boy's eyes were drawn to the little box with the stick by the door, which Clay had manipulated to awaken the sleeping light demons overhead. He glanced to the glowing bulb and back at the command box. He approached the box with reverence and examined it. His heart pounded as he reached out for the small black protruding stick. Shaky fingers pinched the stick and moved it downward. The clinic went dark. Benjad immediately flipped the stick up again and light flooded the room.

Relieved that the light demon had responded to him as it had to Clay, he braced himself and flipped the light off once more. This time, heart pounding, he hesitated a little before he switched it back on again.

A smile pulled at the corners of Benjad's mouth.

He, too, could command light demons.

Emboldened, the boy flipped the switch on and off, slowly at first, and then with gathering speed. He was fascinated with his newfound power.

The steady drone of the monster outside that Eli called a generator ceased and the lights dimmed and went out. Benjad heard groans from the men outside. He ran to the window and saw that all the lights in the camp had gone out.

He had angered the light god by flipping the stick too many times and made him weary. The light god has commanded all his servant demons to punish the village by stopping all lights.

Benjad dove under the examination table to hide from the angry light god and his demons. He had acted stupidly in mistreating the light. Now all the lights of the village were plotting revenge.

His heart pounded as he lay in the darkness awaiting his fate. Then he heard footsteps approaching on the porch outside.

Had one of the men come to check on him, or perhaps one of the light globes had magically grown legs and come to attack and burn him? If only father and mother were here. His father would show no fear and kill the intruder.

He poked his head out from under that table and glanced quickly through the window, A bouncing light swung its head to and fro, surely looking for him. The illumination, though small in size, must have had legs to raise it high enough to be seen in the window. He ducked back into his hiding place and lay still, hoping the light would not find him. The door creaked open and the light entered, first looking at the examination table then swept around the room. The light searched for him—the angry globe in the room had told on him. He could scarcely breathe.

The light saw him and stopped flicking about. A silhouette of legs supporting the light bent to allow the light to be on the same level as Benjad. If he had to die, he would not die easily. He clenched his small fists and readied his feet to kick.

A familiar voice in the darkness spoke his name.

He did not know what the voice was saying, but he recognized it as Clay's. Somehow, he controlled the avenging light.

Clay set the light on the floor and now Benjad could see that the light had no legs. Apparently, Clay had found it by the window and seized it. Now it looked like a big stick with the illumination only on the end. Benjad felt more courageous. He could defeat that short, no-legged light if necessary.

Clay squatted close to Benjad and extended his arms. "Come on. You don't have to hide."

Relief washed over him. Clay pulled the boy into his arms and stood. The child's fear slowly ebbed as the man patted his tense back. Benjad's father used to pat his back like that. When he did, Benjad felt safe.

Clay leaned down and scooped the stick from the floor with ease and did not show any sign of trying to be cautious.

Who was this man who could control demonic lights?

The generator outside cranked back to life with a rat-a-tat sound. Benjad listened to the sound as it settled down to a steady drone.

The light overhead that Benjad had tortured with his flipping of the stick also sprang to life.

"See, everything is all right." Clay swept his hand around the room. Benjad smiled at him in gratitude, and his heart warmed to see Clay smiling back.

The next morning, Clay and Eli went to the dock to work on his boat. Naturally, Benjad tagged along. The replacement motor Clay ordered from Jayapura had been in stock. The prized motor was shipped the same day and arrived in three days by boat.

Benjad squatted on the dock beside them while the two men worked on attaching the boat motor.

Clay stood. "Make sure it's secure to the stern. I can't afford to lose another one."

Eli grunted. "Don't worry. It would take a mountain falling on it for it to break off!"

"I don't want mountains to fall on it either." Clay shook his head in mock seriousness.

Eli looked up from the dugout at Clay, then looked at the water. "I think we should test it. It ran well in the oil drum with water when we tested it, but we need to know it can run in the river water."

"Be my guest," said Clay. "You can play captain and test it out."

Eli grinned. "Ya, Pak. I will do so."

Clay glanced toward the squatting boy on the dock beside him. "Benjad, would you want to go with Eli?" He motioned with his hand toward the boat.

Benjad rose and nodded his head, but Clay detected fear in his eyes. The boy walked toward Eli and whispered in his ear.

A puzzled look came over Eli momentarily, then he started laughing.

Clay glanced from one to the other. "Can you let me in on the joke?"

Between snickers, Eli explained. "Pak Clay, I think when Benjad first saw you and heard a boat motor for the first time, he thought you were being powered by hornets. He is a little fearful of them getting out of control."

Clay laughed as he remembered that first meeting. He laid his hands on the child's shoulders and spoke in slow Indonesian. "No, it is not hornets who give the boat power, and it is not magic. One day you will understand, but for now all you should know is that it is safe for you."

The boy stared wide-eyed as Eli translated Clay's explanation. Benjad's eyes never left Clay's face, but he nodded and uttered, "Ya."

Clay lifted Benjad and lowered him into the dugout to Eli, who seated him mid-craft. Clay untied the ropes securing the dugout to the dock, maintaining his grip on them as Eli primed the motor and started yanking on the starter rope. It took four tries before the motor sprang to life.

Benjad gripped the sides of the craft tighter and looked up at Clay, who nodded his reassurance. The boy returned a tentative smile and relaxed as Clay tossed the rope into the craft.

Eli twisted the throttle, first staying in proximity to the dock, then charging out to the open waters of the river. After about ten minutes the canoe returned to the dock with both occupants relaxed and grinning.

Clay watched from the dock, enjoying the soft warm breeze that licked his face, a smile gaining traction as he realized just what had happened.

"Thank you, Lord," he whispered. "The boy is beginning to trust me."

The next day, Sunday, dawned promising extra heat and humidity. Clay had agreed to preach that day, and surprisingly, four of the Korean workers and three Papuan nationals, including Eli and Benjad, showed up.

Clay had no delusions about being a preacher, but he was a gifted orator and knowledgeable about the Scripture. He preached the brief sermon in simple Indonesian.

Benjad sat with Eli on the bench in a small unused meeting room with a lectern where managers planned weekly activities and dispensed assignments. At first, Benjad squatted on the bench, but then he noted the others seating themselves on the benches and mimicked their positions. Clay smiled faintly when he saw the boy try to cross his dangling legs.

Clay watched the boy as he preached. "This morning, I want to share from the Scriptures about the openness of Jesus to everyone. Mark 10:14 tells the story of Jesus scolding his disciples for not permitting the little children to come to him."

He used the verse to implore all to share God's plan of salvation, but as he preached, the thought pierced his mind he could be preaching to himself.

"As believers, we are responsible for everyone's future with the Lord and—" Clay's eyes settled on the wide-eyed boy, and he lost his focus as he contemplated the child's future.

"Ahem." A noise from the group pulled Clay back to the present. He regained his composure and closed out his sermon, drawing nods of approval.

After the service, Clay gave Benjad permission to visit the dock, promising to bring him something from the dining hall for lunch. As Benjad raced outside, Clay asked Eli to join him. He had been drawn to this rugged, intelligent, and energetic Papuan over the past couple of weeks. He also had noticed the man's evident concern and caring attitude toward Benjad. They ate in silence, which was the custom of Papuans. Food, when obtainable, was to be savored, while conversation could be enjoyed later.

Eli had been gazing at the sizable granules of raw sugar lying on the bottom of his thick glass mug. Eli stopped stirring, removed his spoon, pushed the mug aside and covered his glass with a metal lid that kept out insects.

Eli cleared his throat and spoke quietly, his eyes still fixed on his mug. "Pak Clay, where will the child go? I mean, who will care for him?"

Clay did not expect such directness. Life had clearly been hard for the Papuan. Scars on his body only hinted at the scars on his soul. Clay looked at the man so long that Eli must have thought he had not understood his question.

"I don't know where Benjad will go for sure, but I do know I will make sure he has good care." Clay spoke with firm purpose. "This brings me to a question I have for you, Pak Eli. You said your work with the camp has nearly ended here, but you did not speak of your future plans. What's next for you?"

Clay realized that this might be a difficult question for Eli, because most isolated Papuans only concerned themselves with surviving on a day-to-day basis. Tomorrow might never come.

Eli's response surprised him. "I will go to Sentani, where my uncle lives, and stay with him awhile. I have heard that BP Oil Company is looking for men to service and care for their equipment. They want men who can speak the language of the people, in addition to Indonesian. I'll be a translator."

Then Eli leaned back on the bench and sighed. "I am getting too old to work hard. I can work hard, but if I could use my words instead of my arms, then I would not need to rub camphor salve on them. I do not need camphor for my words."

He grinned, and then chuckled at his own joke.

Clay politely echoed his chuckle. "Well, I want to offer you a job working for me. I cannot pay you like BP, but I can assure you you will never go hungry, and you will have a nice place to stay. You will be around good people, both Orang Barat and Orang Papua."

Clay paused to wait for a response, but Eli just sat, intently watching him.

"Pak Eli, the boy likes you, and I am sure you like him. If he is to survive away from his own people, he needs to learn the languages of the outsiders. He has no mother and father, no blood kin. I would like you to help me with many things. First, to teach Benjad the Indonesian language and help him adjust to the world he has never seen. Second, I need help to keep the generator running at the center. Lastly, we need someone to do small mechanical jobs on boats and airplanes. Of course, you will be given a fair salary—we can discuss it later—and a place to stay."

Eli sat in silence for a few moments, chewing thoughtfully on the remnants of his dinner. Then he stood.

"I need some time to consider your offer," he said.

Clay drew a long breath, "Look, I know I've given you a great deal to think about, and that is all right. Take the night to consider it. If you're still unsure, you can take the job for two months. If you decide it is not for you, you can go your way. I will even give you the money to go back to Sentani and proceed with your original plan."

Eli nodded and left the dining hall, leaving Clay to wonder if he had heard all he had said.

Eli headed to the edge of the river, to a quiet place upstream where the jungle shielded him from curious eyes from the camp.

Clay's offer had surprised him. He wasn't accustomed to such kindness.

Eli had always drifted from job to job. Some jobs were demanding with minimal rewards. He liked the idea of being a part of something more permanent, and he had a good feeling about this big missionary. Besides, he always envied the men who had the opportunity to work on aircraft.

Five years earlier, he had taken his first airplane ride. He had been enthusiastic about these wonderful machines ever since. The pilot not only gave him his first ride, but through this American missionary pilot, he had learned about Christianity. More than a year passed before he understood this new faith and felt the need to accept Jesus.

Although Eli claimed Christianity as his new faith, sometimes old beliefs rose up to intrude on his thoughts.

What if the ghost of Drako had manipulated this situation to place the care of his son into Eli's hands? He found it strange that the father of this boy had been Eli's friend in the past, and now the boy lacked family.

Eli considered the job at the oil company. The potential pay would certainly be greater, but he'd never expected to be a rich man. He picked up a rock and sent it skipping over the river, then watched the ripples until they died down.

His friend Drako needed him.

He raced back to the dining hall and found Clay in the same seat, peering at the last drops of tea in a glass. "Pak, this will be a different job. I will do it!" Eli beamed as the missionary turned around.

"Look, Pak, if you need more time to think ..."

Eli brusquely removed the lid from the tea he'd left behind. He leaned forward, speaking in a conspiratorial manner. "My body may be slowed with years, but my otak ..." he pointed at his head "... is still very fast."

Clay smiled, lifted his glass. "Fine, be packed and ready to go day after tomorrow."

Eli smiled and pulled his noken up into view. The string bag contained his dog-eared Indonesian Bible, a clean T-shirt, a pad and a pen, pocketknife, some small tools, and betel nut.

"I am already packed."

Clay pointed at the exposed betel nut.

"Alice, my istri, is a very nice lady, but she can get very hostile about smoking and chewing betel nut. My advice to you is to stay out of her sight with red lips and teeth." Both men shared a relaxed laugh.

# CHAPTER 8

Clay agonized over how to tell his wife about the boy as he walked to the radio shack for his prearranged chat with Alice. Benjad continued to improve, and he believed she would like him. Eli had been interspersing Indonesian with the boy's mother tongue to help him learn the national language, explaining that Benjad could never return to his people, and that he must learn the world's ways and language. Clay followed Eli's example and spoke to the lad only in Indonesian.

Inside the shack, he found the Sumatran operator dozing, leaning back precariously in a rattan chair, his feet propped on the stained and chipped desk. The hum of electronic equipment and frequent crackles of distant ethereal dialogues, laced with too much static to comprehend, did not seem to disturb the man's slumber.

Clay cleared his throat and feigned a cough to get the man's attention. When that did not work, he reached behind him and slammed the screen door. Still, the operator slept, and Clay repeated his actions only more forcefully.

Bang!

The man jerked, and his eyes flew open. His feet came off the desk, but before they could stabilize the teetering chair, it tipped backward. He flapped his arms to right himself, but to no avail. Clay took a quick step and thrust his hand out, seizing the chair and arresting its free fall. Both men said simultaneously, "Maaf," the operator apologizing because he had been caught sleeping, and Clay for startling him out of a sound sleep. After some awkward seconds, both men grinned, and Clay gave a wave of dismissal.

The relieved operator quickly turned to the radio and set up the necessary frequency for contacting Clay's wife.

Miles away, Alice waited for her husband's call in the little hut attached to the hangar. She had arrived early, as usual. She knew as soon as Daryl finished refueling his Helio Courier, he would enter the radio shack to check his manifest and weather report, but still she worried.

What if distractions kept Daryl from helping her set up the radio? She did not know which buttons to push or dials to turn. Clay had often urged her to learn how to operate the radio in case of an emergency, but she never seemed to have had the time for his tutoring.

She tightened the handmade braided plant fiber that held her light brown hair in a ponytail for relief from the humidity. She would stash the band before her husband returned, knowing he loved her flowing tresses.

Alice brushed imaginary lint off her cotton skirt. Day-to-day chores, walking wherever she went, and playing soccer with the village children kept her in better condition than regular tennis and fitness classes had in the gym back home.

She glanced at the clock on the wall—almost two p.m. She rose from the bench and went to the window. Daryl had just finished closing the valve on the wing where he had drained fuel into a jelly jar to check for signs of water in the tanks. As he lifted the glass to the sunlight for examination, she knew he spotted her peering at him through the window. She quickly stepped back.

Over at the plane, a slight smile tugged at the corners of the aviator's mouth, creasing his already wrinkled skin. His Australian military hat, with the brim folded up on one side, shielded him from the unrelenting sun. Daryl, a lanky rawboned man in his late forties, hid the touch of gray that peppered his crew cut by that ever-present hat. It only came off when he flew. His six-foot-one-inch frame left no room for it in the small cockpit. When the hat came off, the Ray Ban aviator glasses went on.

Although Daryl wanted to load some cargo onto the craft, he decided he had kept Alice in suspense long enough. Satisfied no water waited in his fuel to force him into a treetop landing, the aviator gave instructions to the Korsi helpers who had stacked the cargo by the plane.

"Tungu dulu," he told them, motioning for them to wait. The men were content to squat in the shade of the hangar and swap stories.

Daryl's long legs took him to the radio shack quickly. He opened the door and feigned surprise at Alice's presence, who had reseated herself on the bench.

"What! I didn't expect you here. To what do I owe the pleasure of your company, madam?"

"You know very well why I am here!" Alice met his kidding with equally feigned outrage. "If you Aussies would ever learn to tell time, half the problems in the southern hemisphere would be solved."

Daryl chuckled.

"Okay. Let's contact that wayward husband of yours." He sat down in the creaking office chair and started dialing in the channels and frequencies. At five minutes after the two o'clock hour, the babel of Indonesian, English, Korean, and Dutch languages finally gave way to a familiar voice.

"This is Slippery Earth calling Captain Kangaroo, over." Clay's static-laced voice made Daryl grin. It reminded Daryl of the day he had given Clay that nickname, years ago, when the two of them were trekking up a mountain looking for the remains of a WWII fighter plane. Clay's tennis shoes could not find traction in the slippery steep slope, and he had slid into a deep ravine. Daryl scrambled down the slope and peered into the ravine to find Clay in the process of regaining his feet after the fifteen-foot drop into the ravine.

Daryl had disguised his concern with a good-natured barb. "I see why your mum named you Clay, 'cause Slippery Earth was too long for your report card!"

The name stuck, except Daryl shortened it to "Slippery."

Not to be outdone, Clay had nicknamed his Aussie friend Captain Kangaroo in recognition of his role as an army captain. Clay suggested he must have commanded kangaroos because no one else would listen to him. Despite the mutual joshing, they had become devoted friends who enjoyed each other's company.

Daryl pressed the bar on the chrome microphone and cleared his voice. "This is your captain speaking. We will be cruising at three feet—that is until I stand up. Weather looks good with no turbulence. Alice will be your stewardess, but she prefers not to be bothered by your petty wants. You would do well not to disturb her while the in-flight movie is playing."

Daryl creaked backward on his chair, interlacing his fingers behind his head and turning toward Alice with a grin. Alice just shook her head in mock frustration and returned the smile. The radio crackled again.

"Truth is, she's probably flying the plane while Captain Kangaroo is passing out the peanuts."

Daryl chuckled and pressed the bar again, "How ya doing, mate? You headed home soon?"

After a short conversation, Daryl glanced at Alice, who had been waiting to talk to her husband. "Ok, Slippery, gotta run, so over and out."

Alice rushed forward, "Give me that microphone, you clown."

Daryl feigned the victim. "Clown? You hurt me." He laughed, stood up, and with a sweep of his hand toward the chair said, "I will be outside working, but I warn you to keep the airways free from any romantic prattle."

Alice looked around quickly, selected a clipboard, then pretended to hurl it at him. Daryl scurried to the door. "Okay, Okay!"

Alone at last, Alice smiled and turned her full attention to the mic and speakers. "This is me—are you doing all right?" She softened her tone to the gentle, warm sweetness she used only with Clay.

"Doing fine. What about you? Over."

Alice brought Clay up to date on local happenings and a call from her mother back in the States. Clay listened more than spoke, but she knew he enjoyed the conversation.

"How's your mom managing, since ..." Clay's booming voice softened. "Is she okay?"

Alice's heart sighed. She'd been unable to attend her father's recent funeral because of limited flights out of Irian Jaya.

"Mom is doing fine. She's a real trooper." Reading Clay's silence, Alice continued. "And I am doing fine. I wish I could have been there, and I know you do too. Dad always recognized your qualities, even before you were saved."

Her humorous jab at his youthful wildness accomplished its goal. Clay chuckled, and she smiled.

"Yes, I owe your father a lot. He patiently led this disenchanted, angry vet into salvation when I couldn't see God for the devil."

"He loved you like a son." Alice spoke softly.

"He knew how to approach me. Your Dad knew I held reading and studying philosophy second only to baseball, and he used both to introduce me to Christian philosophers and writers like Platinga, C.S. Lewis, Chesterton, and Adler. Cunning man, your father."

Alice smiled, remembering the times at home when Clay and her father would spend hours in discussion in his study after Sunday dinners with the family.

"Yes, and we'll all miss him. But we will see him again, and you both can show off your baseball skills when you both have your heavenly bodies." She laughed to soften the solemn conversation. She imagined him staring at his scarred forearm and wrist, reminders of wartime shrapnel that had ended any hopes of him pitching.

"I look forward to that day when I can impress him with my fastball."

Alice hoped she had not dampened the conversation by alluding to his injury. "I have seen you play with the kids here. You still throw a mean fastball."

Clay laughed. "You're my best cheerleader. Listen, I have to go and free up the lumber camp's radio. I'll see you soon. The day after tomorrow, in fact."

Before he signed off, he mysteriously added, "Oh, by the way, set two extra plates for dinner. I'm bringing a couple of guests."

Thrilled at the news of his planned return, Alice welcomed the idea of surprise guests. Her husband had a habit of bringing home people he had met. Two days' warning was more than his usual notice.

"Are you going to tell me who they are?"

"Well, if I told you, it wouldn't be a surprise, would it?"

Alice sighed. "That's okay. I still love you."

Miles away in the tiny radio shack in the middle of the camp, Clay glanced around him to see who might be within earshot and then dropped his voice to whisper, "Me too."

Clay rose from the rattan chair, leaving the office and thanking the operator, who had moved outside for a smoke break. He found Eli and Benjad throwing stones at empty tin cans. Clay could not help but be impressed with the accuracy and speed in those little arms.

"I want to talk to Benjad."

Eli discerned the white man's serious manner and nodded, rising to leave them alone, but Clay stopped him.

"Oh no, Eli! I want you to stay and help me translate."

Clay motioned for Benjad to sit with him on a massive tree stump. "I want to talk with you, Benjad. Eli will translate. One day you will learn Indonesian and English and be able to speak with anyone." He nodded toward Eli, who squatted a few feet in front of them, to translate to the boy's clan tongue. Eli spoke slowly and very softly to the boy. When he finished speaking, the boy looked back at Clay.

The missionary drew a deep breath and let it out slowly. "Your mother is no longer living, and so you cannot be with her. We could not find anyone to care for you in your village. And now it is time for us to leave."

A look of pain crossed the young boy's face as Eli translated. Tears ran down each side of his face.

A lump of emotion filled Clay's throat. He extended his arms, and Benjad fell into his embrace and clung to him. The missionary stroked his small back. "It will be all right. You will have care."

Tears misted Eli's eyes, but he turned his face toward the jungle. Clay noticed he patted his noken, likely confirming it still held a small piece of betel nut. When the boy finally pulled back and turned his eyes toward Clay, he continued in slow, simple Indonesian.

"I live with my wife almost two days travel from here. There are children there and other people, both westerners and Papuans. Our village is a happy one with plenty of food. I would like you to be my guest and come and stay with us."

Eli cleared his throat and translated Clay's invitation. The boy looked back and forth between the two men who had become his companions and guardians. Seconds passed that seemed like minutes as the child processed this turn of events.

Clay watched the boy, searching for clues. What could he be thinking? The tragic loss of his mother likely haunted him, and the idea of facing an unknown future must also be daunting. What could a child understand of a world that he never knew existed and of being plunged into a reality not of his making? Finally, Benjad spoke quietly, looking deeply into Clay's eyes as he queried Eli.

Eli paused before he rendered the translation, with a catch in his voice. "Bapak, he asks if he will be protected from evil spirits. Also, will he be able to eat banana pudding?"

Looking down to collect his thoughts before he commented, Clay lifted his head and saw the earnest inquiry in the child's face. "Yes, son, I will make sure that the evil spirits stay away from you, and you will have cool, sweet, banana pudding."

Benjad smiled—Clay couldn't tell whether with happiness or relief. Clay nodded toward Eli, who continued to translate their conversation. "And Eli will come with us. We will travel and stay together."

Benjad lifted his head and grinned at Eli.

Clay studied Benjad's reaction. Did he see a glimmer of hope in the boy's eyes?

Benjad had no personal belongings to pack, but he added the paper and pencil to Clay's pile of possessions so they wouldn't be left behind. For the rest of the evening, he helped Clay and Eli prepare the boat and pack for departure at first light. That night, he stood by Clay's side as his new protector personally thanked all those who had helped them. The doctor gave Clay a fond farewell. The men in the camp, after shaking Clay's hand, each stooped or knelt in front of Benjad and offered him a hand as well.

Benjad mimicked Clay in the strange custom. It could be a way to rid one man's hand of dirt, or to demonstrate one's strength to a potential enemy (some of the men squeezed rather tightly). However, he had witnessed this hand-pumping often at the lumber camp, and it seemed to always be on friendly terms. In some ways, it resembled the customary greeting of his people, who would grab and squeeze each other's fingers, and then pull away, making a popping sound.

Benjad had filled his stomach in preparation for the journey, so much so that he had some abdominal pains and gas. Pak Clay had watched with laughing eyes while he'd stuffed fish, greens, and rice into his mouth. Surely Clay understood that there might not be time to hunt or gather food while they traveled.

The questions kept him awake, or perhaps he'd eaten too much dinner.

It seemed as if he had just fallen asleep when he felt strong hands gently shaking him, rescuing him from uneasy dreams of the spirit world. "Bangun, bangun!"

For a moment he wondered if the spirits were the ones shouting for him to wake. Then he opened his eyes and saw Eli standing over him.

"It's time, Benjad. A new adventure starts now."

Benjad leaped from the bed and followed Eli down the hill to the docks in the dark.

A sliver of light crept across the sky, and the camp had started coming alive when Clay cranked the replacement Johnson motor. Eli untied the heavy wooden dugout from the dock and jumped into the middle of the craft, motioning for Benjad to sit in the front. He no longer feared the sound of the hornets in the container at the back of the boat. At the camp, he had seen many boats with these curious containers pushing them along, and no one ever seemed to get stung.

As the lumber camp disappeared, Benjad fingered his crocodile tooth amulet while his mind raced. What kind of a village were they going to? Would the people look like him or like Clay? Were evil spirits there, or along the way on the river?

# CHAPTER 9

Clay twisted the throttle and swung into the river. He now could allow the current to take over most of the work and just use the motor to steer away from rocky shallows. He wanted no silt build-up in the cooling system as he'd experienced earlier.

The trip downstream promised to be much more relaxing than the way up had been. He rather enjoyed the idea of having companions. In the center seat, Eli dug in his string bag. He pulled out his betel nut and lime, stared at it like a lover, then held it up to Clay.

"I begin." Eli ceremoniously dropped the materials of his habit into the stream.

Clay laughed. "That's one less thing I have to explain to my wife."

The three settled back in the canoe and let the warming sun bathe them as they watched the dense jungle pass.

The further they traveled, the more Clay's brain struggled to relax. How could he tell Alice about Benjad? Surely she'd understand. He'd brought home many surprises, but never a child.

The small boat with its raucous motor plied the waters, intruding on the solitude of the surrounding environment. Nature ruled here. They stopped only to relieve themselves and once to fix a meal on a sandbar. As evening settled in, the lumber camp oasis faded into a memory. Clay and Eli took turns at the helm so they could push on through the night. The moon and stars cooperated to shed light for their journey, so they didn't need to find a village in which to wait out the darkness. By morning, what had been a narrow, fast-moving, angry young river had become a mature, spreading stream preparing to meet its destiny and blend with the salt-laden Pacific.

Around mid-day, Clay started scanning the banks of the river for a tributary marked by an overhanging, oddly formed large tree. It had been struck by lightning and its misshapen trunk and branches formed a caricature of an old lady's face with a hook nose. The dead tree had stood for years as a sentinel, marking the path home.

Clay recognized the high banks with bare craggy rocks on the other side of the river.

They were close.

Their rapid advance threw off his timing. He even thought he had missed the turn-off, but suddenly the tree he had been seeking appeared.

"There it is!"

Eli nodded and Benjad merely stared with curious eyes. The motor's din reached a crescendo as the pilot angled the prow across the current, slightly upstream from the looming tree. The tributary came into view. As they swung into the mouth of the thirty-foot-wide stream, a canopy of trees stretched over them to provide welcome shade.

Clay considered hugging the banks to take advantage of the cool shadow respite, but knew that would be unwise, as the shallow waters hid vegetation traps that could ensnare his prop. Besides, lethal snakes lounged in the foliage awaiting a potential meal of rodent or bird. Sometimes a serpent jarred by a passing watercraft would fall in. The dugout held little room for accidental hitchhikers. Clay removed his sunglasses to search for unwanted guests perched in the dark overhanging branches.

"We are almost there. About two hours." Not that it mattered. Time had no relevance for the boy. "Home village, soon." He attempted to clarify the proximity in Indonesian. Benjad smiled and nodded.

On the other side of the broad Danau Sagu, the locals' name for Sago Lake, Alice stood on the dock near their house, peering out over the shallow body of water for the first sight of her husband and his two guests. She had calculated the estimated time of their arrival but for some reason sensed they would arrive earlier. Still, this was her third trip to the dock.

She pressed the folds of her newest blue skirt and re-tucked her red and white cotton blouse into it. Indonesian tailors did such fine work. Its brilliant colors had not yet fallen victim to hand-scrubbing and the searing sun.

Her feet ached. She had exchanged her usual rubber flip flops and tennis shoes for brown handmade leather sandals she'd dug from the humid confines of her wardrobe. They'd been covered in green mildew. The jungle mold seemed to particularly enjoy leather goods. In anticipation of Clay's early arrival, she had cleaned them up and stored them in the humidity-protecting "hot box."

She wore her hair down, even though it added to her discomfort in the humid climate. Clay always said he preferred the way it framed her soft features.

Alice felt like a school girl on her first date. As they'd grown closer over the years, Clay might have matured and settled. However, he had not changed in the way he looked at her and touched her. He continued to treat her as though he were still courting, and anticipating his return still made her giddy.

She felt a sudden twinge of sadness that she had not been able to give him children. He'd never expressed disappointment. Alice, not he, thought of it as her failure. The doctors she had sought for help proved ineffective. Clay's kindness and patient understanding only increased her grief.

"Perhaps now, God." She lifted her head in familiar petition. "I don't care whether it's a boy or a girl, Lord, please grant us just one child."

Alice sighed, staring across the calm empty lake. Time to shake off her gloomy thoughts and focus on being the welcoming wife. She heard bare feet padding down the path and turned to see her house helper and cook, Anache, carrying an empty basket on her hip.

Anache bore scars on her neck and face where a man in her village had struck her with a machete when she'd been just 12 years old. He had killed her aunt before her eyes. Anache would have died too, had it not been for a nearby mission doctor who saved her life, but his expertise stopped short of cosmetic surgery.

"On your way to the market?" Alice smiled at the thin woman. She and Clay often gave her food to take home, despite knowing she would likely give it to neighbors and extended family members.

Anache looked to the ground and replied almost inaudibly. "Yes, Ibu."

Alice shook her head lovingly at the frail woman, still as shy as the day she started work as their pembantu years ago. Back then Anache had feared men and avoided contact with them as best she could, but years of being around westerners and outside cultures quieted her fears.

"Pak Clay will be bringing two guests, so we need to get more fish and sweet potatoes for the meal," Alice said.

"Yes, Ibu, I will bake Pak Clay's favorite pie." Anache lifted her head and smiled, displaying a missing tooth. Speaking his name always made her smile.

The first year Anache had worked for the couple, she trembled and cowered whenever Clay neared her. Clay's kindness and persistence paid off, and she learned he differed from most men she knew.

Alice nodded. "Pak Clay will like that. He told me he's most anxious to return home and taste your cooking again."

Anache giggled, then hurried on toward the market, somewhat later than she usually shopped. Alice hoped the vegetables had not been picked over.

Alice smiled and took one last glance at the lake. With a sigh, she turned to head back up the hill. She would check the house and ensure all was in order for his homecoming. Along the way, she paused to say hello to the Papuan men and women who lived in the village near the Sago Lake Center.

Missionaries who worked in isolated villages in Papua frequently came to the center for rest and to enjoy some relative comfort they did not have in their work environments. There, they also collaborated with each other on translation work or plans to advance literacy. Most of the long-term missionaries maintained small cottages at the center. They stayed in them to use the resources in the library, to obtain medical help, and, most of all, to socialize among peers.

Alice spotted Essa busily washing blood from his knife. Essa, an elderly man from the Sentani language group, had helped build the Sago Lake buildings. His white bushy hair framed a wrinkled face with intense, watery eyes. She could now see the reason for the bloodied knife. He had just finished butchering a freshwater turtle. Its edible parts were in a battered aluminum pot beside his leg where he squatted. "Good morning, Essa! How are you on this fine day?"

Essa jumped, as though startled to see Alice's shadowy form in the sunlight. He grinned, exposing what few teeth he had left.

"Waw, Ibu Alice, you move so quietly. I am about to prepare a feast for myself. Would you like some?"

"Pak Essa, I think there's just enough for you—besides, I had my fill early this morning."

The old Papuan shifted his weight on calloused bare feet and chuckled. "You remind me of Ibu Katrina, the lady I worked for in Sentani until the Japanese arrived during the big war. She also would not eat my food because she feared I would not get enough." His thin shoulders shook with laughter under his tattered old field jacket. He'd once told Alice the jacket had been given to him by a departing

American soldier in gratitude for his help in providing local food for his men. He missed the days before the war.

"You worked a long time for Ibu Katrina, didn't you?"

The old man stood slowly, wincing. "Yes! They were good days. Then the Americans and Australians came with war machines in the air and on the ground. They fought the Japanese and drove them out. They were good to the Papuan people too, but they also left." He sighed and looked over the lake.

Alice cut his storytelling short. "Pak Essa, I am expecting Pak Clay to return today. Have you heard a boat motor?"

"No, Ibu." Essa's eyesight had faded with the years, but his hearing remained.

"If you hear him approaching, please let me know."

"I will do that. I know the sound of Pak Clay's motor. I know all motors on this lake." Essa beamed. "When Pak Clay is gone, everyone misses him. The Papuans think he is the best Boss Man they have ever had. He is good and fair to all. Even the children miss him."

Alice thanked Essa for his kind words and left him to make the slow, labored return to his home to prepare a turtle dinner. In the interest of time, she decided not to mention Clay had a replacement motor on his craft.

As she headed back up the hill, Alice mulled over the simplicity of their lives here, and of Clay's contributions to its gentle rhythm since they'd arrived. Technically, Clay held the role of the Center Manager of the little community. He kept the generator running, mowed the grass runway, and maintained the guest housing provided for visits from outsiders, both governmental officials and missionaries. He took care of other tasks as well, including mediating disagreements among the clans.

However, he most loved being in the village and working with the people, providing water systems, setting up little supply stores, teaching them how to grow peanuts, and then transporting any extra to the outside markets. He talked wistfully of wanting to improve their lives, saying he saw a need to prepare them for the inevitable approach of civilization.

Clay had found his purpose in life. She thought about how God had led them both. Her heart filled with joy as she returned to her home on the hillside overlooking the lake.

As Clay and his passengers neared the lake, he could feel the slight breeze and smell the decaying vegetation in the tributary tunnel. The coolness of shadowy trees overhead murmured a farewell, ushering the craft out of the channel and into the relative open waters of the lake. The passengers squinted in the bright sunlight. Clay re-donned the sunglasses he had pocketed while going through the dark creek tunnel.

Clay scanned the lake's surface, trying to distinguish stumps from possible living creatures. He did not fear but believed in always using caution.

"Eli, have you ever seen a saltwater croc?"

Eli pondered the question before responding.

"A few, near the mouth of the Mamberamo. They are not something I try to get close to. Why do you ask? There are none here, right?" His eyes darted over the reedy water.

"Well, I have never seen one here." Clay checked whether Benjad might be listening, but the boy in the bow slept soundly. "A few years ago, one wandered into these waters, and two villagers lost their lives. Then a fisherman lost his hand last year, but my wife saved his life. I have been told that this croc is seven meters long. But that may be an exaggeration."

Eli nodded. "They have been known to grow to eight or nine meters, I am told. And unlike freshwater crocs who will hide from men, they will stalk you." Eli continued to look around the waters. "You say someone last saw it a year ago? That could be good news. Still, those crocs live to fifty or sixty years, I am told."

Clay grinned. "Ya, nobody has gone missing since then. They call him Mati Raja, King Death. He has only one eye."

"Ahh, that is in the Bible, Pak! An eye for a hand and a tooth for a tooth." He slapped his leg and guffawed.

Clay rolled his eyes and chuckled. "Eli, you are a comic."

Eli stopped laughing. "How did Mati Raja lose his eye?"

Clay reduced the throttle so Eli could hear him.

"I had just returned from a trip to Sentani about a year or so ago. Scared villagers met me at the airstrip, all talking at once. I finally managed to settle them down and they told me that my wife, Ibu Alice, was tending to a fisherman named Milo who had his hand snapped off by a giant croc. I ran to the clinic and found her working hard to stop Milo's bleeding, and Milo succumbing to shock."

At Eli's puzzled expression when he mentioned shock, Clay did his best to explain the medical condition before continuing.

"Witnesses to the incident, other fishermen in the area, said the croc came out of nowhere as Milo pulled in a fishing net. His brother in the boat grabbed him and kept him from being pulled into the water. The croc had clamped down on Milo's hand with his huge head resting on the side of the dugout." Clay paused while he reflected. "It's a wonder the beast didn't sink the boat."

Eli twisted sidewise and checked on Benjad. Still napping. "So, how did the croc lose the eye?"

"Oh, right. Milo's brother kept beating it with a paddle, which just tickled the croc, but Milo snatched a knife off the bottom of the boat with his good hand and started stabbing the head of the beast. He could not penetrate the tough skin, then by luck he found the eye and caused the croc to release its grip."

Clay shuddered at the thought of that day. "Mati Raja got his hand and Milo got his eye."

Eli nodded. "Even as big as you say he is, there are many hiding places in this lake."

Both men continued to watch for submerged stumps and logs, reducing the motor to little more than an idle. They also looked for the submerged shape of the killer croc. When the little craft cleared the dangerous underwater hazards, Clay twisted the throttle and the dugout resumed its skimming over the waters.

Soon they saw the first village perched on the lake. Men and women near the shore waved as they recognized the man piloting the craft. Normally, Clay would have slowed and exchanged greetings and made small talk as he traveled home, but he had been gone too long and the sun sank low. So, Clay hoped a big smile and a wave would suffice.

A few minutes later, he rounded a bend and saw his home community nestled in the tree-covered mountainside. As he drew closer, he could make out the eight bungalows, the library, workshop, clinic, and the chapel built of local materials. The aircraft hangar had been made from an imported military Quonset hut. He heard the faint rumble of the diesel motor powering the generator. The generator shed had been purposely set away from the rest of the community and shielded by three low hills to dampen the noise. When he spotted the pier with several dugouts tied to it, Clay felt his heartbeat quicken. Closing the distance to the pier was the longest part of the journey.

Eli turned and patted Benjad on the leg. "Bangun, bangun."

Benjad sat up and rubbed his eyes. Watching him, Clay's heart seemed to race even faster as he imagined the conversation ahead.

"Lord, give me the words to present Benjad to my wife," he whispered skyward.

Ten minutes later, Clay cut the throttle and allowed his canoe to drift toward the dock, where it banged solidly against the supporting post. Eli attempted to leap out to secure the dugout, but instead sat down hard.

Clay half smiled. "I know the feeling. I get stiff legs every time. Wait until you see me try to get this big body into action."

Benjad jumped to a ladder and clambered onto the dock. He turned to accept a rope from Eli and deftly secured the dugout as Eli had taught him.

"Oh, to be young again," Clay lamented.

"Saya setuju," Eli agreed.

Clay followed Benjad's exit from the dugout. Eli unloaded the gear from the canoe and handed the items up to Clay on the dock. The two Papuan boys Clay had seen from a distance came running.

"Bapak Clay is home!"

Clay stood up and grinned. In a matter of seconds they were joined by other children coming from all directions, adding their voices to the welcoming chorus.

"This is it, gentlemen. Rumah, sweet rumah."

# CHAPTER 10

Alice had just finished baking cookies in the tin box oven that sat atop the burners of her gas-fired stove. She baked in shifts in the tiny metal box, proud of her ability to adjust the flame and time to produce delicious desserts. Still, Anache was the master chef.

A commotion down by the docks drew Alice's attention from the stove to the kitchen window. Her heart leapt as she saw her husband's canoe, and the local children, both Papuan and Western, noisily clamoring to welcome their beloved Pak Clay.

Alice glanced in the mirror on the wall beside the door. Hair in place. She opened the screen and attempted to walk down the hill without running. It was a game they played called "who missed who more." Both tried to be the last one to succumb to any display of emotions. Clay had won consistently, but she would win this time.

Mostly black faces peered up at Clay, but there were two white faces equally in awe. All spoke Indonesian, even the two white boys, as they peppered Clay with questions.

"Did you see wild pigs?"

"I heard you stayed at the Korean lumber camp. Did they show movies?"

"Now that you are back, can we play ball?"

One little Papuan about seven years old asked, "Did you bring us candy from the camp?" His older brother frowned and poked him with an elbow, chastising him for his poor manners. "Tidak sopan!"

Clay smiled at the youngster and leaned down, setting his hands on his knees, and spoke in a low voice, "Petra, are you glad to see me or only to see candy?"

Petra grinned and shrugged. "Both!"

Clay snorted. "Hmmm. I seem to remember waking up in the middle of the night on my trip and seeing a 'candy angel' putting something in my pack."

The children watched, wide-eyed, as he retrieved a plastic bag containing small chocolate bars from Australia. Although cacao grew here, most westerners preferred the European chocolate or the "down under" variety for its smooth texture and bold taste. So did the Papuans.

Raising the bag dramatically overhead, Clay handed it to Petra.

"Now, I trust you to divide the contents equally with all the children."

Petra nodded and smiled broadly at his important role. He pulled out the candies, one at a time, giving one confection out to each child.

Fina, a little girl on the perimeter, eyed not the bag of candy, but Clay's guests. She pointed at Benjad with her thumb. "Who's that?" She spoke precise English.

Her blunt question reminded Clay that introductions were in order.

"Ah. I want you to meet two people who will be staying with us at the Center." Clay patted his new friend. "This is Pak Eli. He is from the high river country and will be working on our generator and boat motors."

He laid a hand on the boy's shoulder. "This is Benjad of the Koto clan. I want you all to make him feel welcome. He does not speak Bahasa Indonesia, so you need to help him learn."

The children examined the newcomer as if he were a strange bug. Benjad responded by folding his arms on his chest, tilting his head back, and exhibiting a blank expression.

Clay watched the greeting, somewhat bemused. The little barefoot boy, clad in a too-large T-shirt and shorts held up by twine, did not look imposing. However, Benjad seemed determined not to show anxiety to these strange children.

Fina stared at the boy, even after Petra placed a candy bar in her hand. At first, she barely took notice, but then she took a few steps toward Benjad and paused. Their eyes locked as she took a couple more steps and offered the candy to Benjad. He glanced down at her gift and then again to her eyes.

Benjad reached out a cautious hand and accepted the candy. With a curt nod, he used the little Indonesian he had learned to say thank you. "Terima kasih."

Fina smiled and nodded back. The ice had been broken for all. Clay winked at Fina, grateful for her gesture. Fina's adoptive missionary parents, Brian and Cora Yoder, had done well in child-rearing.

Clay finally looked up and saw his lady at the far end of the dock, standing with her head tilted to one side. He knew that look. She wanted an explanation.

But she'd have to wait for now. Clay clapped his hands, assumed military demeanor and declared, "Okay. Some of you big guys grab my gear and take it to my house. The rest of you go play. Tomorrow we will talk about plans to play baseball." He drew out the word "baseball," accompanied by exaggerated widening of his eyes.

All the boys, even the younger ones, tried to seize the packs to identify that they were big guys. This started a minor scuffle. Clay realized his mistake and singled out two of the larger boys to take the packs and supplies to his house. The rest skipped away, talking loudly.

Clay turned to Alice and stepped off the dock with a half-smile.

"It's been a long time," he intoned, as though they were old friends.

Alice shook her head and walked quickly to his waiting arms. They embraced and she kissed him. "Rats, you won again."

"You are the one who won. It's a win-win situation." Clay grinned.

Eli turned his back and looked at the surrounding buildings on the Center. Benjad stared openly.

Alice stepped around Clay and approached Eli.

"I am Alice, Clay's wife." She bowed a little, but did not offer to shake hands, nor did Eli offer his hand.

Eli nodded his head and pointed a thumb at his chest. "I am Eli. I will be helping Pak Clay."

"Ohh." Alice stepped toward Benjad. "And you are?" She bent to meet him on his level and spoke in Indonesian.

Benjad glanced at Clay before he answered. "Koto," he said.

Alice studied the little boy's face then also looked at Clay.

"He is from the Koto clan, but what is his name?"

"This is Benjad. He is not fluent in Indonesian—yet."

Alice smiled and extended a hand toward the boy. "Come with me. Are you hungry? I have some cookies." When Benjad's face lit up, she shook her head at Clay.

"I see you've taught him the important words, at least."

Benjad did not take her hand, but she began slowly walking back up the hill with her arm outstretched and looking steadily at him. He followed with a quick look to see whether Clay was coming too. Alice slowly withdrew her extended hand, but she continued to smile. She, too, glanced back to Clay and in her best Ricky Ricardo accent said, "Lucy, you have some 'splainin' to do."

Her husband shrugged and added a subdued, plaintive Lucy Ricardo wail.

# CHAPTER 11

Benjad had many thoughts to sort through as he walked by Eli's side. Clay had stepped past them to join Alice on the walk up the hill toward a small house. Benjad pondered his words to Alice earlier. He'd identified his clan without thinking. But did he still belong to the Koto people? They had refused to let him stay with them. Maybe he did not have any people. His eyes lowered.

Clay's woman chatted ahead of him in a strange tongue, no doubt filling him in on events that occurred during his absence. Behind him, two of the boys he'd met on the dock brought up the rear, carrying Clay's gear.

Benjad entered Clay and Alice's home with the rest of the group and stared, open-mouthed, at his surroundings.

Clay must be a very important man. Perhaps even a tribal chief. Why would he allow someone like Benjad in this amazing place? There must be many other people living here.

"Thank you, boys. You can leave all that here by the door." Alice thanked each of the bag carriers with a fresh-baked cookie. "You've been quite helpful."

Before leaving, the boys hesitated and looked at Clay. One spoke up shyly.

"Are you going to play ball with us tomorrow?"

"Well, give me a chance to rest and catch up with my work. Maybe in a couple of days. Okay?"

The boys grinned as they ran out the door.

Alice turned to examine her ragtag group of guests. The boy intrigued her. She didn't appreciate having to wait, but there wouldn't be an opportunity to pull Clay aside for an explanation until after dinner.

She had the table set and made everything ready except for frying the fish. The Indonesian Bimoli oil had been kept warm, so now she needed only to increase the temperature.

"Benjad, you must be hungry from your long trip?" She pointed to her mouth.

Benjad nodded slowly, with that expression of wary awe he'd worn from the moment they'd met. Alice smiled.

"First, let's wash our hands." She led him to the kitchen sink with some warm water in a pan and slid a small step stool in front of the counter.

Clay headed down the hallway to the bathroom to clean up himself.

Benjad climbed up on the step stool and placed his hands in the water, then pulled them back, eyes wide.

"Is it too hot?" Alice blew on his fingers to indicate need for cooling. Perhaps he'd never experienced warm water. Here, solar drums heated both the kitchen and bath water—not something typically found in villages of the region.

Benjad returned his hands to the water. She admired his courage.

"How about some soap?" Alice offered a plastic squeeze bottle of dish detergent to the boy.

Benjad examined the bottle with his usual wariness. He rubbed the bottle with both hands, and seemed crestfallen that it wouldn't produce lather.

"Ah. A bar-soap man. Here! Let me show you." Alice took the bottle from Benjad's hands and squirted a little liquid into his hands. The bottle made a slight gurgling noise.

Benjad giggled. The first real smile she'd seen. She watched while he played with the foamy lather and rinsed off, then she handed him a towel. They walked together to the dining table, where she gently placed her hands on his shoulders and guided him to a chair.

"Pak Eli, help yourself." Alice gestured to the sink for her new acquaintance to wash also.

Clay and Eli joined the boy at the table, and Alice listened as Clay gave Eli a short history of the Sago Lake community while she fried the fish in the hot grease. She snuck glances toward Benjad, who sat quietly, his eyes raking over the house and all the activities.

What must he be thinking?

Benjad had learned about tables and chairs at the lumber camp, so he knew how to sit appropriately for dinner. He missed squatting and eating before a welcoming fire in the cool of the evening. He thought about the smell of crispy sago grub worms roasting in the fire, which made him homesick.

Despite longing for the village community, Benjad did feel a sense of pride at being able to sit at a table as these strange people did.

The woman called Alice set the steaming fried fish on a platter in the center of the table. Benjad did not wait for the food to be offered. The aroma wafting up from the table provided invitation enough. He grabbed a filet, but as he lifted it to his mouth, he noticed his fellow diners sitting quietly, watching him. Benjad paused and lowered the filet to the table.

Perhaps they thought he'd taken the biggest fish for himself, instead of allowing the men to have it.

He quickly scanned the fish tray and was relieved to see he had not acted improperly. There were at least two larger fish left.

Eli arched his eyebrows and whispered, "Tidak sopan."

Not polite? Benjad hissed, "It is not the largest."

Then he noted that Eli, Clay, and Alice were sitting with their hands pressed together. Clay did not look irritated like Eli, but he wore an amused expression.

Clay gently pressed Benjad's hands together in a prayerful posture and Eli said, "We thank the Lord before every meal."

Benjad mimicked the curious position as all the diners lowered their heads over their hands and Clay began to speak. What were they were looking at on the table? Now their eyes closed as if they had fallen asleep? Clay even seemed to be talking in his sleep. It was all very odd.

And who did Pak Clay talk to? Surely nobody at the table, and the westerner did not seem disturbed that the mysterious person did not respond. Benjad lowered his head but kept one eye open to watch the group and be ready to escape if someone became violent. When Clay concluded his conversation with the table, everyone looked up.

They all looked at Benjad, Alice moved the fish from in front of the boy and placed it on a flat disk, which she called a piring. So, people in this world ate food placed on the piring and those who did not were considered rude.

It must be to respect the spirits of the animals and not anger them.

Alice spooned rice from a pot onto his plate and topped it with cooked vegetable greens. Then she heaped some strange red morsels in a gooey sauce onto his rice. Benjad leaned forward to take a closer look. He had seen seeds and nuts in his life, but those strangely shaped seeds were new. Benjad had seen similar shaped organs inside of small birds, but how could a hunter have killed that many birds? He took a small bite with the tasty red sauce. Quite good.

"They're called beans," said Eli. "They come from plants."

Benjad scooped another handful of beans and rice into his mouth. Then he noticed that all eyes watched him again. Clay picked up a spoon in his right hand and a fork in his left and held them up for Benjad to examine.

"Spoon." He raised one. "Fork." He raised the other. "Look." Clay lowered them to his plate and scooped the beans and rice onto his spoon with the fork.

Clay stuck the spoon into his mouth and withdrew it empty. He chewed in a vigorous fashion and swallowed. "See?" Clay smiled.

Benjad had been introduced to a spoon in the lumber camp but saw no advantage to putting food on a spoon and then placing it in your mouth. Such a waste of time. And that metal spoon could have been already used for other purposes and might be dirty. However, hunger ruled, and if it took these unnecessary antics to please the white skins, he would comply. Benjad copied Clay's demonstration, to the cheers of his fellow diners.

Despite the strange foods and peculiar procedures, Benjad could understand why Clay had bought Alice for a wife. Judging by her cooking, Clay had received the best part of the deal when he paid her family a bride price.

How many pigs and cowry shells did Clay give Alice's father to buy her?

Alice brought out dessert, the homemade chocolate chip cookies she had baked earlier, along with Anache's pie. She offered the cookies to Benjad first. He glanced at the two men to ascertain they were not offended that she had first offered a child those cookies. They did not seem to mind.

Benjad tried to lever a cookie from the plate onto the spoon, but the cookie fell to the table.

Now what?

Again, the men were chuckling.

Alice reproved them then spoke to Benjad, and Eli translated, "Benjad, you can use your fingers this time."

She held up one hand and demonstrated a pinching motion. She nodded. "Go ahead."

Benjad picked up the cookie from the table and held it in his fingers, and when Alice lifted her fingers to her lips, he followed the example. His eyes widened at the delightful flavor. They were even better than the cookies he'd eaten in the lumber camp.

His hunger satisfied, Benjad studied the house and its furnishings as the men talked. Alice directed the men and boy into the living room where they sat on bamboo furniture with padded cushions. While the men seated themselves in the chairs, Benjad found a footstool and sat on it, where he could observe Alice in the kitchen.

Benjad noticed that Alice washed dishes inside the house instead of taking them to the river. Water flowed out of something that appeared like hollow metal bamboo. A round wheel on top made it start and stop when she wanted. He had seen a similar device in the camp.

The boy didn't trust the water. Were they getting it from a river? Surely they realized that at this time of night, many villagers bathed and used the stream to make body mud. He hoped that they had the sense to get the water upstream from bathers.

As he patted his satisfied belly, a disturbing thought intruded.

What if they were trying to fatten him up to eat him? The meal had been delicious, but did this man bring him here to be used in a ritual?

He glanced around at the faces in the room and the adjoining kitchen. All seemed relaxed and emanated a sense of peace. Benjad decided there were no hostile intentions at this time.

While the men talked, he continued his reconnaissance of the home. The size of this house dwarfed any he had ever seen in his village. However, despite its size, he had noticed when they arrived that large posts elevated the home above the ground. Square openings in the wall covered with some type of see-through material allowed air and light in from the outside.

The bizarre openings first caught his attention when moths and flying insects started bouncing off the barrier, thwarted in their attempts to reach the lights inside.

Fascinating!

Benjad had been mindful of a slightly familiar hum in the distance.

Perhaps it was a beehive? Where had he heard that sound before?

Now, the sound wound down and then ceased. The lights in the house dimmed until they went out—he remembered. Ah. Just like the monster connected to the lights at the lumber camp.

Clay rose and padded softly to a nearby table where he picked up a flashlight that had been strategically placed and switched it on. Benjad watched him use the light-stick to negotiate the furniture and retrieve a lantern from under a table by the doorway.

Alice had already lowered a similar lantern from the ceiling in the kitchen by a rope and pulley system. Eli had taught him about pulleys back at the lumber camp. This one seemed to keep the light overhead at a safe height for people walking underneath. Almost simultaneously, both Alice and Clay lit the wicks and then she hoisted hers back up while Clay strode back to his chair, setting his lantern on the table nearby.

Benjad noted the lanterns did not radiate the light that those little glass bulbs did, but they seemed very helpful. Clay leaned over and pumped a knob that made the lantern brighter.

When Benjad needed to relieve himself, he whispered to Eli, who picked up the flashlight and motioned him to the door of the house.

"Whoa." Clay interceded and pointed down the hallway. After a brief discussion Eli turned away from the outside door and beckoned to Benjad. Clay handed Eli the lantern and took the flashlight from him.

"This way."

Eli walked ahead of Benjad as he checked the three doors with the lantern until he found the right room. Benjad astonishment. He fingered the shiny lever with reverence.

Then Eli showed him how to turn on the water and wash his hands.

Benjad left the room and made a mental note to check under the house at first light to find his excrement and hide it from prying eyes.

Alice stopped him in the hall. She carried a lantern, and, with a nod of her head she indicated a room. Eli said, "She wants to show you where you will sleep."

Benjad entered what would become his room—to him yet another strange place that contributed to his discomfort. The bedroom contained a teak desk and chair and a large bed, over which mosquito netting hung by strings from the ceiling. He'd seen beds in the lumber camp, but never one this large. It had a thick padding, as well as two small, square pads, all covered with material.

Maybe the big pad had been made for adults and the little ones were for babies to sleep on?

The walls were like the rest of the home. Aha! Another opening with that strange barrier over it to keep insects out. He walked to the window and gazed upon some papaya trees and smelled the sweet smell of the nighttime jungle wafting in through the opening. He covertly pressed the material over the window to test its strength and found that it appeared to flex and probably would be easy to tear.

Good to know, should he need to escape.

The faces of Clay and Alice and some unknown people adorned one wall. He stepped closer to examine them by the light of the lantern. He admired the talent of whoever had drawn these pictures. He glanced back and forth at

Alice and her photo showing her playing a game with a yellow ball and large round paddle. What looked like a drying net stretched in front of her.

In the other drawing, Clay wore clothes covered with shiny buttons and decorations. He looked younger, and wore no beard, but Benjad recognized him.

These drawings could come alive. Ajun, back in his home village, could draw people with charcoal and berries on bark, but he could never approach this accuracy. The drawings were so lifelike, but in miniature.

On a small table sat a little square box that glowed and hummed and illuminated strange changing symbols. Such an odd creature. Perhaps it had been left here to watch him. He had become accustomed to strange tools, motors, and lights that the orang barat used, but they still made him uneasy. The white skins seemed to have found a way to control small demons to do their bidding.

He'd have to find some of those little demons and train them for his own use.

Alice watched quietly as the little boy toured the room. She could see his eyes widen at the sight of the clock and the photos. She remembered Clay telling her about an incident when he had taken a photo of a husband and wife among the Walak people in the highlands. The Polaroid film developed in a matter of minutes, and Clay had shown them the photo.

The woman had looked perplexed, the man angry. He said he recognized his wife, but he wanted to know the identity of the man by her side. Clay narrowly averted a scene as he sought to explain to the man that this was his own image in the photo.

"You see Pak Clay here, when he served in the army." Alice pointed to the framed photo.

As she described the photo of herself playing tennis, she wondered how much the boy grasped.

"Well, you must be tired. I know that all of this is very strange to you, but I am your friend." Alice smiled. "And you do not know a word I am saying," she sighed.

Alice pulled the sheet back on the bed and patted the mattress. Benjad understood her invitation and jumped into bed. He lay back, then rose up to push the pillows away. Alice assisted him in his dismissal of the pillow, "Oh, you do not like your head propped up?" She removed the pillows and brought the linen sheet over his body. He still wore his shorts and T-shirt and showed no intent to remove them. "Tomorrow night we will see about getting PJs for you, and you do need to bathe. But for tonight, sleep."

Clay, after showing Eli to the guest room, stood in Benjad's doorway listening to Alice. He decided not to interrupt the moment and silently glided away to the master bedroom, looking forward to a shower from the fifty-five-gallon drum outside that collected rainwater from the roof gutters. Normally, the households timed their showers in the late mornings or afternoons when the sun had heated up the water in the drums.

This would only be lukewarm but refreshing.

Clay shed his sweaty travel togs and stepped into the shower. Water poured from a nozzle that had been improvised from a perforated plastic bottle. The initial cold blast of water caused him to gasp sharply. He'd known what to expect but could not prevent that gasp every time he experienced this abrupt assault. As the water ran it became a little warmer from the solar-warmed drum.

So good to be home.

In the other room, Alice sat on the edge of Benjad's bed humming softly as the child's eyes slowly closed. Then she stood, tucking in the mosquito netting around him, and left the room. She closed the door, leaving a small gap.

She made her rounds in the kitchen and living room, extinguishing lanterns and checking that the gas to the stove had been turned off. Then she walked back down the hallway, past the room where Eli slept. Even the closed door could not diminish the sound of his snores. She peeked in on Benjad.

She didn't know why he'd been brought here, but she had a feeling his was a tragic story.

Alice softly trod into the bathroom and took a wifely inventory of Clay while he showered, his eyes closed as he lathered. She noted the battle scars on his chest and arm, souvenirs from his service in Vietnam. She often wondered how their lives might have been different had he not been wounded there. Alice recalled the anger he had harbored from serving in an unpopular war.

That all changed when he became a believer. Alice had watched his transformation with delight. He had become a dedicated worker for the Lord, repurposing the courage, honor and sacrifice he learned in the military for a higher cause. She loved that in him.

Soap and shampoo covered Clay's face. She took a

plastic cup from the table by the sink and stifled a giggle as she filled it quietly with even colder water than the shower provided. Then she crept up behind him and ceremoniously poured it over his head.

"Hey!" he exclaimed. She giggled and tried to escape but couldn't elude Clay's grasping arms.

He pulled her into the cold shower. "Here's a taste of your own shocking cold medicine."

"Aaah!" she gasped, "You're getting my clothes wet!"

"That's the meaning of wash and wear," he declared.

He gazed into her eyes and she returned it, oblivious to the rivulets running down her face.

They kissed and revived their love for each other. She had asked no questions about Eli or the boy. Tomorrow would be soon enough to discuss them.

Benjad awoke from a brief doze. Clay's wife had left the room. He lay in the bed with the sheet wrapped around him. Something smelled unlike any flowers he could recall. The strange, but not unpleasant fragrance came from the sheets. Even the baby mattresses he had shoved aside smelled like flowers.

The one-eyed glow on the table pierced the darkness as it continued to watch him. In the stillness, he could hear the little creature hum like an insect.

Or could it be sleeping? No, it must have been awake because it was watching me. Maybe the woman left the creature in the room as a guard to prevent me from trying to escape.

He could not sleep while the little creature stared at him. The sleeping platform was too soft, like a stack of bird feathers. Finally, he sat up on the edge and found that the mosquito netting had been tucked in around the bed. Perhaps she had intended to prevent him from getting off the bed. Momentarily he felt a rush of panic, but he realized that the material could be easily parted. He did so.

The boy carefully slid out of the bed, watching the one-eyed creature to see if it shouted an alarm to Alice. When it did not, he leaned in for a closer look, but remained ready to retreat. It just glowed brighter and hummed louder. Relieved, he cautiously stretched his hand out and patted the top of it, gently speaking the word for "friend" in his native tongue. It did not scream or attempt to bite him, so he relaxed.

He dragged the sheet off the bed and pulled it to a corner of the room. The creature continued to watch him. He dropped the sheet in the corner and approached it again. Benjad gingerly turned its face away from him so it looked out the window.

Let the little creature watch for real enemies.

Benjad returned to the corner, lay on the hard wood floor, and wrapped his body in the sweet-smelling sheet. There, that was more like it. Sleep enveloped him, and he succumbed to it as he pondered the day ahead.

What would he see tomorrow in this village?

# CHAPTER 12

Alice awoke before Clay and lay still, cherishing the sound of his soft snores. She rarely woke first.

He must be exhausted.

Remembering her guests, Alice slid out of bed and dressed in the dark. She tiptoed down the hallway, holding her breath when the wooden floors creaked. She paused by the bedroom where Benjad slept. Easing the door open, she strained her eyes in darkness toward the bed.

He was gone!

Her pulse quickened, and she shoved the door open. Then she saw a little huddled mass under the sheet in the corner, sleeping soundly.

Alice exhaled and withdrew, but not before she noted that the clock had been turned to face out the window.

Curious. She did not remember moving the clock. She paused and crossed the room to face it toward the door. She liked things orderly.

She could see only the top of the boy's head among the heap of rising and falling sheets. Alice smiled.

Today she'd learn the story behind Clay's guests.

Is he transporting them here for a flight somewhere? I'm sure Eli isn't the boy's father. Possibly his uncle. They're certainly not of the local Korsi people. Perhaps they're traveling to Sentani.

Alice enjoyed her husband's unpredictability, always adventuresome and eager to try new things. However, she had her limits.

As a planner, Alice occasionally became flustered by Clay's spontaneity. The two rarely argued, but when they did, Clay's unpredictable behavior usually provided the initiating sparks.

To be fair, he did warn her he was bringing a couple of guests. That was a great improvement over the way he used to be.

She shook her head and padded to the kitchen. The first rays of dawn had crept into the room, eliminating any need for lanterns.

Alice tried to be quiet as she pulled out pots and pans for breakfast. She started filling the stove-top percolator with coarse-ground java coffee, allowing some extra for Eli. Clay could and would drink the instant coffee laced with thick cream and raw sugar served in many places, but he preferred fresh-perked and black.

As she placed the pot on the burner and lit the gas, Ibu Anache appeared at the back door carrying a noken filled with fresh papayas, mangoes, and the little stubby, smoky-tasting bananas. The bag had been suspended from her forehead by long strands used as handles and hung down to the small of her back. Alice admired her strength. The weight of the fruit must have been substantial, but years of transporting everything from firewood, mangoes, pigs, and sweet potatoes had enabled the small Papuan woman to adapt to this form of labor.

"Selamat pagi, Bu!" Anache spoke through the screen door.

Alice beckoned her inside. "Good morning yourself. How are you?"

"Oh, what a glorious morning! The market was bursting with ..."

Alice raised her fingertips to her lips and gestured down the hallway.

Anache dipped her head with surprise and spoke in subdued tones, "Oh, Bapak Clay, sudah kembali? Masih tidor?"

"Yes, he has returned and is still sleeping." Alice paused and looked at Anache's expectant grin. "And yes, he brought two guests, who are also still sleeping here."

Alice leaned toward her conspiratorially. "The man is good-looking and about your age."

Anache giggled and waved her hand.

Anache busied herself with putting the fruit and vegetables into bowls of water containing vinegar that destroyed unhealthy bacteria. Alice started preparing the breakfast meal. After only a few moments, Eli wandered into the living room and wished Alice a good morning.

Alice turned and greeted him warmly. "Pak Eli, this is Ibu Anache. Bu, this is Pak Eli."

Anache smiled shyly, then went back to her work.

Alice continued, "Did you sleep well?"

"The bed was softer than that boat." Eli grinned.

The conversation continued as Alice sought to learn more about this Papuan man, his background, family, and character. She caught Anache listening intently as he described his tribal group and his past work.

When Eli mentioned that he had never been married, he stole a glance at Anache as he joked, "It is not that a woman never wanted me ... they just never wanted part of my traveling life."

Eli pursed his lips in a thoughtful manner. "Maybe, one day I will stay put. Traveling has made my legs shorter." He chuckled at Anache, and she smiled back.

Awakened by the smell of fresh-perked coffee, Clay stretched beneath the sheet, ignoring the soreness in his muscles. He bounced out of bed and strode to the bathroom in his cotton sleeping shorts. He had a theory that one who leaped out of bed like a youngster every day would be able to keep leaping, even into old age. Scientific data was sadly missing on this issue, but he believed in time his theory would be validated. He smiled wryly in the mirror.

Alice had set out a thermos of hot water for his morning shave. Her thoughtfulness was not lost on him. He inserted the rubber stopper into the sink, poured the water in and soaked a towel in the liquid. He pressed the hot, wet towel to his face and neck, basking in the soothing warmth before applying lather around his beard.

Neck hair irritated him, no matter what length. Alice would not have minded if he had shaved entirely, but he had worn a beard for years for its protection against insects and sun. Also, it aided him in being accepted by the clans. Many chiefs wore beards, and gray beards indicated wisdom of years. The life spans of the tribal people were commonly short. If anyone made it to a time of life where they wore silver on their heads and faces it was a sign of wisdom and blessing. Clay consoled himself with this thought as he spotted some rogue gray hairs on his temples and chin.

He selected a pair of leather sandals from the hot box and inspected the footwear to see if mildew had grown on the leather. The generators provided electric power only twelve hours a day, but that seemed to be sufficient to hold the spores in check.

Clay set the sandals on top of the hot box and finished dressing. Cargo shorts and a T-shirt advertising the Daytona 500 completed his wardrobe. He picked up the sandals and strode down the hall, dropping them next to the door. Shoes were not worn inside the home.

Clay gave a shallow bow and smiled to everyone. "Good morning!"

After they had exchanged morning greetings, he asked Alice, "Where is Benjad?"

"Still sleeping, I presume," she replied. "Evidently he did not like his bed and chose to sleep in a corner."

"He did?" Clay grinned.

Eli smiled as well. "Too soft for the boy's comfort, I would guess."

Clay cocked his head, "Makes sense." He patted the back of a dining chair with two big hands and said to no one in particular, "Well, I think it's time for him to rise and shine. Permisi." Excusing himself, he strode down the hall.

Clay lightly tapped on the partially opened door and softly pushed it further.

"Good morning, Benjad. Sleep well?"

Benjad squatted in the corner eyeing the clock intently. He glanced at Clay and nodded solemnly toward the clock.

Clay walked across the room and picked up the glowing instrument. "Clock, clock." He searched Benjad's face and glanced around the room trying to find an illustration to describe the timepiece's use. Gesturing toward the rising sun in the window, he pantomimed the trek of the solar day and then hid his eyes to communicate darkness followed by an imitation of sleep accompanied by snoring. He then pointed to the clock.

Benjad's dark eyes were focused on Clay's perplexing performance. Seeing the boy still didn't comprehend, he carried the clock to the youth and offered him the opportunity to hold it. "See, it will not hurt you."

The reassuring tone of the man motivated the boy to accept the little black glowing god and he took it into his hands gingerly.

Unknowingly, Clay's finger had pressed the alarm button as he proffered the instrument. The clock immediately began a staccato loud buzzing. Feeling the vibrations in his hands, Benjad threw the angry little demon in the air and raced back to his corner.

Clay, also surprised, caught the buzzing clock before it hit the floor.

"It's all right, all right!" He tried to soothe the fear of the child by holding the clock in his hand to show that no harm came from the buzzing.

Why did the alarm have to go off right then? The timing could not have been worse.

Clay acted out a sleeping behavior and, as the alarm continued to sound, he stretched and yawned then looked at the face of the timepiece intently, then dramatically in slow motion took his finger and purposely pushed the off button on the alarm. Silence reigned once again. Clay smiled, tilted one hand open and said, "See?" He touched the clock to his cheek with no adverse consequences. "Harmless."

Benjad had stayed in his corner clutching the sheet around his small body as he intently watched Clay's performance.

Clay stretched out his hand to Benjad and used a phrase the boy knew, "Come on. Let's eat." Benjad placed his hand in Clay's. He glanced back at the clock.

"Don't worry. It won't follow you." Clay chuckled.

After breakfast, Clay encouraged Eli to take Benjad outside and explore the little community hewn out of the jungle. Then he and Alice carried their cups of coffee to the veranda overlooking the lake.

The relative coolness of the morning did not fool him. It would get hot soon.

Alice usually completed morning chores in the kitchen before joining him on the veranda for their daily prayer time, but today Anache had insisted on cleaning up, allowing them some rare alone time before the busy day ahead. They seated themselves in rattan chairs and shared the small rattan table between them.

Clay nodded to himself. He treasured this time of the day, when he and Alice watched the morning come alive while they talked and read Scriptures. They also used this time to discuss plans for the day, so each knew what the day held for the other.

He cleared his throat. He had been planning his words for days, yet they seemed inadequate and irrational now that the time had come to deliver them.

"Well, it's good to be home." Clay sighed as he surveyed the lake and the distant activities of the inhabitants of the village. "These trips are becoming more and more difficult. Do you think it's a sign I'm getting older?"

Alice said nothing, but her eyes seemed to peer into his soul. Clay felt like a little boy about to request something that he knew would stir controversy.

He took a quick sip of his coffee, burning his lips in the process, but he fought the urge to wince.

A smile touched the corners of her mouth. He hated it when she did that. It unnerved him, as if she knew something before he said it. She had worn that same smile when he proposed to her.

Clay decided to start with Eli.

"I have been impressed with Eli's skills and aptitude. He knows his way around machinery, and we need someone like him here."

A brilliant white cockatoo landed in the spreading branches of a huge mango tree near them and squawked loudly with a voice that belied his diminutive size. "Haven't seen him since you left." Alice smiled. "I guess you're the attraction around here, not me."

Clay gave the noisy bird an annoyed glance. "Whatever. Listen, Eli is a good man. He is smart and a hard worker. I have offered him a job here in maintenance." Clay hurried on. "There is the little room in back of the hangar. He could also guard the hangar and help with fueling and routine care of the Helios. We have money in the budget for that role. Besides, he speaks Benjad's language, and they have become close."

Clay took another sip of his coffee, cooler now, but still hotter than he desired.

Alice leaned toward Clay, and her eyes narrowed slightly. "Why is it important that he has a good relationship with Benjad and that he speaks his language? Certainly Eli knows that the boy will return to his home or go to live with relatives, right?"

Clay let out a sigh, then reached across the table and took her hands.

"Look, Benjad's mother is dead. The person who killed his mother injured him badly and left him for dead as well. His father died years ago, and he has no close relatives. The people from his village are afraid of his presence. They claim he is a curse." He paused to let the news sink in, then lowered his voice, "If I had left the boy in the village, they would have killed him. I could not have done that. He has nobody." Clay stared into her eyes and did not move.

Alice sat up straight. "What are you planning on doing with the boy? There are orphanages in Jayapura. Were you considering placing him there?"

"Honey, why can't we take him in?"

There, he'd said it.

"We have no children and the probability of having some is pretty remote. He has no parents and I—" Clay had crossed a line. Too late to retract it, though.

Tears welled over the rims of Alice's eyes and rolled down her cheeks. Heat radiated up his neck. He'd reduced all those years spent visiting specialists and kneeling in prayer to one cold dismissive statement.

Such an insensitive idiot.

"Look, baby, I mean that this is an opportunity. The child needs parents. I thought you might see this as something special that God has provided."

Alice pulled her hands from Clay. Without a word, she rose and walked away.

Clay sat for several minutes, drained and discouraged. The idea of taking the boy in had been unrealistic at best, but expecting his wife to embrace the plan? He'd wanted to make her happy, yet he'd ended up hurting her instead.

His coffee had become cold. He flung the brown contents over the rail. They landed like raindrops on the stones below. He left the cup on the table and went down the steps onto the paths. He would give her time to herself. He needed time too.

# CHAPTER 13

Clay strode down the path with mindless purpose—taking care, however, to acknowledge greetings from the people of the small community so that he appeared to have nothing distracting him. Focusing on his role at the center relieved his mind, but his heart remained in the small house on the hill.

The various Papuan clans who called the expat community home amazed Clay to no end. Clans that frequently warred against each other had buried their old animosities here to work and even socialize together. The glue that had brought them to harmony was this "newfound" religion called the Christian faith. It was not a panacea—there were still frequent disagreements that polarized the different clans—but the disagreements no longer ended with a fatality, as all parties strove to find areas of mutual agreement.

Clay passed two women, one from the Dani clan and one from the Korsi clan, on the way to their gardens. They laughed and talked as they walked, balancing baskets on their heads. They smiled at Clay and gave him greetings in their own tongues.

"Good morning." Clay forced a smile and responded to each in her own language.

Most of the Papuans who had taken up residence in small villages on the shores of the lake community had found work in sundry roles in the support of the mission community. They learned about the purpose of money, and that many goods to make their lives better could be acquired with those pieces of paper from the outside.

Remembering the failing air conditioning unit that cooled a small room in the library building, Clay veered off the main path and toward the structure. He entered the building and found Don Cunningham, a linguist from California, seated at a long table with two of his language assistants going over some material.

"Morning, Don. You're getting an early start." Clay waved to the young man in his late twenties, who sat in front of a bulky Toshiba computer.

"Hey, how was your trip?" Don leaned back in the wooden chair.

"Good, with some little wrinkles. I lost another boat motor." Clay shrugged. "I really just stopped by to thank you for taking up the slack in my absence, and to check whether the AC is still working in the cool room." Clay tilted his head toward the small room at one end of the building that housed computers, printers, and valuable books.

"Seems to be working fine so far. Not cold enough to make ice cream, but good enough for midday naps under the tables." Don winked and Clay chuckled, shaking his head.

After chatting a while longer, Clay excused himself.

During his walk to the hangar, he sighted a house that would become the home of a linguistic couple, Steve and

Doris Pickman. He stopped short and stared at the vacant house.

Of course! They had been working for twenty-five years near Benjad's home village. They spoke Eli's language group. If he could speak Benjad's tongue, certainly they would too.

Clay's wheels started spinning and he resumed his walk to the airstrip. He picked up his pace, now eager to reach the hangar. He turned to the airstrip and walked purposefully toward the only extensive flat terrain near the lake.

He had to find Daryl.

Clay couldn't blame Alice for her reaction that morning. He blamed himself for being too aggressive and not giving her more time to develop a relationship with Benjad as he had done. Still, he had to find a place for the boy. Why not here with some caring Papuans with assistance from the mission community?

Clay made his way down to the airfield just as Daryl left the hangar office. Daryl looked up from his clipboard and laughed as Clay performed a series of short hops with his arms in the best kangaroo imitation.

"Does this make you homesick?"

"Sorry, mate, not in the least. The 'roos back at home are far better-looking than you are." Daryl strode forward to grasp his friend's hand.

Clay clapped him on the back, "Aw, and I've been practicing."

"Well, you failed." Daryl laughed. "Glad to see you back. I suppose now we can count on things regaining their usual chaos?"

After exchanging sufficient barbs and quips, the two men settled into a discussion about the needs for the community and the Pickmans' pending arrival. When their name came up, Clay hesitated, stared at the sky, and popped his lips.

"Oh no, I know what that means. Dr. Daryl is in the house, or rather, on the compound. Is something dancing around in the Yank's mind? Spit it out."

Clay half-smiled and then forged ahead. "When you pick up Steve and Doris from their village, could you tell them that Alice and I want to have them over for dinner after they settle in?" He knew that they would quickly immerse themselves in work if he did not get the invitation on the books.

The pilot tilted his head, "You cooking the dinner or Alice? She knows about the invite, right?"

Clay didn't hide his irritation. He had a reputation for his spontaneous invitations. He always repented and offered sincere apologies, but it would happen again, and Alice knew that. It had become a joke in the community.

He sighed, "I am sure she will be fine with it, but no, I have not had the opportunity to advise her of my thoughts."

"Oh, I thought you were with her the past twenty-four hours." Daryl shook his head. "I know how Alice likes surprises. Come to think of it, I think she is surprised that she married you."

Clay made a playful threatening fist at his friend. "Ok. You made your point. I will consult with the queen first. But I am sure she would applaud my request."

Then he became serious. "I brought back two Papuans. One is a man named Eli. He seems gifted in mechanical things, a hard worker, and very intelligent. I think he will make a good addition to the community, both as an employee and just as a good man. In fact, I am thinking that you might consider him as a ground crewman at the hangar."

It was more a statement than a request, but Daryl nodded.

"We could use a mechanical thinker like that. If you like him, I like him."

Clay paused then drew a breath and continued, "I also brought home a little boy about seven or eight. His mother was killed, and he has no family. The village on the Mamberamo has rejected him. They consider him a curse. He was injured by the same person or persons who killed his mother."

Clay tugged at his ear, a childhood habit he used in awkward moments. He looked from the ground into the pilot's focused eyes. "Daryl, he has no one. He would have died of neglect or murder if I had not removed him from the community."

Both men were quiet for a few seconds.

"And you brought him here, to go where?"

Clay shook his head, "I became kind of attached to the boy and thought that just maybe Alice and I could care for him until we could locate a good home with a couple of nationals who would adopt him."

"What you're really saying is that you told her you want to take him in permanently, but Alice is not so sure." At Clay's raised eyebrows, he continued. "Look, I know you well, my friend. Most men who have been through what you have in battle would be hardened, but you have a soft heart under that tough exterior. Don't expect Alice to take orders from tough-guy Clay."

Clay sighed. "It is not that Alice wouldn't want to take him in, but she still wants her own children. I made her pretty upset with me this morning."

Daryl patted his shoulder. "Look mate, I am guessing you were pretty blunt when you sprang this on her. Maybe she's feeling you have given up. What kind of reaction did you expect?"

The slow nod from Clay as he lowered his gaze to the ground said it all.

"Give it time. And in the meantime, I will not extend the invitation to the Pickmans for dinner. I know there is a method to your madness. I bet they are working in the same language program, and you want them to teach English to the boy." It was not a question, but an accusation. Then he added, gently, "Look, I'm doing you a favor, saving you from digging a deeper hole with Alice."

Clay nodded. "Captain Kangaroo, you are probably right this time."

Clay started to leave, then turned. "Say, why don't you bring Betty over tonight for dinner after you get back. I'll introduce you to Eli and the boy."

Daryl threw his hands up. "Didn't you hear anything I said?"

Clay quickly lifted his hands in surrender. "Okay, Okay. I will ask Alice first, then cinch it up. I just wanted to see if you were available. I'll radio you."

"Yeah, yeah, we can make it." Daryl sighed.

Clay grinned and cocked his head to one side, "Are you going to ask Betty first before you commit yourself? After all, she is an emancipated woman and might have ideas and thoughts of her own ..."

Daryl glowered. "Point taken. Look, Slippery, I know the Pickmans are on the flight schedule, but I have not heard a confirmation from them. You and I know they are stalling around, not wanting to leave their people in the village."

"They have not confirmed?"

"Let's check with them right now. Before you make plans, you will want to know if they are coming in. Right?"

"Right."

The two strode off to the radio shack and after a few attempts to reach the Pickman village, Doris's voice broke through the static. Clay stood at the shack's screened window as Daryl sat in the chair manning the radio.

"Doris, we've got you on the schedule to pick you and Steve up today and fly you back to Lake Sago. Can you confirm?" Daryl released the mic button and awaited a response, which took about 30 seconds.

Doris's voice broke the airways again. "Sorry about that, Daryl. We've had a delay on a literacy group coming in to meet with us from some surrounding villages. They didn't show and it's going to be another couple of weeks, I think. Long story short, I believe we need to delay our trip. Sorry I did not get back to you."

Daryl shrugged and looked at Clay through the screen.

Clay shook his head. "Tell them that the director is expecting them to come to the lake as soon as possible."

"You tell them that!" Daryl retorted.

Clay shook his head and entered the building. He leaned down to the mic, pressing the bar. "Doris, this is Clay. Ahhh, we are just thinking of your welfare. You and Steve need a break. It has been almost a year. Over."

"Yes, I know, and we are planning on it. We both recognize we need some down time, and after the literacy session we should be able to work in the comforts of the lake resort." She chuckled but then remembered to say "over."

Clay scored a commitment from her that they would be arriving within the month and, yes, they would be delighted to join Alice and him for dinner.

His plan was coming together.

Daryl stared at his friend. "Get out of my radio shack, you conniver!"

Clay laughed. "I know when I'm not loved. I'm gone."

Clay continued his rounds, greeting and listening to everyone he met with earnest interest and attention. Today, he spent more time on his rounds than usual, putting off his return to the house.

How could he make amends?

He rehearsed various apologetic phrases in his mind, but none seemed authentic, and they all failed to convey his feelings.

# CHAPTER 14

Across the compound, Eli and Benjad were making their rounds too. Eli, although personable and outgoing by nature, marveled at the many smiles they came across in the tiny village. It helped that the community fostered hospitality and greeted them as though they were longtime friends. The children had already informed the adults of the strangers' arrival.

He grinned at Benjad, who walked with his mouth gaping. He seemed to be used to the white-skinned, "ghostly" people who wrapped themselves in soft material. Still, the sheer number of them must be what made him act apprehensive.

Eli gasped when he rounded the corner of the building that housed the massive diesel generator. It had been isolated behind a rise and distant from the rest of the village to reduce noise pollution.

Curiosity about machinery motivated him to approach the door of the building. A slide bolt with a padlock at the top discouraged visitors. However, the padlock hung open, so Eli slid the bolt and opened the door. The noise increased tenfold. Eli stepped forward to examine the yellow Caterpillar engine while Benjad took several steps backward from the growling steel machine inside. Unable to tell whether fear or intrigue held the boy, Eli motioned him to come in and spoke, but the machine drowned out his words. Benjad advanced warily, halting in the doorway.

A lone electric bulb suspended over the beast cast an eerie pale yellow light. The boy stared at it but would not go closer. He seemed obsessed by light bulbs. Eli would have to ask him about them later.

When Eli finished examining the machine, he nodded toward Benjad in the doorway and moved toward the exit. Benjad looked only too happy to leave the presence of the clamoring beast.

Outside, they heard the voices of children at play. Their shouts and animated chatter seemed to be coming from behind the beast building. Eli followed Benjad to the rear of the building where they found a group of children playing games in a flat clearing of grass cut short.

Benjad walked toward the youths, seemingly spellbound by their activity.

"I've heard of this game, Benjad. I think it's called futbol." Eli laid his hands on Benjad's shoulders and they watched together.

Boys and girls, about sixteen of them, were running around the open field, kicking a round white object that sailed through the air and on the ground. It appeared there were two groups competing, each trying to move the object in the opposite direction.

These were the same children Benjad had met when he arrived at the lake, along with some new faces. There was the boy, Petra, who had doled out the candy, and the girl who had wanted to know his name. She played aggressively and seemed to ignore the rough contact delivered by the boys in scrapping over the ball. In fact, she shoved and hit as well as any of the boys. One of the Papuan boys approached her with great zeal and kicked the ball from under her feet. She glared at him.

In the midst of the play, Petra spotted Benjad standing on the sidelines and stood still. The pass bounced in front of his feet and continued out of bounds.

"Hey!" Robert, a tall, lanky missionary kid, shouted across the field. "Pay attention, Petra." Then he looked where Petra's eyes were directed.

Robert called, "Time! Let's take a break."

Robert and Petra walked toward Benjad while the rest of the group halted and watched the two boys approach the young Papuan. Fina recovered the ball from the sidelines and joined them. She paused as she passed near another Papuan boy whose attention was fixed on Benjad and quickly bounced the ball off the side of his head. The hit elicited a grunt from her opponent.

"Now we are even!"

He scowled at Fina as she passed.

"Benjad, is it?" Robert stopped several feet from him. Benjad nodded. The children conversed in Indonesian. Eli and Clay had been priming him with simple Indonesian and he learned quickly.

After a brief silence, Petra indicated the group on the field with a nod of his head and took the ball from Fina. "Want to play?" Robert nodded also.

Benjad remained silent, just staring at the two boys. Fina noticed the awkward silence. "He doesn't understand Bahasa Indonesian." Then she turned to him. "Do you?"

Benjad held his thumb and fore finger tightly together to indicate a small amount, "Sedikit."

"Well, come on." Robert raced off.

Fina placed her hands on her hips. "Do you even know how to play futbol?"

"Maybe not," Eli said. "But you can teach him. I know he is a fast learner, and a good athlete."

Fina looked down and softened her expression. "That's fine. We all had to learn. I learned a long time ago."

Eli hid a smile, as if she'd been on the earth for decades instead of seven or eight years.

At Benjad's questioning glance, Eli nodded. "Go ahead. You have fun." Turning to the three children, "And could you see that he gets back to Pak Clay's rumah before lunch?"

The three new playmates bobbed their heads in unison. Eli watched from the sidelines as the children rejoined their teams and started their game. They did their best to explain the objective of the game, but quickly realized that only by playing it could the boy pick up the principles.

Benjad soon learned he couldn't use his hands to pass the ball. He already had rudimentary skills in using his feet. In his village they'd often made a game of keep-away, maneuvering a coconut or homemade rattan ball using only their feet. The manufactured ball at Benjad's feet had a different feel and texture to it, but he soon adapted. The rules were confusing, but he was getting the hang of it.

He found Fina fascinating. Although young boys and girls played together in his village before puberty, girls were less physical. They tended to spend their time preparing for their roles as clanswomen, which did not call for aggressive behavior.

However, the three girls here matched the boys in roughness and competitiveness. Occasionally Fina jostled

Benjad. After a couple of times, he decided to retaliate, and sent her sprawling to the ground. The surprise on her face turned to anger. She leapt to her feet and thrust a hand into Benjad's chest. Benjad, thinking it part of this game, responded by thrusting back. Fina's eyes widened in disbelief, and she almost lost her balance again as she staggered back.

Robert leapt between the two. "Easy, Fina!"

"But he pushed me down—and I did not even have control of the ball!" Fina wailed.

"Look, he is just learning. He thinks this is the way the game is played. You can see from his face he doesn't think he did anything wrong." Robert tilted his head to the curious expression on Benjad's face.

Petra chimed in. "Yeah, Fina, he thinks futbol is played that way. He is just stronger than you." He took a step back as Fina flashed him a look of irritation.

Cora, the only other missionary girl and Robert's sister, defused the situation, speaking English. "Fina, boys will be boys, from wherever they come. They sometimes have the manners of a pig. We girls have to give them a break."

Petra snorted like a pig and ran around in small circles. This broke the tension and even Fina found it amusing. She nodded and smiled as the rest of the group laughed exuberantly.

Benjad laughed as well. He didn't understand the conversation, but Petra's pig imitation needed no translation. Afterward, the children used some elaborate pantomiming to explain when jostling was and wasn't permitted.

This strange group of children included him in a way that the children from his village had never included him.

Eli left the field, satisfied that he'd left Benjad in good hands. Children always seemed to find a way through challenges. If adults could borrow some of their social skills and wisdom, the world would be a better place.

He strode down the path returning to the center of the village already at home in this peaceful place. People greeted him warmly, as if he'd been there for years.

Two men beached their dugout. One was driving the heavy craft with powerful thrusts of his paddle. The other was culling out dead fish and casting them into the rushes so not to contaminate the fish intended for the market. Eli grinned at the boatmen as he waded out into the shallows to assist pulling the dugout ashore.

Eli's grin evaporated and he jerked erect his eyes scanning the bank. Mati Raja. This is a place for a giant croc to wait for a meal.

Eli jumped back on the bank and regained his composure. He spoke Indonesian to the men as they unloaded their boat.

"Ahh, it was a good morning, I see." Eli gestured to the contents of the buckets.

The men agreed that it had been profitable, and Eli proceeded to introduce himself. They shared their backgrounds then Eli approached the subject that was haunting him. "I hear that there is a giant saltwater croc that sometimes appears in this lake?"

The men halted their work and looked around. The older man with a bushy gray beard fixed his attention on Eli. "What? Have you seen him? Mati Raja, he is called."

"Oh no, I just heard about him from Pak Clay."

The men were visibly relieved. "Yes, I have seen him from a distance, but that was many seasons ago. I don't care to see Mati Raja up close."

The men shared stories about the giant croc. Some he thought were true, and some probably had gained weight at the many retellings.

Eli said his farewell to his new friends and resumed his walk to the carpentry shop.

At the workshop he peered through an open window and gave a low whistle. The inside had been well-equipped for carpentry, metal working, and mechanical repair. He could hardly wait to start work.

Clay walked up the slight incline toward Eli with his head down. Not wanting to risk being run over by his new boss, Eli spoke. "Pak Clay, you have a grand operation here."

Clay jerked his head upward, then smiled. "Thanks, Eli. It is the effort of many people who came before me and those who are carrying on the work at this time. Now I want to add another worker. We need a mechanic to take care of all our machinery."

He motioned Eli to come with him. "Come on. I want you to meet our shop foreman, Simson." Then he stopped short. "Where is the boy?"

"Don't worry. He is fine. He is getting to know the children through playing futbol."

"He knows how to play soccer, er, futbol?"

Eli grinned. "He is learning. Some of the children have made him their special project."

Clay breathed a sigh of relief. "Kids. They can work things out better than governments."

Eli knew that the English term "kids" referred to children, although he also knew that young goats had been given that nomenclature in English as well. How could westerners see goats as similar to children?

Clay escorted Eli back into the shop and introduced him to Mr. Simson. He left the two men to get acquainted and reminded Eli to return to the house for lunch, promising to show him the rest of the village and orient him to his potential living quarters.

"Wouldn't miss it." Eli winked. "I'm looking forward to some more of that wonderful cooking."

He watched Clay head back down the path, his shoulders still slumped. He'd never seen Clay so preoccupied.

# CHAPTER 15

Anache sorted the wash, taking advantage of the brilliant midmorning sunshine before the inevitable afternoon showers. She squatted on the stones of the back patio separating colors, darks and lights into three tubs. One tub contained a washboard, lukewarm water, and an imported Australian detergent. She needed no bleach. The sun would take care of that task.

She scrubbed, shooting occasional glances upward at Alice, who had retreated to the deck attached to her bedroom. Anache hid her concern by humming while she worked. She had lived and worked with the Burris household for years, and the close contact had given her more than a glimpse into their private lives. The typically upbeat Alice rarely gave in to moodiness. Upon Pak Clay's return from his village trips she tended to dance about the house.

Anache held a genuine interest in Western culture and held the Burris marriage in high regard as a Christian model. She dreamed of finding a mate who shared similar values.

This behavior, however, had her stumped. What could have happened?

Anache stood and deftly balanced on one bare foot as she used her other to scratch a pesky mosquito bite on her calf. She stole another glance, but quickly averted her eyes when Alice looked her way. She picked up a cheap plastic basket filled with soiled clothes from Clay's recent excursion, dumped the contents into the tub of water, and crouched down again with the washboard.

Up on the deck, Alice watched a cockatoo in a nearby mango tree belting out a raucous alarm. The white bird had raised his feather comb as he hopped from one foot to another, repeating his warning. She searched for the cause of its agitation but saw only thick green foliage.

Probably a snake sunning himself.

He is really in no danger—he can fly away. Alice sighed. What about me? Am I seeing or hearing something that also is not there?

"Be anxious for nothing." Words from that morning's Bible reading swirled around her mind. Alice wrung her hands. The boy's needs are the important issue, not mine.

"Oh, Lord, please forgive my selfishness."

Alice pulled herself from the chair and smiled weakly at Anache as she saw the house helper steal another look at her. Anache flashed a full grin back without breaking her rhythm on the washboard.

Alice reentered the house. She needed to prepare for Clay's return.

On the futbol field, Benjad was catching on to the game, and he'd translated quite a few new phrases through association and guessing. Physically, what he lacked in skill, he made up for in enthusiasm. As the sun's rays baked the athletes, the children slowed their pace, except Benjad.

"Time out!" Fina shouted, and the players retreated to a banana grove to escape the harsh sun.

Fina rummaged under some banana leaves and pulled out a red jug and a plastic sack containing small paper cups and a box of cookies. The kids all sat, jockeying for a position near Fina. Benjad could tell she controlled the treats. He looked from face to admiring face. They surely looked up to her.

Fina pulled the plastic cups from the sack with a dramatic flair and addressed the group. They all nodded. Although he could only make out a word here and there Benjad sat mesmerized, drawn to her coy smile and the way she commanded their attention.

Fina poured the drink from the red jug, which she called a thermos. Benjad noticed that the thermos rattled as she poured. A couple of clear square rock-like formations plopped into the cup along with the blood red liquid.

After filling the cup, Fina thrust the cup toward Benjad. He had been taught it was impolite for a guest to refuse anything offered. However, he hesitated to drink what looked like blood with floating rocks.

Surely the cup was not filled with blood. No children would be allowed such a thing.

The floating rocks rattled as Fina shook the cup in front of him. His hesitation must have embarrassed her, judging from the frown on her face.

Robert tipped his head back and laughed. He pointed to the cup. "Kool aid." He made a drinking motion. "Go ahead, Benjad. Fina did not make it. Her mother did, so it is not poison."

Fina gave Robert a dirty look as he grinned at her.

Benjad understood Robert wanted him to accept the drink. He took the cup, studying the contents. Their eyes were all on him and he steeled himself to take a sip of the bloody rocks. He tilted the cup and the unfamiliar liquid rolled over his lips and tongue.

What was this? The liquid and rocks were colder than anything he had known, even the pudding Clay had brought him at the clinic. Evidently coldness could come in many forms.

His raised his eyebrows and poked the ice cubes with his finger. They bobbed up and down. And the sweetness! Certainly not blood.

Benjad lifted his head and grinned at Fina and the rest of the children. He repeated the word he had learned in Indonesian for thank you, "Terima kasih!"

The children started chuckling. Benjad joined in on their amusement. He had learned a new game, lots of new words, and had found a new taste. Most of all, he had discovered new friends.

Then the cookies came out and Benjad showed no reluctance to accept that offer.

"You better stay alert, Benjad." Petra said. "Fina might be trying to get you to relax so she can have a chance to really poison you!"

Fina lightly punched Petra's shoulder and he rolled on the ground as if he were mortally wounded. The group laughed loudly. Benjad did not know what Petra had said, but he understood that they were teasing Fina, so he joined them in their laughter.

Petra rose stiffly and looked around. "We have time before lunch to finish the game."

Bejnad knew "the game." It was all he needed to hear.

All the children joined him and rushed to the field and began their game, refreshed.

It seemed they had only begun to play again when he saw Robert stop, hold up his arm, and study the bracelet on his arm.

He looked up from the curious bracelet and said, "Well, it's lunch time."

Benjad had seen men in the Korean camp wear similar bracelets on their arms. The Koreans frequently consulted them before they started an activity. So, when Robert framed his decision based on the apparatus for lunch, Benjad understood that this metallic thing had advised all of them that they were hungry. He did not know how the instrument knew that, but it was correct. Perhaps the instrument related somehow to the one that shared his bedroom. It had similar markings and tiny sticks that rotated.

Robert evidently controlled the little demon on his arm. Perhaps he could learn to control the demon in his bedroom.

Benjad hesitated as the rest of the children picked up sandals, snack containers, and other items, then moved off to their respective homes. Robert turned to Benjad. "Come on. My house is near yours."

"Mine too," Fina contributed.

The three left the playing field and walked along the beaten path toward Clay's house. They chatted in

Indonesian and included Benjad in the conversation as much as they could. Fina and Robert asked questions about Benjad's past. Unfortunately, or fortunately, Benjad still struggled with the language.

They parted company at the path to Pak Clay's home. Benjad climbed the steps to the back of the house, lured by the pleasant aroma of frying meat.

"Come in!" Anache motioned to him from the doorway with a spatula in her hand. "Are you hungry?"

Benjad did not need to be encouraged anymore. "Yes, Ibu."

Alice entered the room and gave him a warm smile. "Come on. Let's get washed up." She extended her hand and he took it. The disturbance of the air as she moved floated her fragrance to his nostrils. She always seemed to have a flowery essence. He found her closeness comforting.

They walked down the hallway to the bathroom.

Alice placed a stopper in the sink and ran some water into the bowl. Before she could stop Benjad he thrust his hands into the water expecting coolness to greet him.

"Yow!" Benjad exclaimed, more out of surprise than pain. The water felt like fire.

"Ooh, darling." Alice grabbed his hands. "Panas! I should have warned you."

She turned the other tap. "Here, we make it comfortable like this." She added cool water then allowed him to experiment with the taps to adjust the temperature.

When his hands were clean, Benjad took the towel she offered, not sure what to do with it. After a few awkward moments, he offered it back. Alice playfully seized both his hands and the towel and rubbed them vigorously together, "A drying we will go, a drying we will go . . ."

She looked into the mirror and saw Clay standing behind them in the doorway with a strange grin on his face. Alice's face reddened.

"How long have you been standing there?" She laid her hands on Benjad's shoulders and gently steered him toward the doorway.

Clay stopped her and Benjad watched their gazes lock.

"I am sorry for laying this on you the way I did." Clay bit his lip slightly.

Alice stepped closer to him. "Shh. I'm the one who is sorry." She kissed him.

Benjad wondered at the interplay. These were strange people, always wanting to press their mouths together. However, just watching Alice and Clay kissing gave him a sense of security.

But for now, he had seen enough. He uttered a simple question in Indonesian. "Eat now?"

They both chuckled. Alice sighed, "Little man, or big man. Food is their main focus."

Clay stuck his chin in the air and announced, "Come on—yes, we eat now."

That evening after supper, Alice watched as Benjad drew illustrations using his newfound skill with crayons and paper. She smiled at Benjad's efforts in the living room to capture his new home in pictures.

Oh my! Did I really think that? His new home.

She turned to observe her husband as she washed dishes and he dried them. The focus on drying caused his sun-burned features to knit in concentration. The last plate clattered into the cabinet, and he turned.

"You must be the most helpful husband that ever lived," said Alice.

Clay bobbed his head from side to side. "I learned to listen to my forefather, Adam—even though it did not work out well for him. When the woman speaks, you must listen."

"You toot! I'll get Benjad ready for bed."

Alice playfully swatted Clay's backside as she passed by him on the way to the living room.

"Are you ready for bed?" she asked.

Benjad looked at her with sleepy eyes and nodded.

# CHAPTER 16

Alice stood in the hallway watching Benjad. Over the past month, Benjad had gradually adapted to his new life. He ate a lot of food. More than she thought healthy. Eli had explained that since Benjad had grown up in a land of feast or famine, he likely worried that the cornucopia of food would disappear, so he made it a point to gorge himself whenever food appeared on the table. His greatest vice seemed to be pork and beef fat. She knew the Papuans relished the fat, something rare on wild-caught game, but she could not wrap her mind around the attraction.

She had tried to limit how much he consumed at one meal by serving smaller portions and warning him that if he ate too much, he would become sick. Still, he ate like a horse.

Today it rained, and Benjad had stayed in the house, as had his playmates in their own homes. Alice approached the boy as he squatted in the middle of the living room, immersed in playing with a wind-up train set on an oval track Clay had given to him. A missionary couple had left the toy behind.

Alice watched the boy, who evidently had not seen her yet, as he stared intently at the miniature toy that raced around the track making a clacking noise. He had perfected the winding process and repeatedly recharged the locomotive by turning a key. Benjad seemed proud of this newly acquired winding skill. Eli told them his village environment had been devoid of wheels requiring circular motions. Thrusting and pulling seemed to be the routine dynamic action there.

"Ahem." Alice didn't want to startle him. "Benjad, let me talk to you for a moment. Then you can continue." He had made incredible progress in both Indonesian, compliments of Eli, and English, through his home life.

He watched as she sat cross-legged on the floor across from him.

He looked up at her with questioning eyes, and she chose her words with care. "Benjad, we have some visitors coming to our house tonight. They are very nice people."

She paused, not knowing how to communicate the next thought. "Um, you need to be polite to them and well-behaved. That means no scratching, eating fast, grabbing food, or burping." Alice acted out the related behavior for each instruction.

Benjad looked puzzled.

He smiled and duplicated her demonstration enthusiastically.

To her chagrin, Alice recognized the miscommunication, "Oh no, no, these are things that you do not do." She shook her head and waved her hands palms down in a circular motion like a pair of erasers.

"Oh, never mind, sweetie. I guess you will catch on soon enough. Just so you know we have guests coming for dinner. Their names are Steve and Doris, Daryl and Betty."

Benjad recognized the word "dinner."

There will be more feasting tonight.

Why was she reminding him to eat well and pass air from his throat to compliment the food served? Did she think he had no knowledge of polite behavior? Was he a sago grub?

He determined that he would not lose face, nor cause her to lose face by forgetting to use his manners—he turned his attention back to the train set.

Clay had shown him a magazine photo with a train in it. This strange machine had stopped and people were standing beside it, but there were also some people inside! How fascinating that somewhere there were men and women who were small enough to be able to get inside the train. He looked at the reverse side of the page, but no one appeared. It seems they had magically disappeared and would reappear when he flipped the page back.

These little people were smaller than he was. He could be a great warrior if he went where they lived and fought them.

An older man and woman arrived at dinnertime, bringing loud, joyful chaos into the house with them. Benjad stood in the living room, a little uncertain, as Clay and Alice welcomed them warmly. Alice pointed a finger at them repeating their names—Steve and Doris. A few moments later, Pak Daryl and his wife Betty arrived. Benjad knew Pak Daryl. Pak Clay had brought him to the place where the big bird lived and Pak Daryl talked with him. He found Daryl a bit intimidating because he had the magic to control the big bird. He had watched Pak Daryl crawl into it and make the big bird leap into the sky with great noise.

The guests' behavior at the dinner party confused Benjad. They laughed and talked when they should have been focusing on feasting. His people, even in celebratory times, focused on the food when it came time to eat, considering it rude to talk while partaking of a meal. Plenty of opportunity would come to talk and share stories after bellies had been filled.

The time for sitting down to dinner came none too soon for Benjad. After someone said grace (that one-sided conversation to the food), he accepted a platter of fish from Alice, seated next to him. He was busily trying to disengage the flaky meat from the rib cage when the man named Steve, who had been watching him, spoke.

"Benjad, did you eat much fish in your village?"

Benjad froze, and his eyes opened a little wider as he looked at Steve. This white, wrinkled man had spoken to him in his language. The man smiled as he returned Benjad's look. How had this man come to speak his language?

"You know my language. Did you know my mother and father, Kalita and Drako?"

The dinner table quieted. All eyes were on the boy and the elderly man. The two other couples did not know what was being said, but they knew the dialogue was sincere and heard the boy evidently asking an earnest question.

Steve responded gently, "I learned your language from some people who were from another village near yours. And, no, little one, sadly I did not know your mother and father." He paused to let this sink in and then added, "But I would like you to tell me about them sometime in the days to come."

Doris smiled and nodded, brushed some stray gray hairs that had escaped from her headband, and reached across the table to pat the boy's hand. "Yes, we would both like to learn about them from you." She spoke his language too.

After dinner, the adults, except Steve Pickman, seated themselves in the living room to chat. Steve had noticed a checkerboard on a corner table. He invited the Papuan to sit on the floor and told him he would teach him a new game.

Benjad sat and watched the old man slowly lower his body, wincing as he folded his legs. When they were eye-to-eye, the man said, "Now we play."

He caught on to this strange game called checkers in a short time, pulling off a win in the sixth game. Steve clapped loudly.

"I think we have a budding checkers champion on our hands!"

Nobody had ever clapped for Benjad before. A strange warmth rose in his heart. He whispered, "Terima kasih." But his simple thank you seemed too small for such a hearty celebration.

For the first time, he believed that this village of white people accepted him and had no ulterior motives. When Alice announced his bedtime, Benjad said a polite good night to the guests and told Steve he hoped they could talk again.

Before settling on the floor with his linens, Benjad made sure to turn the glowing eye of the clock around where it could not watch him, thus ensuring an undisturbed slumber.

Clay led his guests out onto the porch where they could talk without disturbing Benjad in his bedroom.

"So, what did I tell you, Steve? Quite a young man, is he not?"

"Yes, indeed."

The Australian pilot seated to Clay's right leaned close to him whispering, "Get that smug look off yer face, Slippery."

Clay spread his hands in innocent pretense whispered back, "What? I just know things. Yankee ingenuity."

Daryl shook his head and chuckled.

Clay cleared his throat and assumed a serious look. "Steve, you and Doris speak the language of Benjad?"

"Well, we do speak a related language."

Clay ignored his response and continued. "Look, the boy has no family and has been rejected by his community. They were going to kill him, I am sure."

Doris gasped. "Kill him?"

"Well, probably by marginalizing and not caring for him. Possibly starvation. And there is a shaman who wanted to obliterate him."

"What is going to happen to him now?" Steve inquired.

"We are not sure, but we would like to give him a chance. We will take care of his physical needs, but I would like you and Doris to consider helping to educate him. You know his language and culture, and you need to stay out of the village for some recuperation time anyway. You can continue your language work here in the comfort of the community."

Clay thought for a moment. "Listen, you are both models for serving the Lord. But God wants us to make sure we take care of ourselves. Alice got the reports back from blood and stool samples. I hate to lay this on you, but you both have malaria, giardia, and dysentery, and you need to treat this. You haven't taken a furlough in four years. You can stay here, work with your helpers, and regain your health. Alice will help you get whole again. You can still take short trips out to your village to check on things and let your helpers get back to their families. What'dya say? You'll be helping your program and Benjad."

Steve leaned back in his chair and stroked his chin as all eyes stayed on him.

"Seems like a plan. What do you think, Doris?"

"He is a sweet boy, and we can help."

Steve nodded at Doris and turned to Clay. "When do you want to start?"

"Tomorrow!"

All laughed except Clay.

"Dear, let these folks get unpacked first." Alice chided.

"Okay, okay. Patience is not one of my virtues."

"You can say that again!" Daryl chimed in.

The laughter again came at Clay's expense.

However, Clay sat back, satisfied. He had communicated the need, and Steve and Doris had risen to the challenge. They talked for over an hour before all the conspirators on behalf of Benjad ended their discussions and ultimately outlined a plan of action.

The next morning, Benjad ate breakfast and hurried off to meet his friends at the soccer field. To his puzzlement, he discovered no one there. While walking back up the path, he met Eli leaving the generator building, wiping his greasy hands on a rag.

"Benjad, I have not seen you for a day or two. How have you been?" He spoke first in Indonesian and then repeated it in Benjad's tongue.

Glad to see Eli, Benjad responded in halting Indonesian. "Pak Eli, how are you? I have been busy. But now I am not busy."

Eli did a double-take and opened his mouth in exaggerated surprise. "Wah! You are speaking Indonesian like President Suharto!"

Benjad did not know who that was, but assumed that the named individual spoke fluent Indonesian, so he grinned at his former caregiver. "Thank you. I have been learning from Pak Clay, Ibu Alice, Ibu Anache and my friends."

"Oh, you have friends now?" Eli winked.

"Oh, yes, I was to, to ..." the child knitted his brow as he searched for the appropriate word.

"To meet them." Eli supplied the rest of the sentence.

"Yes, yes, but they are hilang."

"Lost?" Eli smiled at the boy's choice of words. "No, they are not lost. Robert, Cora, and Fina have school in their homes, and Petra and the others are attending the government school now."

Benjad filtered the word school through his meager Indonesian dictionary, trying to ascertain what kind of game Eli described. A few seconds elapsed, then he spoke. "They did not invite me to play. I think they know I cannot play school."

Eli laughed. Benjad felt heat rise up his neck.

"No, Benjad, it is not a game. School is where people go to learn things. They learn to read and write and increase their knowledge so when they grow up, they can work and live among many people who are in this world."

Benjad looked up into his eyes and proclaimed, "Then, I want to do school so I can learn how to grow up with my friends."

Eli led Benjad over to a stump by the path. Instinctively, they both checked for ants or hostile insects. Benjad sat.

"I need to tell you more about this thing called school."

Benjad listened attentively while Eli spoke, and he frequently interjected questions. By the time they finished, he wanted to go to school more than ever. He returned to his house to discover Steve and Doris seated on the veranda with Clay and Alice enjoying conversation and tea.

"Hey, Benjad!" Clay beckoned. "You have returned at the right time. Steve and Doris are here to see you."

The two linguists smiled a greeting and Steve spoke in his mother tongue. "Good morning. I hoped I would see you again this morning, but I knew you had important things to do."

"I went looking for my friends, but they are all doing school." Benjad sat in an open chair.

Clay cleared his throat. "Benjad, about school, do you understand the meaning of school?"

"Yes," he said proudly. "Eli told me all about school."

Alice interjected, "Would you like to go to school the same as your friends?"

Surprised by Alice's words, Benjad could only nod. Then Steve twisted his position in his chair and leaned forward. "Would you allow Doris and me to introduce you to school?"

Benjad grasped the Indonesian meaning from the context and again nodded vigorously. "So, you would teach me to play checkers better. Maybe other games?"

There were peals of laughter from the group and Steve said, "Yes, among other things you will learn." Then he made a serious face and switched to Benjad's mother tongue. "You will have to work hard if you want to succeed. There is much you need to learn to become a man."

"I will work hard. I already know many things that I need to know to be a man." Benjad crossed his arms.

"I am sure you do know many things. What you will learn in school are things you never learned in your village. However, these other things you need to learn are important if you are to live in this village and other villages. In time, you will understand."

After speaking briefly with Clay and Alice, the Pickmans took their leave. Alice extended a plate of mango and papaya left from the morning refreshments to Benjad, and he accepted. It had been almost an hour since breakfast, and he felt empty.

Benjad looked up from his fruit plate long enough to fill them in on his latest news.

"Eli said I am speaking Indonesian good."

The boy moved to a corner of the veranda to watch a cat ferret out a mouse under a log. While he watched, he stuffed himself with mangoes.

Clay and Alice sat quietly, conversing in English.

"He doesn't really know what's in store for him," Clay said.

"What choice does he have?" Alice smiled. "I think he is just in survival mode."

"For now, yes. But he will do more than survive. Just give him time and he will excel. I am certain of that."

Benjad wiped an arm across his mouth, and Clay grinned as Alice leaned toward him with a napkin. He knew they both wanted the boy to do more than survive. He had shown a gift for learning languages, and Clay hoped it would continue in English. Benjad needed life skills for a world beyond the village. Language could help him acquire a great part of those needed skills.

Glancing at his watch, Clay said, "Listen, I have to go down to the hangar for the translators' check-in. I had to send Daryl yesterday to make a flyover and check on Dave and Angel when they did not come up on their radio. Turns out their batteries were bad. They signaled Daryl by using tarps on the runway. Daryl is air-dropping some fresh batteries as we speak, and they should be up and running by check-in time."

Alice nodded and walked with him to the steps to the veranda, where they paused and lightly kissed. Benjad watched, then shrugged and resumed his snacking.

Alice turned to Benjad. "You can go out and play, but tomorrow you start school."

Benjad acknowledged both bits of information and hurried down the steps onto the path. Clay and Alice smiled at each other.

"See you at lunch," Clay said. Then, grabbing his baseball cap from the rail, he trotted down the steps.

The Aussie pilot circled above the grass airstrip. Clay knew he had to ensure there were no pigs, dogs, or people to interfere with his landing. A pilot could forgive pigs (they don't fly), and overlook dogs intent on sniffing out a potential meal, but Clay never understood why people did not comprehend the danger to themselves and the aircraft. They thought nothing of crossing the airstrip while a plane took off or landed.

Clay had spent a great deal of time trying to teach people to stay off the airstrip and keep their livestock off it too. He once refused to fly out a fish cargo for the market because people wouldn't keep their dogs and pigs off the runway. After that they cooperated for a good length of time.

Daryl had been fortunate in his many takeoffs and landings. He had only had one mishap, when a suicidal chicken darted in front of his plane as he took off and flew directly into the prop, covering the windshield in a mass of blood and gore. This had occurred in a remote mountainside village where flights into the village were rare. Daryl told Clay he now made sure to buzz the airfield before landing to warn all trespassers.

Clay walked out of the hangar to greet the airman as the bouncing craft slowed and the propeller grudgingly rotated to a stop. The clicking of the hot engine became lost amid the insect orchestra.

Daryl opened the door, stuck out his long legs, and slid to the ground. He removed his headset and hung it on the steering yoke, then thrust his hand back inside, retrieving his signature Aussie hat, his clipboard, and his logbook.

Clay approached the pilot, who stood by the craft busily making notations. "You get the batteries dropped?"

Daryl halted the exercise and straightened. "Slippery, I am fine, thank you. No troubles, and, yes, I delivered the batteries, as I am a responsible person."

The pilot's sarcasm came through loud and clear. "Okay, sorry about being so pointed. I guess I've worked around you too long."

"Grace and peace be to you, my son. I forgive you."

"I can survive without your absolution." Clay laughed.

Behind a palm tree, fifty yards from the hangar, Benjad squatted. He had seen the strange machine take off and land several times since he had been at the village. It always fascinated him. However, it scared him as well.

How can such a big machine jump into the air and fly like a bird? How can one man control it like Pak Daryl? He can't be a spirit because he grasped my hand the night we feasted. His hand was warm, so he is human like Clay.

Benjad watched the men for a while, trying to ignore the heat of the late morning sun. Clay entered the hangar and Daryl took a bucket of water with white foam and proceeded to give the mechanical bird a bath. Eli joined him. They talked briefly and then Eli drew another piece of cloth from the bucket and helped bathe the bird.

That bird must like the attention it receives.

Benjad stood and inched toward the men, keeping a watchful eye on the bird. If it accepted Eli and Daryl as friends, perhaps it would extend friendship to him.

The sun glistening off the lake caught his eye and he paused. Then again, the heat was nearly unbearable. A swim at the lake might cool him off. He looked back and forth, from the bird to the lake path, and then convinced himself that a swim should take priority. He trotted back down the path to the beckoning lake.

Benjad wished his new friends could join him. He liked his strange new acquaintances. He found Robert especially interesting. And Fina, although a girl, impressed him with her athletic skills. She treated him nicely too, most of the time.

The lake looked inviting, like one of Fina's cold drinks. Benjad stood on the dock, appreciating the scene before him.

A little way offshore in a cluster of water hyacinths, Mati Raja watched the boy approach the water. The croc had returned to the lake after he had satisfied his primal urge to mate. Now he wanted to sustain his massive appetite. Waterfowl, smaller crocs, and wandering village dogs that paraded along the shore—they'd be easy prey, but the small boy on the pier held his attention now.

He lay with only his eyes, upper snout, and nostrils showing about sixty yards from the pier, invisible to all but the most discerning creatures. The croc slowly turned his body so he could use his good eye to study his potential meal. Despite his huge body's maneuvers, he generated no sound, and no ripples.

Benjad debated whether to shed all his clothes to swim or keep his shorts on, even though wet shorts were uncomfortable. He decided to keep his shorts on in respect for ways of this new culture that had accepted him. He discarded only the T-shirt on the pier and then assessed the shallow water. No point risking a bloody skull. He leapt into the water, feet-first.

The water enveloped him in a cool embrace. Benjad turned to float on his back, listening as the birds sang and chirped, accompanied by the buzz of a saw in the lakeside carpentry shop, forming a musical backdrop interrupted only by his splashes.

Such a calming escape from the strangeness of his new life.

Across the lake, the watching eye of the reptile saw the boy's splash and reflexively inched his rough gray body forward in the shallow mud. Because of his size, Mati Raja had learned to be patient and move slowly toward his prey. Only when he came within striking distance would this hulking killing machine cast stealth to the wind. Then it would be too late for the hapless victim to escape.

Back at the house, Alice had finished filling a blue plastic shopping bag with slices of banana cream pie in Tupperware containers brought from the States. She headed down the steps, planning to meet Clay at the hangar to bring him a snack. Certain that Benjad would be on her path as she made her way to the hangar, she had packed a snack for him as well.

She would stop at the carpentry shop on the way, in case Clay had finished his radio schedule early and moved to the shop.

As soon as she saw the lake, Alice noticed the dark-skinned boy shimmering as he frolicked in the water. The hair on the back of her neck bristled.

Something was wrong.

The air stilled, and except for the splashing of water and sporadic subdued buzzing from the shop, she heard no sound that could account for this unease ...

The birds were quiet. Yes, that was it!

In the lake, a large creature was cutting a 'V' in the water, heading directly toward Benjad. Time seemed to stand still before an uncontrollable scream escaped her lungs.

"Benjad! Benjad get out of the water!"

The basket fell from her hands as she sprinted down the path to the dock. Her heart pounded as she watched the semi-submerged leviathan closing the gap to Benjad.

At her scream, Benjad stopped swimming and treaded water. He scanned the shore and spotted Alice racing down the trail.

Alice frantically waved toward the water and screamed again. "Behind you, behind you!"

Alice became aware of running steps overtaking her. As the runner swept by her, she saw only Clay's back. His long strides outdistanced hers.

In the lake, a puzzled Benjad had now turned to see what Alice's frantic behavior was all about. The grayish shape looked like a huge log cutting the water toward him. It took only a split-second to identify the threat. He sucked in his breath, ingesting a little water with it. Fear seized his stomach. He coughed out the water. His survival instinct kicked in and he began to swim with deep, fast strokes accompanied by strong kicks. The pier looked far away, but he had to reach it.

The croc surfaced, exposing all twenty feet-plus of his muscular body.

Benjad did not waste time looking back. If the croc traded stealth for speed, Benjad couldn't hope to out-swim him. He pulled as hard as he could toward the makeshift wooden ladder attached to the front corner of the dock. He'd nearly reached the ladder when something bumped his foot, sending ripples of terror sweeping through him. Surely the long teeth were about to crush his legs.

With his last ounce of energy, he propelled himself through the small opening between the rough pier post and the ladder. Immediately, he heard a violent crash behind him, and the entire pier shook. Benjad finally turned to look. The croc, too big to fit through the small opening, had rammed the dock and ladder with his gaping mouth, causing the whole structure to shudder and groan.

Clay hit the dock and slowed briefly to scoop up a boat hook. He had witnessed the close call between the croc and the boy, but he couldn't tell where Benjad had gone. He ran to the edge of the pier, searching for the child. Reflexively, he jumped back when the beast broke the water's surface with an enormous thrust upward, his head rising a couple of feet over the quivering dock. Despite his fear, a strange sense of relief washed over Clay at the sight of the cavernous empty mouth and rows of sharp teeth.

Clay thrust the boat hook into the gaping maw of the carnivore with all this strength. The hook hit solidly on a five-inch tooth, glancing off into the soft palate before the crocodile snapped his jaws closed.

Mati Raja shook his head from side to side, wrenching the shaft of the hook from Clay's hands. The protruding shaft slammed against the upright post of the dock and snapped into two pieces. With the croc preoccupied by the oversized toothpick, Clay spun around to the opposite side of the dock, dropped to his knees and searched for the little boy. Benjad's head surfaced, coughing and sputtering, his eyes wide.

"Got you!" Clay seized one of Benjad's arms and yanked him from the water like a hooked fish. When Benjad's feet hit the deck, his rescuer did not stop to assess his condition, but grabbed the boy in his arms and raced off the dock to solid ground.

The croc had managed to free himself of the remaining half of the boathook. He circled the dock and appeared on the opposite side in search of his young prey. Clay, knowing the croc could continue an assault on land, did not stop running until he reached the main path and thrust the boy into the waiting arms of Alice, then spun around to locate the killer.

Alice clutched Benjad to her chest and sobbed, checking the boy over with her eyes and hands. "Honey, you all right? You okay?" She kissed him on the forehead.

The boy gasped, still trying to catch his breath. Clay, satisfied that the threat was terminated, knelt with Alice and the boy, but remained vigilant.

The three huddled forms on the hillside path watched from a safe distance. Mati Raja raged and returned to the other side of the dock searching for either the boy or the man who had assaulted him. Clay could not be sure who was the object of his search. Finally, they watched as the angry croc hissed and slid backward under the surface. Only a few bubbles and disturbed ripples testified to what had happened there.

"You're safe now." Clay whispered into Benjad's wet hair.

Benjad pulled himself from Alice's embrace, looked from Alice to Clay, and let the emotions welling up within him escape.

"Terima kasih." His voice broke. He wrapped his arms around Clay's neck, sobbing.

Alice's eyes filled with tears as Clay looked at her over the shoulder of the clinging child. "I guess we are a family now," she said.

# CHAPTER 17

Shaka pushed aside the foliage downriver from the Kota village. A small clearing revealed itself with a small thatched hut in the center. In front of the hut was a pole stuck in the ground with a weathered human skull atop it.

The man surveyed his surroundings and allowed himself a small smile as he rested his one good eye on the leering skull.

*Ahh. It is as I left it. No one will enter this territory and touch what is mine.*

"My friend, you have done your job well."

The shaman took special pride in the skull. The owner had succumbed to his curse long ago and died an agonizing death by the bite of a death adder. He had angered Shaka by refusing to do his bidding. He had forgotten the specific offense, but he remembered his refusal to obey.

Now, he continued to serve Shaka in guarding his goods and his special place where he communed with the spirits.

Shaka grunted. "No time to waste."

With a glance at the hut, the big man strode to the tree and peered into the branches. Two buckets camouflaged with leaves and suspended by a vine over a branch remained undisturbed. The other end of the vine was tied to the buckets and secured to the tree trunk.

The shaman dropped the string bag he carried on his shoulder and proceeded to untie the vine and lower the buckets to the ground.

When he bent over to open a bucket, pain shot through his empty eye socket. He gritted his teeth and slipped a finger under the crocodile-leather patch to wipe out the pus excreted by his wounded eye. His magic potions had not been able to stem the infection. He realized he had to find an outsider from beyond the great waters to give him back a pain-free life. That was tomorrow's business. But tonight was the time for summoning the spirit world to place vengeance on his enemies. He would start with the boy who had taken the light from his eye.

Shaka returned to his efforts to remove the lid from the bucket and ignored the pain in his head. The bucket was well sealed to prevent moisture and marauding ants from reaching the contents.

He worked his fingers around the stubborn lid until it gave way to his strength and popped loose. The contents were also just as he had left them.

He removed the items and laid them on the ground. When he finished, he admired his display of boar's tusk with a cord, human teeth, feathers, several candy tins containing dried mushrooms and other plants. He pulled a notebook out of the bucket and paused. He opened the book and looked at the scrawled letters in the pages. On the first few pages, there was his name written over and over again. Shaka nodded his head at the progress he had made on writing his name in Indonesian. He would spend some time tomorrow with the government teacher, Widoba, in the village of Darma. He had learned much about reading and writing, but he needed more to fit into the outsiders' world.

Shaka squatted and imagined what he would do with the power he gained. He already had gained power in his community and surrounding villages. But the outside world had riches beyond his reach.

I will one day live in both worlds. I will have power in both worlds.

Shaka remembered what he had brought to add to the operation in casting spells. He opened the string bag and removed a bamboo hair pick. It had belonged to Kalita, the devil woman he had killed. He had given it to one of his wives in the village. He would use that to curse Kalita's ghost, who interfered with his plans.

Another thought entered his mind. Since my wife has used this pick, the curse might plague her too. No matter, I have other wives.

It was getting dark. Shaka removed the coil of rattan with sticks on each end from his bag, along with some dried grass. Using another short, dried stick from the bucket, he uncoiled the fire-starter and placed it under the dry stick with the grass tinder and stood on the ends of the stick. He began a brisk sawing back and forth with the uncoiled rattan. In a few minutes, wisps of smoke floated upwards. The smoke gave way to small flames. Shaka threw the coil aside and cupped the tinder and stick. He blew on it gently until he had the fire going.

After gathering additional firewood, he arranged the contents of both the bucket and what he had brought in his bag in order of need. It was important to have everything ready when he was in the heat of frenzied spirit summoning. The sun had already slipped below the jungle trees and the flickering firelight made the grinning skull come alive.

Satisfied with everything in place, he reached in his bag and brought out a hollow gourd filled with palm wine. Conscious of the pain in his head, he ate a handful of mushrooms and washed it down with liquid.

*May the spirits of my ancestors reward me with the breaking of the spell of Kalita, the death of her son ... if he isn't already dead ... and the death of the white devil who rescued him. Give me success for my plans.*

A sense of floating was erasing Shaka's pain. He pulled a wooden bowl from the bucket and placed a variety of plants in it. The man hovered over the bowl and rocked back and forth on his haunches. He removed the big knife from his belt and drew the blade across the palm of his left hand. Blood flowed and he dripped it into the bowl.

*Someone is humming. It is me! The fire, it is brightening. Now it begins.*

Shaka rocked harder. He tilted his head upward and laughed.

Shaka awoke the next morning with the sun peeking over the treetops splashing onto his face. He had not made it to the interior of his hut and the sleeping mat. As the fog rose from his brain, he became aware of himself curled up in the position with mosquitoes feasting on his body.

His one eye began to focus, and his breathing came in ragged doses. The shaman sat up and held his pounding head in his hands. As he looked at his immediate surroundings, the night before returned. Only partially though. The fire was now ashes and the various artifacts for spell casting were scattered around the campfire's perimeter.

*Yes, I was talking with the spirits. They will do my bidding. It is worth the pain.*

Shaka glanced at the knife wound in the palm of his hand. It was sensitive but had scabbed over. He lunged to his feet, and the effort made his head swirl. The gourd that had been full of palm wine lay on its side like a sleeping drunk. He bent over and snatched it, lifting it to his lips for the last drops.

*I have to get going. My plan cannot bloom until I get to Darma. I hope Widoba is there.*

Shaka raked some still-warm ashes from the fire into the wooden bowl that had been used for mystical purposes the evening before. He trotted to the riverbank and stripped off his shorts and the ragged T-shirt he wore. He waded out to just below his waist and began washing. Once wet, he dipped his fingers into the bowl that floated next to him and proceeded to smear his body with ashes. It relieved itching mosquito bites and helped to cleanse oils and sweat from his body. He rinsed off and returned to his campsite.

Shaka approached the other bucket that had hung from the tree and struggled to remove the lid. He peered into the bucket and removed a pair of cotton pants and a batik shirt with Papuan decorative designs. Donning them, he looked into the bucket once more, removed a pair of rubber sandals, and slipped them on.

Shaka replaced articles he had used in casting spells in one bucket, then raised both buckets back into the tree by the vine and tied it off. He picked up his string bag and slung it over his shoulder. Looking around the area he observed that the skull was no longer on the pole, and the cassowary bone knife was lying a good distance from it. He frowned, then a grin creased his face.

*The spirits danced with me. It is well.*

Shaka replaced the skull on the pole and thrust the bone back through the eye socket. He took two steps back, nodded his satisfaction, and spun to find the path near the river.

*I must hurry. The sun will be high in the sky. There will be food in Darma.*

Shaka's mouth watered in anticipation.

Widobo dismissed the Papuan children to return to their homes at midday from the thatched-roof platform that served as a school. The school emptied as the chattering students rushed to their village homes for meals and afternoon naps.

The small man from Sulawesi now lived in Jayapura. He had been here for a month now and was anxious to be rotated to his home in the city. He missed his wife, hated the jungle, and loved the social life with his friends. He wasn't so anxious as when he was here alone. This time he had the company of two government officials. One from the provincial office and one from the Department of Social Advancement. They were good company and provided a sense of security here. If help was needed, the men had a radio and could call for it. They also provided better food than he could obtain on a teacher's salary.

The sun was at its zenith. Widobo was ready for a meal and a nap. He turned from his rustic table to wipe the whiteboard clean of the morning's lessons. Something attracted his attention on the path into the village. He stopped wiping the board and squinted through his thick glasses into the distant approaching figure.

Who would be out at this time of day? All the villagers would be eating, napping, or sitting in the shade socializing.

The figure came closer. He is not headed to the village compound itself, which means he is not looking for family or friends.

Widobo suddenly straightened, trying to make-out the lone Papuan figure through the unwalled schoolhouse. His heart pounded in his rib cage.

*Shaka. It is him. Allah, protect me! Bless Allah.*

Widobo turned and ran to the edge of the platform—ignoring the steps, he leaped to the ground and sprinted to the only modern wooden structure, about twenty-five yards from the school.

Widobo was winded when he thrust the door open to the small office/dormitory. The two men seated at the table jerked back in surprise, the older one spilling his warm tea.

"He's back!" Widobo finally found his air.

The heavy-set man of Papuan and Javanese descent busily mopping up the spill was the first to speak. "Who's back, Pak?"

"Shaka!"

The older man, Subota, stopped his mopping and look into the wide eyes of Widobo. Subota tried to appear calm. As the field leader for the government's development program he did not want to show concern.

He continued to clean the spilt tea. "I had thought we had seen the last of that man. Stay calm, both of you. Don't be such cowards. He needs to understand my authority and what I can do for him or to him."

Widobo looked at Karim. The youngest of the three had frozen like a statue, with a spoonful of greens poised to enter his open mouth.

"What do we do?' Widobo implored.

Subota leaned his heavy frame back on the rattan chair. He scratched his short graying hair and spoke slowly.

"It's like this, something has to be done about him. He is always using and taking from his people. Even provincial officials fear him and give him what he wants."

Subota rose from the bench and peered out the window. Widobo moved to the window beside him. Shaka had climbed up the steps to the school and was looking around. He picked up a literacy book and was examining it. He did not seem to be in a hurry.

Subota turned from the window and studied his companions. "The leaders from the villages fear him and they want him gone from their communities. They say he has killed men--and women, and some of his wives. They also say he gets strength through eating his enemies."

"Protect us, Allah," Widobo said.

Karim switched from watching Subota and looked at the anguished face of Widobo.

"He wants me to teach him how to read, and also about the outside leadership," Widobo wailed. "He said he wanted to have a place in Jayapura or Sentani so he could protect his people from invaders. I don't understand."

Subota faced the two men. "He is coming this way. Quickly, just listen. The leadership in the province are trying to develop the people from the hutan, from the interior. But they are looking for someone who can pull them all together and control the troublemakers."

Subota had the attention of both men. He reseated himself and looked at his roommates. A slow smile crept across his face. "I have an idea. Shaka will get what he wants, and he will not bother the people, or us. The government will get someone who can control this area, and Shaka will not want to come back here when he finds the luxuries outside the hutan."

Subota picked up what was left of his tea and raised his glass to his friends. "In the meantime, teach him. Make him qualified to fit the needs of this province. Who knows, he might even leave his old ways of black magic."

Widobo was puzzled by Subota's words, but he nodded. Karim also nodded.

"When he gets to the door, let him in. He will be hungry. Befriend him—for now."

There was no knock, but a deep cough sounded at the door. Shaka had announced his presence.

Subota whispered, "He is requesting entry. No, he is demanding entry. Let him in."

# CHAPTER 18

"Benjad." Doris smiled when her student did not look up. Their weekly reading sessions seemed to be his favorite activity. In the six months they'd spent working together at the small desk Steve had made for him, Benjad had made amazing progress in both Indonesian and English. Today, an English version of "Thomas the Engine" held his reading focus.

"Benjad!"

He looked up and grinned sheepishly.

"Yes, Ibu?" Benjad closed the book.

"What do you think about the story? Is there something to be learned?"

Benjad sat quietly for a few seconds. "I liked the story. Thank you for letting me read it, but—" He gave her a puzzled look. "Are there trains with faces, that talk? My train never talks, and if it has a face, it does not show it until I am asleep and cannot see it."

Doris laughed and slapped her worn cotton dress at the hip. "No, son, trains do not talk, nor have faces. It is just a story for entertainment." She looked into his puzzled eyes. "Don't your people tell stories in the village about things you know did not happen, just to make you smile or wonder?"

Benjad stared blankly, then shook his head.

Doris sighed. "Look, I am sure that some reports in your clan are true, but others are not true. They are told to teach a lesson or just to have fun. Right?"

Benjad considered what she said. It might be true in some circumstances. When people did not understand supernatural events, they interpreted those events as a lesson or truth, and shared them in an entertaining fashion.

"So, books are not true, but only for the mind of children?" Benjad thought perhaps he now understood the place for books.

Doris sighed. "Books are written for both children and adults, and can be entertaining imaginary stories called fiction, or they can be truth, and then they are called factual." She sat on a chair beside him. "It is important to know the difference. Also, now that you can speak English and Indonesian, we are going to start learning more about numbers and how they are used."

His eyes brightened and Doris felt his excitement.

"Would you like that?"

Benjad nodded. He didn't completely understand, but he had learned to trust her.

"What time is it, Benjad?" Doris pretended not to see the clock on the wall.

Benjad quickly looked at the clock and announced with a smug grin, "It is ten minutes after three."

"Yes, it is, and that means time for school to end. You can take the book with you, but you need to run along home. Alice and Clay will be expecting you."

"Yes, I will see you again soon." Benjad excused himself and bounced out the door, glancing back to smile at his teacher. She waved.

Benjad wanted to meet up with the other kids and play, but he knew he must first check in with Alice. Ever since the thwarted attack by Mati Raja, he noticed Alice watched him a little more closely. He did not mind. His mother used to do the same thing.

From a distance, he saw Clay and Alice seated on the front porch engaged in what appeared to be a serious discussion. How strange that Clay talked with this woman as much as he did. He often even asked her opinion or allowed her to order him to do something. Although Clay had big, strong arms, and Benjad had seen photos of Clay as a warrior, he found him surprisingly gentle with Alice. Perhaps Alice, like Fina, had earned the respect of those around her at an early age.

He had never seen Clay beat her, even when she broke his favorite coffee cup. Alice had tripped and banged the cup on the doorway trying to right herself. It had broken off at the handle. She had uttered, "Oh, dear," probably expecting a beating from Clay, but he acted more concerned about whether she'd been hurt. He even said he was due for a new cup.

Such a strange response. The men from his village often beat their wives for more minor infractions than that—not brutally, which could prevent them from working in the gardens, but just a little slap or a strike to their backsides with a wooden paddle made for that specific purpose. Wives expected it. Some wives even interpreted the discipline as an indication that the husband cared for them.

Father had been more like Clay. Despite his status as a great warrior, he did not strike Mother.

As Benjad considered this odd behavior, he neared the steps to the veranda. Clay called out, "Hey, little man, come on up here. We want to talk to you."

He climbed the stairs and slowly walked toward the couple, who rose to greet him. Clay grabbed him under his arms and effortlessly swung him up and seated him on the heavy small table that functioned as the cup and snack holder. Clay pulled both chairs around to create a semi-circle, and the couple resettled in front of him. Clay leaned forward with a half-smile, looking into Benjad's eyes. Then he sat upright and nodded toward Alice. "You go ahead, honey."

Alice took the little boy's hands into hers. "Benjad, you have lived with us for many months now. I know you faced difficulties getting used to a new world. But you have done fine. I want to ask you, are you happy staying with us?"

Benjad stared at Alice, not sure where this line of questioning would lead. "Yes, I am happy. It is easy to stay with you now. Before, I did not know."

"So, do you miss your people or your village?" Alice peered into his eyes.

Benjad looked down while he fingered his crocodile tooth amulet. He looked back at Alice and said, "I think I did, but now I don't know if I want to go back. My mother and father are both in the world of their ancestors."

Clay cleared his throat. "Benjad, we understand you still feel pain, and we are sad for you. We want to help you. We care for you." Clay spoke softly and slowly. "We want to raise you to become a man, and then you can make decisions for your own life."

Alice squeezed Benjad's hands lightly and blurted out, "Benjad, we want to become your mother and father in this world."

Benjad said nothing but continued to stare at her intensely.

A deep red color crept across her face.

Clay broke the awkward silence, "Listen, son, it is not that we can ever take the place of your mother and father. We will not even try to fill your memories of them. It's just that you need someone to care for you and help you learn the ways of the world. We would consider it an honor to be like second parents to you. We would not want you to forget your parents."

Benjad looked from one to the other. He spoke in halting English at first, but then more easily as the need to express his feelings increased.

"At first I feared you." He nodded toward Clay. "Then you treated me kindly. You took me from my village that no longer wanted me."

Benjad turned toward Alice. "After I arrived, you took care of me. But I was scared. Sometimes I had bad dreams. Sometimes I wondered why you gave me all the good food. I thought maybe you were preparing me to be eaten, because you were making me fat. I did not know if you were spirits or monsters."

Alice gasped, but Clay just chuckled.

"I've been called worse," he said. "I'm glad you've changed your mind."

Benjad looked down and twirled the tooth hanging around his neck. When he looked back up into the faces of Alice and Clay, he spoke with an unsteady voice. "I knew for sure you only intended good for me when the buaya almost ate me. You both hugged me like my mother and father used to hug me. I saw the light and rain in your eyes."

Alice reached out a hand and caressed his cheek. Her eyes reflected that same light and rain he remembered.

Benjad searched through the words his teacher had taught him. "You were afraid for me to get hurt. You were at peace that I had not been harmed." Benjad frowned for a moment and then brightened as he found the appropriate English word. "You were relieved!" He smiled broadly.

When Clay and Alice both nodded, he continued.

"I think my mother and father, if they could speak, would say I should be with you. I would like for you to become my father and mother."

The rain in Alice's eyes spilled over. She gathered him in a bear hug. "Thank you, Benjad. Thank you so much."

Clay patted the child on the back, then lightly pinched his arm.

"Great. And we promise not to eat you. That is, until you get more fat on you."

"Clay! Stop that." Alice gave Benjad a quick kiss and quickly assured him, "You know he's only joking, right?"

Benjad grinned. "I know. He is my funny father." Then he thought for a moment.

"I do have one question." He pulled away from Alice's hug. "What should I call you? Father and Mother?"

"You can call us what you want, but maybe you want to keep those titles for the ones who gave you your life," Clay answered. "You can call her Mom and me, Dad." Then he added, "Or you can call me Pop."

"I like Pop!" Benjad rocked on the tabletop. "It is the sound you make when you are thinking hard!"

Clay gave Alice a quizzical look, and she laughed. "It is quite fitting."

"What are you two talking about?"

"Dear." Alice placed her hand on his. "You don't even realize it, but sometimes you make a popping noise with your lips right after you reach a decision and before you make it known."

Benjad mimicked his new father, smacking his lips. Pop, pop, pop!

"I do not do that!" Clay's expression betrayed his denial. Sheepishly he said, "Maybe I do ... sometimes. Okay, Pop it is!" Clay took a sidewise look at Alice. "I guess it does seem fitting."

"Let's celebrate!" Alice stood and started into the house.

Benjad nodded vigorously. He knew this word 'celebrate' meant food. The three went into the kitchen to enjoy the fresh mango pie that Ibu Anache had baked.

Benjad talked more than he had ever talked at one time. His new parents listened as he chatted and they ate their pie. That evening, both Clay and Alice tucked him into bed. When they wished him a good night, he returned the wishes. "Good night, Pop and Mom!"

He knew they were pleased. It pleased him also. As they lingered in the doorway, he turned in bed, pulling the mosquito netting open, and rotated the once-evil-eyed clock around so he could see the time.

Clay thanked the Lord silently for dissolving Benjad's fears over the past. He whispered to Alice as they turned and walked down the hall to their own room, "Now, for the hard part. Formal adoption in this country is not an easy task for a foreigner."

"We just have to trust that the Lord will take care of all the details." Alice's voice sounded confident, but her eyes revealed doubt.

"You know what Fina's parents went through to formalize adoption. It took three years and lots of meetings and money before the missionary parents were granted their daughter."

Clay sat down on the bed as Alice followed him and sat down beside him. She folded her hands and looked at his face. "I know, I know."

"It will be all right." He took her hand and squeezed it.

Suddenly the day's events hit him hard and he sat on the bed. "Man, I'm tired. Good times can be as draining as bad times."

"Yes, but it is a good tired." Alice placed a hand on Clay's shoulder as he started removing his sandals. She leaned down and kissed him on the back of his neck. The two new parents fell asleep excited about the days ahead.

Clay rose the next morning earlier than usual. He had a lot to do. He left Alice sleeping soundly and crept into the hallway, peering in at Benjad, who also slept. The boy's dark features contrasted with the sun-bleached sheets.

Clay picked up a flashlight on his way out the door so he could see any snakes before they saw him. Snakes unnerved him. He did not fear them so much as respect their lethality. His Vietnam experiences with deadly serpents were etched firmly in his memory.

Clay unlocked the hangar office door and entered. The distinctive scents of paper, mildew, oil, and aircraft fuel mingled with the early morning dampness, something Daryl called pilot perfume.

The Coleman lantern suspended on a light spring just above his head groaned slightly when he pulled it down. He stuck his flashlight in his pocket and primed the lantern, then felt around on a nearby shelf for the Zippo lighter. A skilled flip of the lid, followed by thumbing the wheel, brought a flickering flame to life.

Settling into the creaky wooden chair, he perused the flight schedule for next week. A planned flight on Wednesday showed no passengers, only freight. He penned a request form for Alice, Benjad and himself to travel to Sentani, the small town closest to Jayapura, seat of local government. Sentani's major airport had paved runways, courtesy of the occupying Japanese forces during WWII, that were still in use.

Clay left a note for the Korsi dispatcher to radio the airport to request a rental vehicle. He sat back in the chair then remembered something else. He added a note to request reservations at a guesthouse run by a mission group for when they arrived.

He smiled slightly, knowing these arrangements would elicit numerous questions from Daryl, and soon after, from the rest of the mission community. He needed to announce their intent to adopt Benjad, not only to satisfy their curiosity, but to obtain their prayer backing for this challenge. However, he wasn't ready yet.

His joy dampened as he thought of the inherent obstacles of a cross-cultural adoption. He made a mental note to send a letter on the next Sentani-bound flight to his friend, Pak Darsono, a Christian lawyer in Jayapura. Darsono had studied abroad in Australia before studying law in Jakarta and passing his certification exams. He had traveled to Irian Jaya with his wife of Papuan heritage to set up a practice.

Clay would announce their plans at the Sunday morning chapel service at the Center and request prayer for this endeavor. With a deep breath, he leaned back in the creaky chair placing his hands behind his head. "Pop, pop, pop." He made the noise thoughtfully, then chuckled out loud.

The rising sun had just peered through the gray clouds when he left the hangar office to return home. He whispered a small prayer of gratitude and handed over control of all details.

"Lord, the die is cast, but you're in charge of all dice."

# CHAPTER 19

Benjad awoke before daybreak and wondered why. As his sleepy fog began to wane, he bolted upright.

*Of course! Today I will go inside the big bird! I mean the airplane.* He laughed aloud at how he used to think of the airplane as a living creature.

He turned to his side and read the luminous dial of the clock that had now become his friend. Only four a.m. His new parents had told him they would have to be at the hangar by six a.m. He could barely contain his anticipation when Pop told him about the impending trip to Sentani. He'd asked so many questions Clay was prompted to say he shouldn't have mentioned the subject to Benjad a week in advance.

Benjad kicked off the lone sheet on the bed he'd learned to accept, parted the mosquito netting, and lightly touched down on the floor. He scurried to the bathroom clad in his sleeping shorts and started preparing for the trip. Standing on a wooden box that had once contained an aircraft fuel pump, he washed his face with the invigorating cold water.

Benjad took special pains to brush his teeth the way Mom had taught him. It took many tries before she convinced him that toothpaste was not a delicacy to be consumed. He savored the lingering flavor of peppermint after he had cleaned his teeth. He concluded his ablutions and brushed his tightly curled hair. Then he examined his face and upper body in the mirror. He had given up trying to move faster than the image in the mirror. No matter how quick or erratic his movement, the fast and clever mirror captured his actions simultaneously. It had taken him time to realize the image he saw belonged to him and not his ghost.

The boy wrinkled his brow, causing the small scar above his eye to dance. He touched the mark he'd received the day his mother died. He briefly relived the feeling of deep waters covering his body as he'd fallen into darkness after the evil shaman, Shaka, had struck him.

Benjad shook his head to rattle the memory away. The past belonged in the past. He had a happy future now. He stepped off the box and pushed it out of the way under the sink. Then he padded back to his room. Mom had already laid out clothes on a chair.

He went into the living room after glancing down the hallway. The yellow candlelight glowed under the door to Pop and Mom's bedroom. He could hear the rumble of Clay's voice and the higher pitched voice of Alice as they conversed, but he could not make out the words.

At least they were up and about. They wouldn't miss the airplane.

It was still dark in the living room, so he darted back to his bedroom to retrieve a small flashlight. Finally, he could control the tiny light spirits. He whacked the flashlight on the open palm of his hand before sliding the switch forward to turn it on. He had seen Pop discipline the flashlight like that. Benjad decided that this action jolted the spirits into submission before sliding the switch to allow them to exit the tube and run around in their newfound freedom. If you did not whack them, they might lose their fear of you and not return when the switch shut off.

He returned to the living room and settled down to play with his train. As soon as Mom and Pop were ready, they would be on their journey. The journey intrigued him, but he could not imagine what to expect. He tried to concentrate on the train to drain his nervous energy.

Alice came down the hallway dressed for travel, excited about the idea of seeing friends, shopping, and taking in a restaurant meal. It was almost like a vacation. She stood in the doorway watching Benjad play with his train in the beam of his flashlight. He had laid the light source on a footstool and had set two books on top to secure it in place.

She had a very inventive son.

She reflected on those words that had come so naturally. Her son.

*Please Lord, let that come true in the strictest legal sense.*

She felt Clay behind her. His arms embraced her waist as he leaned over her left shoulder and kissed her lightly on the cheek, his soft beard tickling her neck. She had become used to his beard, and even liked it a bit, although she continually threatened to cut it off while he slept. He would respond as an anguished Samson. "What, and remove all my strength so I can be bound by my enemies?" His imitations always made her chuckle.

They stood quietly, Clay's arms around his wife, observing the boy. Benjad turned and leapt to his feet, smiling. "Mom, Pop, you ready to go? I will put the train away. I am ready."

"Whoa, whoa, slow down. Don't you think we should have breakfast first?" Clay grabbed the boy for a hug.

"I am not hungry. Shouldn't we be at the hangar to meet Uncle Daryl? If we are not there, he might leave without us."

Clay laughed. "Don't worry. He'll wait for us. We are the only cargo he is carrying. But if we don't eat breakfast, then I might have to eat you for breakfast on the long flight." Clay licked his lips and made a low, threatening growl.

Benjad grinned. "I know now you don't find me tasty. Besides, I would taste like soap!" He offered his freshly washed arm for inspection.

Alice and Clay laughed. "Come on. We will have a little breakfast." Alice started for the kitchen.

"A little?" Clay held his belly. Alice playfully jabbed her elbow into it and he groaned.

Clay lit a lantern and Alice set the table with bowls and poured homemade granola into them. She placed a bowl of fruit on the table and turned to fill a pitcher with purified water so she could mix up some powdered milk.

Benjad ate a mango, a banana, and a bowl of granola before requesting another bowl. Clay eyed him. "I thought you said you're not hungry?"

"It is wise to fill yourself before a long journey. I remember that from my father." Benjad held up his bowl.

"Certainly, your father was a wise man," Clay responded with a serious tone. Alice knew he wanted to show Benjad that he respected his father and would not interfere with his memories of him.

Benjad, still clutching his spoon, looked up into Clay's eyes. "Pop is also a wise man. I have the joy of having two fathers."

Clay smiled and nodded. "Eat, in case I need you for a snack."

"Benjad, ignore Pop. He is teasing again." Alice gave Clay a soft poke.

"I know. Pop is a tease man—a joke man."

"The proper term is comedian. And I plead guilty." Clay tousled the boy's hair.

They finished breakfast and left the dishes for Ibu Anache. Clay went over what they needed to take for their trip, including his and Alice's passports, photos, copies of their visas, and a surat jalan, which permitted travel, in case Clay needed to travel to other areas of Papua while in town. Then the threesome set out for the hangar.

They found Daryl readying the paperwork for the flight, and Eli busy fueling the aircraft by cranking the hand pump from a fifty-five-gallon drum to the hose inserted in the wing tank of the Helio Courier.

Eli spotted the travelers first and greeted them with an exuberant welcome. Benjad ran to Eli and offered to crank as he had in the past.

"No, you need to stay clean for your travels."

Benjad puffed out his chest. "Yes, I am traveling far away. Pak Eli, I will bring you oleh oleh."

Eli chuckled. "Gifts, I do not need, but I will pray for your safe return."

Daryl looked up from his clipboard and peered out from under his weathered hat. "Morning, Slippery. See ya brought Alice from Wonderland." He paused and turned toward Alice. "I wonder what you see in this bloke."

Clay just grinned and shook his head.

Alice gave him a smile. "Good morning, Mr. Daryl. I trust you had a good night's sleep—if you are going to be flying us."

"No, as a matter of fact, I did not. But if I get tired, Benjad can fill in for me."

She watched Benjad's expressions waver between fear and elation. Knowing her ambitious, literal boy, he was probably assessing whether he could perform the task.

The pilot completed his walk-around, checking the aircraft, and then invited his passengers to board. Alice expected him to put Clay, being the heavier passenger, in the copilot's position, but he surprised her.

"Benjad, you can sit beside me and help me fly the airplane." He winked at the boy. "Be sure to tell me if I am doing anything wrong."

They all laughed at Benjad's astonished expression.

A strange mix of joy and fear surged through Benjad's heart. Not only was he preparing to take his first flight, but the pilot was permitting him to take a position of importance. He frowned at Daryl's suggestion. "Thank you, but maybe I do not know enough that I can find your mistakes."

Daryl and Clay chuckled. Benjad found nothing funny in his words. It must be something that men held secretly.

Alice squirmed her way into the passenger seat behind the pilot. Clay held his hands up behind her. "You wanna push?"

She glanced backward at her husband and scowled. "No! Don't touch me unless you want broken fingers."

Benjad watched the exchange. "Pop will not push that hard. He does not want to break his fingers."

Clay burst out laughing. Alice shook her head at her boys.

"Oh, you guys. Partners in crime." Alice finally settled into the seat.

Clay followed Alice, seating himself beside her, an action made more difficult because of his size. However, he moved quickly. "Whew, so glad I'm young and agile enough to do this."

Alice shook her head. "You are a brat!"

Clay grinned and winked at Benjad, still standing beside the plane. "Uncle Daryl will help you get in." He nodded and waited patiently.

Daryl placed his clipboard under his seat on the left side and then came around to the front of the aircraft pausing to seize the prop and try to move it on the shaft. "Seems tight to me." He lifted Benjad into the copilot seat.

While Daryl adjusted the seat belt for his small body, he asked, "Now, you don't have to go to the bathroom, do ya?" But the boy did not hear. He was staring in awe at the copious dials, gauges and switches on the panel. Above the panel was a window that was too elevated for him to see out. Daryl finished buckling the boy in his seat. "Did you hear me?"

Benjad directed his attention to the pilot, and he repeated his question a second time. Benjad assured him he would not make water in his bird.

Clay called from the back seat, "You better ask my bride the same question."

Alice delivered a sharp elbow to Clay's side. "Knock it off. If you are going to be like this for the entire trip, you can stay here."

His passengers secured, Daryl returned to the pilot's side of the aircraft. He removed his hat and placed it between the seats. He started to retrieve the flight helmet from the dashboard, then paused. "Be right back." The mission pilot spun around and jogged back to the hangar office. He returned with another helmet, and leaning across his seat, said to Benjad, "If you are going to be my copilot, you need a helmet."

Benjad could barely contain his excitement as Daryl fitted him with the helmet and inserted the radio plug wires into the cockpit intercom system.

The giant helmet fell down over his eyes, but that did not matter. Benjad turned to look at Alice and tried to look at Clay, who leaned forward.

"Looking good, looking good!"

Alice clasped her hands. "Oh, my little pilot!"

Daryl climbed in and seated himself, leaving the door open to allow cooler air to flow into the cabin as he prepared to crank the Helio.

Outside, Eli removed the chocks in front of the wheels and then walked backwards. He waved at the passengers and they waved back.

"Awas!" Daryl called out loudly to anyone in the range of the lethal propeller.

The prop started to turn grudgingly, then faster, as the engine coughed to life, spewing white smoke from the cowling. The aircraft shuddered in tempo with the loud power plant. Daryl ran through the check list mounted on the instrument panel adjacent to a set of red plastic tabs.

As he checked each item—oil pressure, manifold pressure, magneto, etc.—he would flip the corresponding red tab down to cover the item. Benjad watched with fascination. The pilot looked around the cabin. "Everyone secure?" He gave Benjad a smile and thumbs-up signal.

The monster motor drowned out his thoughts. Benjad fingered his amulet. It was louder inside the belly than standing near the airfield watching. Periodically, Daryl would push a stick into the panel, and it roared louder. He gave Benjad a confident smile. Clay reached forward and patted Benjad's shoulder, reminding him that Daryl held them in capable hands.

Benjad tried to pretend that he felt no fear as Daryl spoke on the radio in Indonesian to Eli, who had gone inside.

Daryl rolled the plane onto the runway and taxied to the upper end of the inclined grass airstrip. At the end of the runway, the pilot toed the right pedal and revved the engine to turn into the wind and look down upon the runway to the lake, only a short distance from the end.

Benjad could not see out the front, but he observed the passing jungle from the side windows. He watched everything the pilot did with a sinking heart. He would never remember all the required steps for taking to the air.

The pilot placed sunglasses on the bridge of his nose and radioed Eli. "Cleared for takeoff?" The voice through the helmet startled Benjad for a second. Daryl pressed both pedals down and closed the door, to Benjad's great relief. He had worried that the pilot could fall out if he forgot to close the door.

Daryl pushed the stick he held, increasing the noise of the motor as the bird shook. Suddenly the bird lurched forward and cast itself down the inclined runway toward the lake. Faster and faster it raced, and then the bumpy ride smoothed out.

Benjad looked out the window. The ground dropped away and soon they were higher than the trees. As the lake water came into view, his heart pounded—no longer from fear, but from excitement. They gained altitude, and the aircraft dipped its wings to the right and started to turn. The green jungle and languid streams slowly became obscured by the smoky thickening clouds. The temperature cooled as they rose, and the steady roar of the engine penetrated the cabin.

"How do you like this?"

Recognizing Daryl's voice, Benjad looked at the pilot, who now seemed relaxed.

"Can you hear me, Benjad?" Daryl readjusted the intercom on the panel.

Benjad nodded, conscious of the helmet's weight, and then croaked, "Yes, I can hear you in my hat!"

The pilot chuckled, "That's because your 'hat' is a helmet that has radio communications in it, so I can talk to you and you can talk to me directly without the noise of the loud motor."

Brilliant sunlight filled the aircraft as they topped the cloud carpet. Benjad redirected his observation from the outside to the inside as he watched the pilot deftly adjust the controls. It seemed contrary to the way he had seen the man perform actions on the earth. Daryl's rough, sunburned hands danced smoothly over controls and dials. He talked to Benjad as he worked, explaining that the levers allowed him to adjust the fuel mixture and reduce the throttle. The noise dropped to an even hum.

Benjad could not see Daryl's eyes through the dark glasses, but he could tell the aviator was focused and serious, unlike his manner on the ground. His lips moved rapidly while speaking into the microphone connected to his helmet. He had explained to Benjad he needed to switch channels to communicate with the Sentani Airport, so Benjad could no longer hear him. Benjad sat extremely still, afraid any sudden moves might disturb the stability or the complacent hum of the aircraft. Summoning courage, Benjad turned his head slowly and peeked around the high back of the seat to see his adopted parents.

Alice returned his smile and leaned forward, patting him on the shoulder. Clay leaned sideways to view the boy and nodded reassurance.

The pilot switched back to intercom mode. For the next hour, he taught Benjad about the complex cockpit and occasionally pointed out sights below. He identified the sluggish Mamberamo. From this altitude, the ribbon of water wound through the green foliage as far as Benjad could see. He could also see a couple of villages reflecting sunlight off their metal roofs and one premodern village with thatched roofs. Benjad wondered if it could have been his village. A lump rose in his throat as an image of his mother flashed before him. He wanted to see his home again, but he knew it was not possible.

The cottony clouds were solid, and Benjad could hardly see in front of them. Daryl grew silent as the bird descended through the thick vapor whiteness.

"Okay. We will be landing soon, Benjad. Your ears may feel plugged. If so, hold your nose and try to blow it." Daryl demonstrated the action, and then turned his full concentration on the landing procedures.

# You Cannot Grasp the River

The plane now floated through a thick white soup. Disoriented, Benjad tried to establish in his mind whether they were flying forward, descending, ascending, or turning. It gave him almost a panicky feeling, trying hard to pierce the whiteness all around. He looked at Daryl's face, which remained fixed—not outside, but on the instrument panel. The pilot must be trusting his instruments to tell him what to do rather than his eyes.

They burst out of the whiteness to blue skies. The land below appeared with green cultivated fields, clusters of small metal roofed homes and buildings, and narrow dirt roads. As they dropped lower, Benjad became aware of the heat reflecting from the ground. He could smell earthy fragrances—a mix of floral scent, disturbed soil, and composting vegetation.

On the horizon, at the foot of a group of mountains, Benjad glimpsed the town for the first time. He had never seen so many buildings before—more than in his newly adopted community. Roads crisscrossed between the buildings. He'd never seen anything so big or so strange. What would happen next in this new world?

# CHAPTER 20

Daryl obtained approval for landing as he flew parallel to the runway. The runway ended and shortly their small plane flew over Lake Sentani. Fishing boats dotted the surface, but they were few and far between. He banked sharply to line up the aircraft for the final approach, as his eyes swept the instrument panel and his hand rested on the throttle. He smiled at Benjad's wide eyes. Poor kid must be thinking the runway was rather small for a landing.

Daryl reached down and ascertained that Benjad's seat belt remained secured, and he quickly scanned the backseat for the same reason. Clay gave a thumbs-up sign. Daryl squirmed in his seat, positioning himself for the transition from air to ground. He cut the throttle a little more and adjusted the flaps for the slower airspeed.

Daryl smiled. The oversized helmet moved as if on a swivel as the little boy tried to watch his every move. Benjad must have taken seriously his request to fly this bird.

The runway rushed up to meet them, demanding Daryl's full attention. Landings and take-offs were never casual events.

# You Cannot Grasp the River

As the little plane sailed across the end markings on the runway, Daryl expertly crabbed into the wind to maintain the presence of the craft over the middle of the strip. Satisfied with his altitude above the runway, he flared the Helio by pulling the nose up and cutting the throttle. The wheels gently touched down and the tires squeaked their greeting to the earth. The pilot slowed down by toeing both pedals' brakes.

From his copilot seat, Benjad could only gaze in wonder at the parade of objects that zipped past his window. Airplanes of all sizes, shapes, and colors populated the grounds, some of them many times larger than the one in which he rode.

People were everywhere—Papuans, brown-skinned men, and a few white men milled around, some walking to and from buildings, some loading carts, and some talking to each other.

Daryl pointed out the control tower. Inside, people moved around high above the ground. They were looking out—some were peering through those handheld instruments that caused things to race closer. Binoculars, Pop had called them. Benjad recalled looking through them and being so surprised he dropped the gadget before the distant trees and buildings could run up and collide with him. Pop had quickly caught them and roared with laughter.

The plane rolled near to a hangar, roaring briefly during a turn and coming to a halt. The engine went silent after a few coughing protests, and the propeller stopped turning.

Daryl removed his helmet and grinned. "We be here! Last stop, all deplane."

He patted Benjad on the leg, then unsnapped his seatbelt and removed the oversized helmet.

Benjad gave an ecstatic grin. "Waw! I feel like a bird!"

After Daryl had helped Benjad out of the plane, the boy still couldn't relax. He had never seen so much activity in his life.

Despite the early hour and the already sweltering sun overhead, the landing field seemed alive with energy and purpose. Men that Clay called baggage handlers pulled their luggage out of the cargo area in the bottom of the aircraft and loaded it onto a cart. Other men were walking, running, carrying, loading, or offloading. Some worked on other aircraft on the concrete and in hangars like the one back home.

Alice took his hand, and they walked toward a hangar. A loudspeaker on the terminal startled him as it proclaimed a flight from Jakarta soon to arrive. Benjad swiveled his head to the source of the voice, then tripped on a swollen line of tar filling a gap between concrete slabs.

"Whoops!" Alice clutched his hand tighter and helped to right the youth. "You have to look down sometimes," she said with an affectionate smile.

In the relative cool of the hangar sanctuary, the group paused to greet the aviation workers and a family of four. During the conversation, Benjad learned they were waiting for a return flight to the village where they worked as linguists.

"I'm going to head over and sign for the rental." Clay said, moving toward a counter. Benjad walked back outside with Alice to the line of vehicles in a small lot.

"I think it's this one." Alice stopped at a red van. "Clay said we had a Mitsubishi van with a carrier rack.

A woman approached from the entry gate.

"I don't believe it." Alice waved excitedly. "That's a friend of mine."

Benjad examined the woman, blonde, middle-aged, and wearing a long blue skirt, dark blouse, and bonnet.

"Myra!"

Myra flashed a smile and called out a greeting in Indonesian as she approached with a bouncing stride. She carried a small box.

"Well, if it isn't Alice from Wonderland."

Alice rolled her eyes. "Yes, Daryl's nicknames do seem to stick. And do my eyes deceive me, or is this Ad-Myr-able Myra," She gave a slight curtsey. "You look lovely. It's been so long. How are you?"

Benjad stood patiently as both women hugged each other and chatted for a few minutes, but his eyes were drawn to the red van Alice had said they would be using. He approached the auto with curiosity and wariness. He had seen cars in books and knew they were a form of transportation, but he did not know how to use one.

He circled the van as a hunter would approach his wounded prey, and then patted the shiny red side with the tips of his fingers. It stung like a heated pot on a stove and he yanked his fingers back. The darkened windows didn't seem as hot, so he cupped his eyes and tried to look inside, but he could see nothing.

He spotted a familiar apparatus on the rear of the van leading to the roof, a ladder that led to a box-like rack on top of the vehicle. Seeing no obvious openings in the sides of the van, he climbed it to the roof and squatted on the rack to wait for Mom and Pop to join him.

Two Papuan baggage men arrived at the vehicle, pulling a cart filled with the Burris family baggage and other boxes destined for some local mission offices. They looked at Benjad questioningly and he nodded his head and wished them a good morning.

He heard Myra chuckle and looked toward her to see her pointing at him. Alice turned to look. Her hand flew to her mouth, which he could tell was an attempt to hide her mirth.

"Oh, Benjad, honey, come down and I will show you what to do." Alice walked toward the van, smiling.

Clay arrived and also laughed. Benjad realized he had made a mistake. Embarrassed, he slowly descended the ladder.

Suppressing his amusement, Clay said, "It's okay. But it is a hot day and you can ride inside."

Benjad watched as Clay pulled a lever on the side and slide a door open.

"Go ahead and get in."

Benjad hopped into the van and seated himself. Clay had disappeared from the opening but reappeared at the back of the vehicle. Benjad watched as he opened another door, but this one lifted upward.

The baggage handlers loaded the contents of the cart into the van. When they finished, Clay thanked them and returned to the open side door and buckled Benjad's seat belt.

*I wonder if he is afraid that I will jump out?*

"There. You're all set to have your first automobile ride."

Clay slid the door closed, opened the front passenger door, and Alice seated herself. He circled the front of the van to climb into the right-side driver's seat.

Clay turned to Benjad and smiled. "From here, we're going to the town of Abepura," Clay said. "It's about a thirty-minute drive to the guest house."

Benjad nodded from his seat behind Alice and turned to watch and listen to Sentani through the open window. The city bustled with activity. Food carts, people hawking their wares, and shoppers going in and out of little shops filled the main street. Monstrous vehicles Clay described as "dump trucks" spewed smoke as they chugged along.

"They're probably helping workers repair the road. Since this is the only paved road connecting Sentani, Abepura, and Jayapura on the coast, it requires a lot of work," Clay said.

The shops and stores were filled with activity. Outside the stores, a plethora of merchants vied with one another to tempt customers with their diverse goods—everything from books, T-shirts, leather goods, flip flops, plastic combs, buckets, piles of fruits, betel nuts, and soap to toys and games. The sellers squatted on mats, sometimes barking out the qualities and descriptions of their products if they saw any eyes fixating on their goods.

Clay dodged people and two-wheeled food carts as he shifted the gears of the van up and down, responding to the traffic.

Benjad stared out, occasionally catching the aroma of cap cay, an Indonesian style of chop suey and other delicacies grilling over coconut shell charcoal fires.

Clay had to focus on his driving, but he pointed out changes and new stores to Alice as he drove.

Benjad tried to listen to Clay's conversation but only understood a smattering. He marveled at so many new things as they drove past one unusual sight after another. Finally, the vehicle slowed.

"This is the entrance to our guesthouse," Clay announced. "The security guards will recognize our van because it's owned by the mission organization."

As if on cue, the gates opened wide. The guards dipped their heads and saluted as Clay waved.

Benjad could hardly take it all in. The house was enormous.

Clay introduced him to their hosts, an older couple named Charles and Penelope from a place called the UK. Charles limped and carried scars on his face, which piqued Benjad's curiosity. He must have been a warrior once like Clay had been.

"Well, welcome!" Charles extended a hand to Benjad. "Did you have an uneventful trip?"

Benjad accepted the hand, nodding politely.

They strolled toward the shade of a giant spreading mango tree, where the adults caught up on recent events.

Penelope suddenly clapped her hands and exclaimed, "Oh dear, how we run on. Charles, our guests must be tired. Let's see them to their rooms so they can freshen up and rest before tea."

Clay and Alice exhaled in unison, then Alice patted Benjad's shoulders and pointed to the open doorway. The managers seized their luggage and led them into the two-story building. A refreshing coolness greeted them, a benefit of the block and stucco walls. One side of a large hospitality room housed the dining hall. On the other side, a long hall led to individual rooms and suites.

"There are more rooms upstairs," said Penelope, "but you'll be staying down here on the ground floor."

She led them into a suite, showing Benjad to an adjoining room.

"Rest up a bit," she said. "Tea is at five o'clock."

From his bed, Benjad could see his adoptive parents through the open door between their rooms. He watched Clay kick off his shoes and collapse on their bed. Soon, Clay's soft snores filled the air. Alice lay down beside him and stared at the slowly rotating ceiling fan over her bed. Benjad tried to watch the fan as well, but sleep overcame him.

He awoke to the sound of traffic and horns honking on the street in front of the guesthouse. Benjad bounded off the bed eager to see new things. He found his future parents seated at a table talking in low tones.

They looked up and greeted him with a smile.

"Well, well, sleepy head. You almost slept through tea," Alice said.

Benjad wrinkled his brow. "I hope they have more than tea to drink. I am hungry."

Alice and Clay looked at each other and burst out laughing.

"Benjad, Charles and Penelope are from another country. They are missionaries like us, but they are serving by giving missionaries a place to stay while they are traveling. But even missionaries are different people. We call the evening meal supper or dinner in English. They call that meal 'tea,'" Clay explained.

"Oh. So, there is food there?"

"Yes, indeed, but it will be all gone if we do not get over to the dining hall. After that, we can take a walk and see some sights. But we do not want to tire ourselves out. Tomorrow is a big day for you." Alice gripped his shoulders and her eyes danced.

Benjad nodded. *Yes, tomorrow I get new parents!*

# CHAPTER 21

Benjad awoke early the next morning, eager for adventure. He had absorbed many new sights and experiences the day before, and he knew more surprises lie ahead. Pop had already showered and stood by his bed, packing the well-worn canvas bag he usually carried slung over his shoulder.

The boy raced to his side and stood on tiptoes, trying to peer into the bag.

"Do you want to see what is in there?" Benjad nodded, and Clay removed the contents, setting them on a nearby table, one item at a time, explaining their purpose. "A pen and a notepad for writing things down. Some Chapstick for sore lips, a pocketknife, water purification tablets, tweezers, sunglasses, a bag of peanuts, and a Bible."

Benjad slid the Bible closer. He had seen this little one before when he was in the logging camp and Clay had preached.

"You already have a Bible, a big one. Why do you need this little one? It seems less important."

Clay smiled. "A man, or a boy, cannot have enough Bibles. And all Bibles are important. This one is just easier to carry when I travel."

Benjad looked deep into his eyes. "Have you read the whole book?"

"Many times."

"Why? Did you not understand it the first time, or was your mind unable to hold all the things it said?"

Clay laughed, but Benjad didn't join in. He wanted answers about this mysterious book. He stuck out his chin.

"Teach me."

Clay's face sobered. He paused, as if trying to decide how to start.

"Come here, Son," he sat down on his bed, patting a space beside him for Benjad to use. The boy had to hop up to get on the bed.

For the next half hour, Clay explained the Bible and the story it told, emphasizing God's love illustrated in its pages.

As Clay finished, Benjad touched the cover with reverence. He didn't understand everything Clay had told him, but he knew it was more than a book.

Clay gently cupped Benjad's chin. "Son, this is a lot of information. I don't expect you to keep it all in your head, but just think on it and know you can ask me questions any time. Okay?"

Benjad pursed his lips, "Okay."

*This book is very important to Pop, and to Mom. I need to learn more about it to see why.*

Pop reloaded the bag, which he called his "possible" bag, because it was possible he might need something from it. Clay paused before placing his worn little Bible back into the bag. He thumbed through some pages until he found the page he wanted.

"This is from the book of Psalms. Psalm 20:4." He cleared his throat. "'May He give you the desire of your heart and make all your plans succeed.'"

Benjad looked up at him, listening intently.

Clay turned to put his hands on Benjad's shoulders. "You know this is an important time for you, and for all of us."

Alice joined them from the bathroom, vigorously drying her hair with a cotton towel. At Clay's words, she seated herself on the bed beside Benjad, sandwiching him between them.

Benjad looked from one to the other. "I know. I think I know."

"Benjad, in order to make it official that we are your mom and pop, we have to go to some important people, and they have to give us permission to adopt you." Clay paused, then started again. "If they do not agree with us, or they want you to have another mom and pop, then we have to give you up."

Benjad felt a tightening in his chest, and Alice gasped.

"He needs to know the truth about what could happen," Clay spoke to her over Benjad's head. Benjad looked up at them.

Alice lowered her eyes to Benjad and said, "But that is not going to happen. Pop is just telling you what happens with some children. There is no reason why you will not become our child. We just need to pray for all things to work in the Lord's timing."

She grabbed Benjad's hands, closed her eyes and spoke quietly. "Dear Lord, you can make this happen. Please give us the blessing of Benjad." She continued her prayer, but her voice quavered on the last few sentences of the petition. When she looked up at her husband, her eyes were full of tears.

Clay laid his large hand atop their smaller ones, still clutching Benjad's shoulder with his free hand, and said,

"Okay, and I will add another 'amen' to that prayer."

Benjad spoke up loudly. "Amen too."

Clay stood. "Now, who is ready for breakfast?"

Benjad leaped off the bed. "Amen to that too."

Clay and Alice laughed as she wiped the tears from her eyes.

---

Clay ushered his family out of the guesthouse before seven o'clock, planning to arrive in Jayapura for the meeting with the attorney, Darsono, at nine. While there, they would also go to the customs office to see whether any packages had arrived from the States for their community.

Clay's parents and friends often sent them care packages, boxes filled with treats and useful items from home. He wondered what Customs would charge him for the Christmas gift he had ordered from a friend for Benjad, or whether it would even arrive.

He smiled, imagining the puzzled faces in the customs office when they saw the baseball glove. He doubted they'd know its purpose, as baseball hadn't yet been introduced to this remote area.

They'd probably search for its mate, thinking it was some sort of protection. Not finding another, they would probably conclude there was a one-handed giant of a westerner living in Papua. They wouldn't want to anger the man who wore a glove of this size—one-handed or not. He found it even funnier to imagine what they would think had the glove been not a boy's size, but a pro size.

Clay could not suppress his comedic thoughts any longer and chuckled aloud.

Alice turned to him. "What's so funny?"

Clay shared his creative scenario, being careful not to be overheard by Benjad from the back seat. Then it was Alice's turn to laugh.

"You've got quite the imagination."

Once in town, Clay had to circle the block several times before finding a parking spot near the attorney's office. As they stepped from the vehicle, Clay and his family were met by a Papuan man in a bright orange T-shirt who handed Clay a smudged piece of paper with a number on it. Westerners who were not tourists knew that these parking attendants were not legitimate, yet they played the game to avoid potential damage to their vehicle in retaliation for refusing to pay. Clay did not resent these guys, nor the few rupiahs he'd have to pay to keep his van intact. In fact, he applauded their entrepreneurial spirit and work ethic. Instead of begging for money, they were earning it. As a plus, they did guard the vehicles in their care.

The party made its way to the second floor of the old whitewashed office building and entered an inner office. An oversized plaque screwed to the door announced that someone of importance worked here. Once inside the room of modest furnishings, they saw a graceful young woman of Javanese background seated behind a heavy teak desk. She rose, bowed slightly and smiled a greeting. "Selamat Pagi, Bapak dan Ibu." She then noted Benjad and cordially greeted him as well.

Clay and Alice returned the perfunctory greetings, introduced themselves and asked if Bapak Darsono was available for their appointment. She invited them to sit and stepped away. Alice and Benjad sat on a couch made for smaller people. When Clay joined them, the couch sank and groaned in protest. Embarrassed, he quickly rose to his feet again, glad that the secretary had already entered the adjoining office.

Benjad turned to Alice with wide eyes. "Ummmm! Pop is almost as big as Mati Raja!"

Alice laughed and gave him a hug. Clay just grunted, showing his displeasure, and sat gingerly in a more substantial wooden chair, wiggling a bit to test its structural capabilities.

"There is no need for laughter." Clay tilted his chin upward. "This attorney caters to a poorer, underfed clientele. I vetted him for his humanitarian instincts, and that is why I chose him. Perhaps he cannot afford stronger seating."

Alice giggled. "Maybe it's just an indication that someone needs to go on a diet."

"You forget you were sitting there too."

"But it did not scream in agony until you sat down." Alice gave him a smug smile.

Even Benjad grinned at the teasing. He tittered as he pointed a thumb back at each of his potential parents.

Clay turned his attention to the partially open office door and watched the attorney busying himself with some files on his desk while his secretary waited for him to acknowledge her. Clay knew it would have been rude for her to call out to him to gain his attention. He finished shuffling and looked at her. "Apa?"

The girl spoke at a low volume to the dark-haired, middle-aged man. Clay could not hear what she said, but her words galvanized the attorney into action. He jumped from his chair and strode to the door. "Ahh, Pak Burris and Ibu Alice, you are here."

The meeting lasted almost an hour as Clay brought Darsono up to date on the events that had led Benjad to be in the custody of the westerners. Then Alice explained their desire to adopt Benjad, with Clay interjecting occasional endorsements.

Darsono sat silently until they finished, then asked, "Does he understand bahasa Indonesia?"

Clay and Alice both nodded. Benjad also bobbed his head and grinned.

Darsono smiled, rose, and went to the office door, patting Benjad on the shoulder as he did so. "Nona, please come in here," he called. The secretary appeared. Darsono addressed the boy. "Benjad, would you like to draw?"

Benjad looked at Alice and Clay who nodded, then back to the lawyer and said, "Yes." Darsono turned to his assistant. "Take Benjad and let him show you what he can draw." The girl took charge of Benjad and closed the door behind them.

Darsono returned to his chair pulling it closer to his clients and spoke to them in a conspiratorial voice. "I did not want to disturb the anak." Taking a deep breath, he continued. "Although you would think this would be easy, the boy has no parents and no relatives. He has no home with his own people, and besides that there is an educated western couple willing to give him a good home." Darsono lifted his arms in a shrug. "However, the government scrutinizes every detail, and an adoption is a long, drawn-out process, especially for westerners. It can be and has been done, but I want you to know it is a long battle, and it is expensive."

At Clay's raised eyebrow, Darsono explained, "It is not my fees, but the government fees and"—he raised his fingers to make quotes—"'helper' fees."

Clay looked the attorney in the eye. "Pak Darsono, we appreciate your honesty, but we also are aware of others who have been through this process and were successful. Besides that, in the United States, the process is equally frustrating. So, your country is not the only one in which it is difficult for well-meaning people."

The Indonesian relaxed. Clay knew his words had enabled the man to salvage some national pride for his candid appraisal.

"Okey dokey," Darsono's American euphemism eased the formality between the men. "Now the work begins. I will need funds to get things rolling, and please forgive me if I cannot produce receipts for every action."

"No problem." Clay brushed aside his concern. "We just want the boy to become our son to raise."

They spent the remaining appointment time filling out forms and discussing next steps. When they finished, Clay discreetly handed a retainer payment to the attorney, and they left the inner office.

The receptionist looked up when they entered her office, but Benjad sat absorbed in drawing on pieces of typing paper with multicolored markers. She had pulled her chair beside the boy as he stood drawing at her desk.

"He is very good, and what imagination!" She stood, bowing. "I hope you succeed in your efforts to help him."

After an extended farewell, Clay and his family retraced their steps to the van. Benjad started asking questions as soon as the van doors closed.

"What happened? Do I belong to you now?"

Clay swiveled around in the front seat. "These things take time, little man. You have to be patient."

A look of confusion crossed Benjad's face. "Okay," he sighed, and settled back in his seat. "Maybe we'll know by tonight."

Clay only smiled at him. He knew the answer and did not want to put a damper on the boy's excitement.

# CHAPTER 22

Clay enjoyed watching Benjad drink in the sights and sounds of Jayapura.

"Pop, I've never seen anything to compare with this. So many people, all fully dressed, cars, trucks, motorcycles, and scooters, and so many people sounding their horns! It's like a language only cars know!"

The trio stopped at a restaurant on the bay that specialized in fish and sate, chunks of chicken or deer, grilled on a coconut charcoal fire and coated with peanut sauce. A young girl came to their table and asked for their orders. Clay ordered for the three of them. He paused, leaned across the table and said to Benjad, "I think we will get you an all-American Coke to drink. I am sure you will like it."

Clay then nodded to the girl and she noted that on her pad with the rest of their drink order and walked away. Soon she reappeared holding a tray with two hot teas in mug-shaped glasses, one empty glass and a cold red can. The waitress placed the Coke can beside the empty glass by the boy, smiled, then disappeared again.

Benjad lifted the can and shook it lightly. Alice quickly seized his hand. "Oh no, little man, don't shake it. It might explode."

He gave the can a concerned look.

"Here, let me open it," Clay reached for the can and lifted the tab on top, very slowly.

The hissing noise that came out of the can caused the boy to leap out of the chair, shouting to Clay, "Awas, there is a snake in there!"

Clay chuckled. Alice seemed amused too. She tried to stifle a laugh, but it ended with a red face and shaking shoulders.

Clay finished opening the can and poured half the contents into the glass. "See, no snakes," he said. "Just a delicious drink."

The soda gurgled into the glass and then sizzled like a green log on a fire. Benjad warily reseated himself eyeing the bubbling drink carefully. "It is hot, yes?"

"No, it is not hot. Try it!" urged Clay.

The boy lifted the glass, peered into it, then slowly touched the contents to his lips. The sweet liquid tasted unlike anything he had ever experienced before. It danced on his tongue.

"Pop and Mom! This black water has many bubbles in it and is sweet like honey."

He smiled, and they laughed, as he tilted up the glass and consumed what had been poured. He then quickly grabbed the can and poured more. Not bothering to wait for the effervescence to settle down, he tried another gulp of this strange liquid. However, this time the gases raced up his nostrils, causing him to sneeze.

When he recovered, he announced, "I have to be careful and wait for the bubble dancers to tire themselves, so they do not jump up my nose."

Clay smiled and pulled the can of Coke back a little. "That's enough for right now. Your food is coming, and we don't want you to ruin your appetite."

Benjad gave Clay a puzzled look. "It will not poison my hunger, will it?"

Alice explained the finer points of savoring the Coke. Then she talked about dining in restaurants. The waitress delivered their food, and after Alice said the blessing, Benjad devoured his grilled fish on a bed of greens.

"See, it did not poison my appetite."

After the meal, the threesome drove to a cluster of buildings that housed the Provincial Police, Customs, Immigration, and the Kantor Kebupatan (regional administrative office). Clay purchased Benjad a small plastic airplane at a store adjacent to the restaurant. Ecstatic, the boy sat in the back seat playing with his new prize. He imitated his own flight, complete with sounds.

Clay needed Alice to help carry some packages for their Sago Lake community colleagues. Benjad insisted he wanted to stay in the van and play with his newly acquired toy. Both adults hesitated to leave him alone in the vehicle, even if they could view it from the customs office. However, Clay and Alice knew that Papuans loved children, and they had never heard of a child being abducted or injured, so they decided to allow it.

"Okay. But do not get out of this mobil," Clay made his sternest face. "We will be right in that office, and I will leave the windows down to keep you cool." They left the boy and entered the government building.

The missionary easily read the stares that met him when he entered the office. The officials were sizing him up for the potential negotiations. This part always annoyed him, but he drew a deep breath, smiled, bowed slightly to the head official, and exchanged greetings. "Selamat sore, Bapak. Apa kabar?"

Alice stood in the background while Clay conducted his business. This procedure could be lengthy or short, but he had no way of knowing. Clay brought a list of goods expected by his coworkers and friends, who liked it when Clay picked up the packages from Customs. He always struck the best deal, and no one ever questioned the final cost. Clay was fortunate this time. The newly appointed Customs official turned out to be honest and pleasant. By the time he left the office, Clay and the official had established a warm relationship.

From a second-floor window across the street, a large Papuan peered out at the street below. He stood in the office of the Bupati (head of the local district in the province of Papua). The Papuan had been attending an annual planning meeting with local leaders. Now the meeting had ended and the group of fifteen officials were engaged in informal group discussions consuming tea and cookies.

He had struggled to squeeze his large frame into the brown uniform of a government worker. He knew his size and the black leather patch covering one eye made the others in the room uncomfortable. He liked it that way.

Shaka towered over the other men—Papuan and Javanese alike. They had to look up at him. He permitted himself a slight smile. It was good fortune to obtain a position like this. It did not pay well, but there were benefits. He could use his power over the people under him for favors, food, and women.

Shaka had assumed the role of kepala desa, or village head, in the Mamberamo region through pressures of various clans and chiefs. He held no notions that it was due to his popularity. They just wanted him out of their villages. They were even agreeable to allow him to have multiple villages under his care. However, they had not reckoned with him being granted more power than they expected. The plan had come together.

Pak Satono, technically Shaka's senior and the official bupati, or district head, frequently glanced toward Shaka. However, while he could clearly see the man in his peripheral vision, Shaka ignored him and stared out the window.

Let him squirm. Although Pak Satono had personally asked him to be an official representing the clans in the Mamberamo region, that offer had been out of necessity, not a choice. Shaka owed the man nothing. In fact, he'd already learned how to make the man do his bidding. Senior, perhaps, but not his superior.

In the street below, Shaka observed the arrival of a western family. Westerners were rare here, but something else interested Shaka besides the couple's mere presence. The man opening the car door looked vaguely familiar. An attractive woman exited from the passenger side, but for now he focused his gaze on the bearded man.

No one talked to Shaka, which suited him fine. As soon as he could, he would collect his pay, pick up some supplies, and take a taxi to a boat waiting to transport him back to his village. He then would regale all who would listen to him about the business he'd accomplished. In the village, he was, indeed, important.

"Ahem."

How long had Satono been standing behind him?

Pak Satono rattled a piece of paper and looked down at it, as if pretending he had just approached.

Shaka turned his head and gave Satono a disdainful sneer, allowing a few seconds to pass before he spoke to the man. "You have something for me?"

It was not so much a question as a demand.

The Bupati cleared his throat again, but when he spoke, his voice cracked. "Yes, Pak Shaka. I have a letter from Jakarta requesting our assistance in arranging transportation, accommodations, and guides for a botanical research team from an international company."

Satono paused, but Shaka said nothing, imagining his cold dark eye boring a hole through Satono's nerves.

Satono shuffled his feet slightly, then continued. "It seems the area of interest is the Mamberamo region stretching to Sago Lake. They want to examine some plants that have medicinal purposes and are native to that region."

This got Shaka's attention. "What plants and what do they do with them?" Magic plants had power, but more importantly, an international company could mean wealthy visitors.

"I don't know the details, but as kepala desa in that region, perhaps you could take an active role in the arrangements. They could set up their command post at Sago Lake. It is run by orang barats who work under the Department of Social Development and a part of the University Cenderwasih. They have a plane and a landing strip. Also, they often have visitors from the government in their guesthouse."

Shaka's mind worked furiously. White-skinned interlopers ran Sago Lake—they lived, worked, and worshipped their god there. He never visited the place because he did not want their Christian god to block his magic. Perhaps though, he now had reason to visit. Perhaps such a place might enrich him with western comforts and pleasures.

A man could get used to the power that a government position had to offer.

Shaka softened his tone and gave the Bupati his well-honed false smile. "Yes, I will certainly help where I am needed."

Satano's eyebrows raised, but he seemed relieved.

"Fine. When I receive more information, I will contact you, and you can assist them with their needs." Shaka stiffened. Was he giving an order? However, the man quickly added, "I appreciate your willingness to do this. You are well-qualified."

Shaka allowed a slight smile exposing unnatural sharpened canines. "I will be waiting. Now, I must go to take care of other business."

They exchanged farewells. Shaka strode through the door, closing it loudly behind him.

Leaning against the closed door, Pak Satano exhaled heavily.

"Good riddance."

He didn't trust that man.

The Bupati, a Javanese and a faithful Muslim, sensed an evil about Shaka, and resented that he feared this employee.

He regretted being talked into appointing Shaka as kepala desa, but the chiefs from the villages demanded that he consider him. Even some government officials and teachers had lent their voice to his appointment.

He would have to keep an eye on that shaman.

Shaka left the coolness of the block office building and crossed the street, intent on cashing his paycheck and buying supplies before he returned to the village. His route led him past the parked vehicle belonging to the white man and woman. All the windows were lowered—something never done in an unoccupied vehicle, as it invited petty theft. He glanced around. No bystanders, and no "security" attendants. The couple was probably at the customs office picking up overseas packages, something westerners often did.

He slowed his walk and approached the vehicle still searching all directions to see if anyone guarded the car. Then he looked through the rear side window and saw the small figure engrossed in playing with a plastic toy airplane.

The man and woman had left a child in the car.

Another surprise. This child was Papuan.

He stepped closer to the vehicle, detecting something familiar about this boy. Then Shaka spotted the crocodile amulet suspended outside of his T-shirt on a leather cord. His eye narrowed as angry memories flooded his consciousness.

Not many years ago he'd stood over the body of Drako, watching him bleed out from multiple wounds. His stealthy ambush had been perfectly enacted. The stab wounds in his back were intended to look like the result of pig tusks. However, the wounded man still moved, so he had used a nearby rock to strike a blow to the back of Drako's head. The man had been hard to kill.

Ultimately, although the blow killed him, he did not succumb to it until he was carried back to the village. Shaka recalled turning Drako's still body over and noticing the missing crocodile tooth amulet that Drako usually wore as protection.

Could this be the same amulet? It looked the same. A puzzle piece fell into place in Shaka's mind. This had to be Drako's child. The man he had seen exiting the vehicle was the westerner who had rescued the boy. Now it all made sense.

Yes, that's why the man looked familiar.

Shaka felt his gut tighten and anger rise up within him. This was the boy who had struck the light from his eye with a stone. The man who had challenged him at the village had become the boy's benefactor, and now both turned up here. Shaka reached into the car and seized the tooth, pulling the cord tightly around the boy's neck.

Yes. Drako's.

In the car, Benjad gasped as a giant hand burst through the open window and closed on his amulet with a violent wrenching. The nightmare of the man who had killed his parents became a vivid reality. He dropped his toy and grabbed Shaka's massive arm, struggling to free himself. Repeatedly he struck the man's arm, but Shaka only twisted the cord tighter.

Then a muscular white arm encircled Shaka's throat in a choke hold. Gasping, he released his grasp on Benjad's cord and grappled with the tightening arm.

All his Vietnam training returned in an instant. Clay maintained pressure on the boy's assailant's throat as he shoved him against the van. He applied enough scissor pressure to the sides of his neck to control him but not kill him.

The Papuan pulled and clawed against his arm, but Clay's other hand snaked out and bent back the struggling man's index finger, forcing him to release his grip. He bent his finger until his arm surrendered to an outstretched position.

He then deftly released his choke hold and shoved his hand behind the attacker's elbow joint, all the while maintaining pressure on the bent index finger. The unfortunate man hissed a low growl but was trapped and unable to move. His strength was no match for Clay's martial arts training.

When Clay knew that the combatant had no other choice but to stop resisting, he loosened the armlock—a little—and addressed the man. "Why are you attacking the boy?"

The strange calm of the Papuan's voice contrasted sharply with the rage written on his face.

"The boy threw a rock at me, and it struck the back of my head. I was just trying to get him to tell me where his parents were, so I could report him to them. Then he started attacking me, and I merely held him off."

Clay did not believe that Benjad would deliberately throw a rock at someone, but still, he thought, he did have a certain prowess with rocks. He glanced into the car. The boy looked all right, just frightened. He quickly scanned the gathering crowd and noted there were many boys milling about.

"You sure it was this boy who did it? You were hit on the back of your head. Did you see him? Maybe it came from one of these boys here."

Shaka gritted his teeth. "It could be. I did not see him."

Clay slowly released his hold on the man's arm, stepping between him and the vehicle door. He turned sideways, still monitoring Shaka, but took a quick glance at Benjad. "Did you throw a rock at this man while he walked past?"

Benjad opened his mouth but no words escaped. He shook his head.

"The boy says he did not do it, and I believe him."

"Maybe I got the wrong boy." Shaka tilted his head to the side and massaged his sore elbow.

Clay examined Shaka closely. A formidable man, larger than most Papuans—and that eye patch ... something clicked in his mind.

Could this be the man from Benjad's village? No, it could not be. He wore a brown official uniform. The Indonesian government did not usually give positions of authority to unsophisticated Papuans. And Clay had no desire to create an international incident with any government official, no matter their office.

The danger abated—Alice raced to the other side of the vehicle to check on the boy. "You okay?" She ran her soft hands over the child to assess any injuries. Benjad nodded.

Alice pleaded in English. "Clay, let's go. We're finished here."

Clay tipped his head toward Benjad in the vehicle and addressed the attacker. "You made a mistake. Don't make that mistake again. Good afternoon."

He turned to a wide-eyed boy at the edge of the gathered locals, whom he had recruited to carry the packages from the Customs office. He directed the lad to the back of the van and opened the rear door for him. Clay carefully monitored his former opponent while he arranged the packages inside the van. The boy's assailant had taken a few steps into the crowd. He turned and looked back at the westerner, massaging his sore arm as he glared.

Clay tipped the boy. Then he climbed into the van and backed out of the parking place, still eyeing Benjad's assailant in the crowd of onlookers.

He did know this character!

Alice checked one last time on Benjad before she seated herself in the front and closed the door. "Thanks for letting me operate and not distracting me. And thanks for letting me know that we were finished here." Thankfully, Alice had broken into his thoughts and urged him back to the present.

"Let's go to Abepura to eat." Alice patted his arm. "We need to sit somewhere still for a bit."

Clay nodded and watched the menacing figure in the rear-view mirror until he disappeared. He tried to relax, but the encounter troubled him. He didn't know how he knew, but of two things he was certain.

He'd seen that man before.
And he would see him again.

# CHAPTER 23

The Burris family rode to the restaurant in silence. Alice knew the man she had married had come close to stepping back into his old life, but thankfully he had restrained himself and taken minimal action to protect the boy. She said a prayer of gratitude for so great a protector.

His lips were pressed closed and he said nothing, gripping the wheel tightly and staring at the road ahead.

What could be going through his mind?

Alice turned to check on Benjad in the back seat. He, too, stared out the window, clutching his forgotten airplane. She undid her belt and scooted toward the middle of her seat to reach toward him and gently pat his knee.

Benjad looked from the window to Alice, and she saw tears welling up in his eyes. She could not help tearing up as well. Benjad nodded and smiled slightly, then redirected his attention back to the window. She turned around in the seat, noticing that Clay had observed the scene in the rearview mirror.

❦

Clay mentally reviewed the incident with the Papuan. Things started clicking.

Could this be the dreaded Shaka, the murderer of Benjad's parents?

He had to know for sure, but he did not want to put the boy through the trauma again. There would be a time. Out of the corner of his eye, Clay saw Alice staring at him. When the human and machine traffic thinned, he held her hand and gave her a long, reassuring look.

"It's over for now, and we can talk later." He looked at Benjad in the rear-view mirror. "Let's enjoy the rest of our stay. For his sake too."

They arrived at the restaurant and entered the dark confines. A frigid breeze blew in from a vent. When the family's eyes adjusted to the dim interior, Clay led them to a table.

A young waitress approached them shyly and handed out menus. She waved her hand at the ceiling. "We have new air conditioners for our western patrons. Please enjoy." She waited with pen and pad until they had decided on their food, then bowed slightly and retreated into the kitchen where an older woman and man were banging pots and pans as they prepared dishes.

Through an open rear door, Clay observed a young man smoking a cigarette. Its clove scent wafted in on the afternoon breeze.

He smiled. The concept of keeping portals closed for more efficient cooling by the air conditioner had not yet seeped into their thinking. When they received their electric bill, it would.

The waitress brought their drinks to the table. Hot, sweetened teas in glass mugs for Alice and Clay, and another Coke for Benjad. The boy sat in the wooden chair staring at the red can with a protruding straw but did not make a move to drink from it. When the food arrived, the Coke had not been touched. Clay noticed now that the child had brought the airplane with him, but just ran his fingers over it. Clay said a blessing over the food and omitted any reference to the incident involving the boy.

Alice and Clay began to eat slowly, but Benjad sat stroking his toy.

"Go ahead and eat your food. I know you will like it," Clay urged. He'd never had to coax the boy to eat.

Benjad lifted a somber gaze toward Clay. Then came the thunderbolt from his lips.

"That was Shaka. He killed my mother and father."

The boy's shoulders shook with sobs. Alice quickly pulled him into her lap and held him, murmuring, "Okay, okay, go ahead and let it out."

Alice looked at Clay imploringly. He felt his chest constrict and fought to control his anger. Clay rose, touched the boy on the head and walked toward the kitchen. He requested a box and paid the check. The young waitress brought a box to their table and proceeded to pack up the uneaten food. Alice continued holding and gently rocking the boy while he cried. The girl gave them a puzzled look. "Ada anak sakit?"

Clay sighed heavily. "Yes, the child is sick, but he will be better in time."

Benjad fell asleep on the way to the guesthouse. Clay carried him in and laid him on the bed and tugged Alice gently as she hovered.

"Best thing for the boy is sleep," Clay whispered. They both walked out into the living quarters and sat down on the rattan couch.

"I had a hunch I knew that guy—bigger than the average Papuan, missing an eye, filed teeth—those things should have been a dead giveaway." Clay reprimanded himself for not putting the pieces together, then slapped his head. "I missed it. The government uniform threw me. I never expected to see a remote villager in Jayapura."

Alice rubbed his shoulder. "You could not have known. And probably it was best you didn't know at the time. Maybe the Lord blinded your recognition because he knew what you might do."

"The glass is always half full, right, lady?" Clay half-grinned. Alice had a disarming way of making things brighter.

"The glass is half full. Benjad is safe. Healing for him can finally begin, and you did not get us kicked out of the country for starting an international incident. So, I would say the half-filled glass is blessed."

Clay cocked his head to one side. "Sometimes, you are right. Maybe this is one of those times." He drew her into his arms and kissed her before she could frown at him for the last comment.

Alice woke first, and stroked her sleeping husband's hair, worried he might have nightmares after this step back to his military time. She'd just started to believe those days might be behind them.

While they'd dated in high school, Clay had been a happy-go-lucky boy with a passion for baseball. He and his close friend, Steve Mancuso, played on the same team—

Steve as catcher and Clay as the star pitcher. Clay had been awarded a full-ride athletic scholarship to the state university. Steve enlisted in the Marine Corps and tried to persuade Clay to join with him on the "buddy" program. Clay had vacillated, but finally told Steve he needed to take advantage of the scholarship.

Clay had been in his sophomore year, playing ball and even dreaming about a professional career, when he received news that Steve lost his life in a rice paddy in Vietnam. Telling her he felt overcome by guilt for not being there for his friend, Clay dropped out of school, despite his parents' pleas, and enlisted in the army.

After saying goodbye to the shell of a man who had been Clay at Steve's funeral, Alice enrolled in nursing school, and he spent six years in the army. When he returned, they renewed their relationship, but Clay returned very different from the boy she had known. The combat scars on his forearm only hinted at the emotional scars he suffered for years.

A shiver went through Alice as she looked at her husband, knowing that below the surface of the man she loved lurked a violence held in check only by his newer Christian nature. He would go to all lengths to protect his loved ones and had vowed never to fail them as he felt he had failed Steve.

He stirred, bolted awake, then seemed to relax when he saw her sitting near.

Alice reached out and laid her hand over his. "Do you want to talk about it?"

Clay glanced up at her with a bit of surprised look. "Talk about what?"

Alice chose her words carefully. "All these years we've been together, I know that sometimes the memories come back. You have nightmares. You have great control, but sometimes—despite your efforts—the anger comes out. Much like what happened yesterday."

Clay pulled his hand away, rose and crossed over to the window. He stared out, but she knew he was not really seeing. Alice waited.

Across the room, Clay sighed. "Sometimes I think I've forgotten about past events. I can even talk about them without bitterness or my heart rate increasing. Then things like yesterday happen, and I fall off the wagon."

Alice listened intently. Clay had never been so open. For the first time since she'd known him, he seemed vulnerable.

Clay sat on the bed next to her. He was quiet for a time, staring at the floor. "I don't know why I thought I needed to get even when Steve died. I don't know why I feel guilty about killing people who wanted to kill me. I don't know why I get so angry about people who demonstrated against the war when I returned home. People showed no gratitude, no sense of honor, no understanding. Then I consider, they were not there, so how could they understand?'

Alice took his hands in hers. "Darling, I know that I can never understand fully what you experienced. But I can understand how you feel somewhat. I compare my feelings of not being able to give you a child to your feelings of guilt. I know it's not the same, but I tell you, those feelings have evaporated since taking in Benjad." She tightened her grip. "It is time you released your feelings of guilt and anger too. God has applied all your experiences, good or bad, for the mission he has for you now. He has given you grace, and it is time to give yourself grace."

Clay swallowed hard and met her eyes with a deep, intense stare. "Did anyone ever tell you you're a wise woman? I needed that, thanks. I cannot guarantee that never again will I feel that anger, but I guarantee that at those times I will remember your words."

He hugged her. They both turned around when they heard a creaking of the bedroom door. Benjad slowly entered the room with sleep still in his eyes.

"Hey, Sport. Did we wake you?" Clay patted the bed beside him.

The boy padded over to the bed and Clay lifted him on to it. "No, Pop. I had a bad dream."

"I think we'd better talk about this man Shaka. Where do we go from here?"

The boy looked fiercely into Clay's eyes and hissed, "I have to kill him! I will avenge my mother and father."

"Benjad, will that make it right? Will that bring your parents back to life? Yes, he should be punished for the evil he has done, but it is not for us to judge. Punishment is for God to give out. Do you understand?"

"God has not punished him." Fire flashed in the boy's eyes. "God has not taken his life to pay for my mother and father. I don't have them anymore."

"Benjad, God's ways are not our ways. We do not always understand why God allows things to happen, but know this—he loves us and wants to take care of us." Clay paused. "I know you do not understand, but in time you will. God has brought you into our lives to help you with your pain and loss. We know we will never replace your mother and father, but let us care for you and love you. I think that is what they would have wanted."

Clay could see by the boy's eyes he was trying to make sense of things. Enough had been said for now. Benjad needed a distraction. He looked at Alice. "Hey, I saw a swing set and playground out back. Why don't we go test them out?"

"Swing set?" Benjad puzzled.

"Come on, we'll show you."

The playground took Benjad's mind off the encounter with Shaka for a while. He even laughed as Clay pushed him high on the swing. He could believe Clay and Alice cared for him, and he appreciated the diversion. However, the sight of the shaman could not be tamped down for good. As they returned to their room for the night, he couldn't shake the image of the frightful killer of his parents. The episode made the past all too real.

Benjad prepared for bed while his guardians talked in the other room. He stood on the footstool, brushing his teeth. He spat toothpaste into the sink and raised his head and eyes to the mirror. Benjad paused and rubbed the back of his head, fingering the welt raised by stitches. An image of his mother lying on the jungle floor flashed across his mind.

*I know it is all real. It is mixed up, but it is real.*

A familiar guilt rose in the pit of his stomach like bile as the buried memories continued to rush into remembrance, now even further back in time. He pictured another morning, when he had been playing in the village with a little bow and arrow, shooting grasshoppers. His mother had turned from cooking sweet potatoes on the wood fire built on banana logs when Benjad heard her gasp—and hunters entered their thatched-roof house, carrying his mortally wounded father.

Leaping to Drako's side, Kalita had worked frantically to stanch the flow of blood, while the hunters backed out of the home. They nervously looked toward Shaka, who stood across the village center sharpening his steel knife.

The memories of that night were frightening. Some parts were a bit foggy for the five-year-old, but he could still recall his father's last words. "Shaka!" The dying man turned his head slowly to Benjad, his eyes barely able to focus. "Avenge me!"

His father sucked in air and made a rattling sound as the child stared wide-eyed at the terrible scene. Then Drako ceased fighting for air and his fading eyes stared at his son.

Jolted back into the present, Benjad dropped the toothbrush and rushed into the room where Pop and Mom were sitting.

He slumped into Alice's arms crying as she sought to console him.

Benjad looked at Clay. "I need to kill Shaka! I am not a bad boy because he killed them. I was there when he killed my father too."

Clay placed his hands on Benjad's shoulder. "We don't believe you are a bad boy. You want to tell us what you saw? You are safe."

Benjad felt safe. He could tell Mom and Pop. With tears streaming down his face, he shared the lost memories with these westerners. He stopped when he uttered the words of his father. "Avenge me!"

Falling into Clay's open arms, Benjad cried until his tears were spent. The three sat quietly until Benjad, with a huge sigh, stood and announced, "I am better."

Benjad heard softness in Clay's voice, "For now, my little warrior. The memories will return sometimes, particularly when you're reminded of the violence you witnessed. I cannot fix the past, but Mom and I will always be here to talk or just sit with you when the past invades your thoughts. One thing I've learned to do at times like this is to think of things I'm grateful for, and to thank God for those gifts."

After a few moments of silence, Clay added. "I know something I'm grateful for. Ice cream. How about we all go out for a treat?"

Benjad shrugged and scrutinized his palms. "I will need much time to grow. I need to take revenge on Shaka. His leg is bigger than my whole body. I will need ice cream to get stronger. I will get bigger, and then I can find him once again."

Clay sighed. "Enough talk about revenge for now. We will discuss things more later. Understand, if you want to talk to us about anything, we are here for you."

The next morning, Clay woke his family before daylight, and they packed the rental car to return to Sentani airport. They arrived as the dawn promised a beautiful day and gathered in a small waiting room adjacent to the mission radio shack. The airways were already crackling with short, clipped voices, mostly Indonesian, with occasional intermittent English.

Clay greeted Yubo, the Sumatran load master, who was busy totaling the weight that would be loaded into the aircraft. Clay placed luggage and boxes onto the scale, with the assistance of some Papuan helpers. Yubo noted the weight in kilos.

Finally, the time came for the passengers to be weighed. Alice remarked, "I hate this part. Turn around, you guys."

Clay could never figure out women. They were so concerned about people knowing their weight. Even their own husbands. The pilots had learned to require a weigh-in for everyone, because even sincere Christian ladies would often underreport their weight, despite knowing precise weights were critical in these small aircrafts. It impacted passenger seating, fuel loads and how much cargo could be safely carried.

He could see no reason for Alice's concern about her weight. She still had the same petite build as when they first married.

Daryl greeted them on the flight line and directed them to board in the same seats. On the flight home, Daryl taught Benjad more about flying the big metal bird. The boy's eyes twinkled with joy the entire flight. Clay offered up a silent prayer of thanks.

Perhaps this would help Benjad put yesterday's traumatic event behind him.

# CHAPTER 24

The Burris family had just finished dinner, and all of them took seats around a makeshift Christmas tree. Benjad patted his stomach appreciatively as he sat. He couldn't remember eating a more delicious meal.

"We have two celebrations today," Clay announced. "Not only is this the day we celebrate the birth of our Savior, but we will also always celebrate this as the day Benjad became an official part of our family."

Benjad beamed.

The adoption process had taken more than three years to formalize. Benjad's parents said this was speedy by all counts in any country. The journey had not been easy. He had Mom and Pop as his staunch supporters, along with the mission community. However, the events of his earlier life sometimes clashed with who he was becoming.

The Pickmans had reported they were pleased with the progress he'd made at school. They called him a voracious reader. Benjad read books years beyond his grade level.

Clay gave Benjad a regulation Little League baseball bat marked "Louisville." Benjad marveled over the smooth grain of the wood. While he turned the bat admiringly in his hands, Alice picked up another box, which had been behind a chair.

"Here, this goes with it," she declared with a smile.

Benjad eagerly unwrapped the box to discover a youth league glove. His original glove no longer fit his hand and had become worn from use. Benjad had viewed video tapes of baseball games sent to Clay by friends in the States who were also aficionados, so he had a good understanding of the game. He also joined his friends playing improvised games.

"Thank you, thank you!" He jumped up and kissed Alice on the cheek and then hugged Clay, almost throwing him off his stool.

"Whoa!" Clay laughed. "Come with me." He rose and headed for his study with the boy in tow.

Alice smiled. "Darling, it is Christmas and we are celebrating."

"I know, I know. Just ten minutes to try it out." Clay walked to the office, talking over his shoulder. He came back holding up his old, well-oiled leather glove. Benjad watched him put on the glove and give it a resounding smack with his fist before grinning at him. "Let's go outside and try your new glove."

Clay admired Benjad's natural athletic skill. Years of throwing rocks at targets had prepared him for the manufactured ball he had received on his first Christmas. The first time the boy threw it, the ball had sailed true and fast into his adopted father's glove.

252

The two had spent many nights together throwing and catching the ball after that. At first, the activity served to help train Benjad in baseball skills, but over the years, their time spent playing catch had developed into something deeper. It created an atmosphere for the boy to ask questions and hear Clay's stories. Several times a week, the two could be found at the side of their home on what passed as level ground, hurling a baseball back and forth. Clay cherished these practice sessions.

This brief Christmas practice session had such a purpose, so it appeared. Benjad seemed quiet and distracted. Clay kept quiet too, allowing him to volunteer what was on his mind. Finally, Benjad caught the ball and stuffed it into the pocket of his glove. He stood erect and asked Clay, "Pop, do you like my name?"

Clay wiped the beads of perspiration from his forehead with the back of his hand. "Sure. Don't you?"

Benjad hesitated, then spoke with authority. "Benjad is a name given to me in a different life. I don't think it fits anymore. I would like to be called 'Ben' from now on, like Ben Franklin."

"Well, if you feel more comfortable with Ben, I could get used to it myself. Why don't you think about keeping your birth name, but your family and friends could call you Ben?"

Benjad considered his suggestion, but still didn't toss the ball.

Clay said, "Let's talk about this with Mom. She would like to be involved in any decision you make. Right?"

The boy nodded his head. "Yes, that is good. We will discuss it with Mom. I will do that now!" Benjad tucked his glove under his arm, spun around and ran into the house, leaving Clay standing there alone.

Clay smiled to himself and shook his head. Then he looked up as he thought he caught a faint sound of aircraft approaching.

That's puzzling.

Daryl was not due back for another couple of hours. Clay walked slowly toward the front porch. "Ben, could you come here?" Ben bounced out of the house grinning as his new name reached his ears.

"Sir?" He approached Clay on the porch.

Clay continued to scan the heavens as he spoke. "Here, could you put my glove back in the hot box with yours? And tell Mom I'm going to the hangar. I think we're having company."

Ben glanced up. He could hear it now. He could identify various aircrafts by the sound of their engines. "That's Uncle Daryl."

Clay did not think it was an emergency because no one manning the radio had come to tell him. Still, he had an uneasy feeling about Daryl's unscheduled return. "You stay here at the house."

Disappointment registered on the boy's face. He had become very fond of both the pilot and the aircraft. He regularly met incoming flights and saw them off when they departed.

Clay handed the glove off and turned toward the hangar. Now he could see the approaching aircraft. To his relief, he detected no sounds from the engine evidencing problems. He reached the hangar in time to see the Helio making its final approach. He glanced toward the open window where Eli sat at the desk, talking on the radio, presumably to Daryl. The Papuan looked toward Clay and widened his arms in a gesture that communicated, "I don't know what's going on." Clay nodded.

He shaded his eyes with his hand as the small plane cut power and drifted toward the uphill grass runway. He could see Daryl leaning forward in concentration and flaring the plane as it gently touched down. It continued its uphill course until the speed reduced and the left brake turned the craft around. Daryl raced the motor to complete the turn and headed back to the hangar.

Clay could now make out two passengers, a large man occupying the copilot seat and a smaller man in the seat behind the pilot.

More curious than ever, Clay waited. Guests were rare and always scheduled their arrivals. And Daryl was typically good about notifying Clay of potential visitors.

The Helio came to a halt with the pilot's door facing Clay—and Eli, who had emerged from the radio shack and stood beside him. The motor cut and silence reigned as Daryl extricated himself from the seatbelt and helmet. He saw movement on the passenger side as the visitors disembarked. Daryl swung his long legs out from the aircraft and hit the ground walking, clipboard in hand. When he neared Clay, he gave a tight-lipped shake of his head. Something had happened. Daryl had even left his Aussie hat in the cockpit.

Clay could not be quiet any longer. "What gives?"

"Well, I was just about to leave Sentani when a government car pulls up and two official looking chaps approach me. They said it was critical they get to Sago Lake on this flight. I told them I had other scheduled flights, but the big Papuan says to me, 'This is government business and you need to change your plans.'"

The irritated pilot shook his head.

"The other guy, who is the Bupati for this region, did not seem pleased with the Papuan's abruptness and tried to make amends for his rudeness. Still, it seemed to be urgent, so I rearranged my schedule. Sorry, I didn't get a chance to let you know."

Clay waived his hand. "No harm, no foul."

Pak Satono walked up to Clay, smiling. He extended his hand and introduced himself, and apologized, "Minta maaf for our sudden arrival. However, we urgently need assistance of this community."

Clay looked over Pak Satono's shoulder and stopped cold at the sight of the large man with an eyepatch. The missionary clenched his teeth. Narrowing his eyes, he glared at the Papuan. "Why is this man here?"

Satono glanced at Shaka. "This is Bapak Shaka. He is the kepala desa for this region."

Neither man offered his hand in greeting. Shaka returned Clay's steely gaze and said nothing.

"We have met before." Clay spoke through tight lips.

Pak Satono looked uncomfortably from man to man.

"Bapak Burris, I understand you are the director of this community, so we need to talk. However, we will make it brief and leave this afternoon."

"Daryl, would you show this man to the waiting room while I use the radio shack to conduct a meeting with Bapak Satono?" Clay never took his eyes off the shaman.

Shaka stood his ground. "I am over this region. You are the visitor."

Clay snapped, "I am a guest of the Provincial Governor, President Suharto, and the Director of DEPSOS, the agency concerned with social development. They issued the invitation to me long before you held your position. So, allow me to discuss business with your superior." Clay's pointed retort was not in keeping with Indonesian protocol.

Pak Satono looked stunned, and even Eli and Daryl's faces registered surprise. Shaka's good eye flashed a curse.

For a few tense seconds, time stood still. Clay's lips curled slightly at the corners as though he were ready to smile. His calm demeanor belied his words. Daryl looked at Satono, whose mouth hung open as he blinked rapidly.

Daryl stepped in to defuse the situation. Ignoring the tense standoff, he placed himself between Clay and Shaka as if this exchange were just friendly bantering. "Bapak Satono, right this way. It is much cooler in the radio shack. Eli, would you kindly show Pak Shaka to the waiting room and bring some tea for our guests."

Pak Satono, eager to escape the confrontation, gladly accepted guidance to the small room attached to the hangar. Eli walked up to Shaka and flatly commanded, "Follow me." Eli spun around and walked briskly to the waiting room.

A violent rage etched across Shaka's face. He slowly walked behind Eli but turned his head toward Clay. "Another time you will see you need to listen to my voice."

"Only when your voice is saying goodbye." Clay calmly walked away.

In the relative darkness of the hangar waiting room, Eli turned and indicated a bench for Shaka. He now stood face-to-face with the man who had killed his friend, Drako, and Drako's wife. Eli chose his words carefully.

"We have never met, but I think you know a friend of mine—a good friend. His name was Drako. Unfortunately, a cowardly shaman killed him while he was out hunting."

Shaka jerked his head up at Drako's name. However, the shaman recovered quickly and crossed his muscular legs in a calm manner.

"No, I don't think I know him … Oh, yes, I do remember him. It seems he also took a wife from another clan, which angered his people." Shaka ended his remark with a slight taunting smile.

Eli stiffened. "He was a good man and a good hunter. Both he and his wife were killed and left a young son in need."

Shaka stared at Eli for a few seconds before he spoke again. "How did they die?"

"You have heard the stories, I am thinking."

Shaka shrugged. "I hear many stories. Some true, some not."

Eli leaned forward slightly when he spoke. "I wish I had been there. Then my friend's story might have had a different ending."

Eli drew himself up. Without the customary Indonesian polite phrase to excuse himself, he left the room before things could ignite further. He walked to where Daryl stood servicing his aircraft and picked up a bug sponge from a bucket of soapy water. He began to vigorously scrub crushed insects off the horizontal stabilizer.

Daryl watched his animated motions and then stepped closer to him. "What's going on, Eli?"

Eli paused and looked at the pilot. "Shaka is the man who killed Benjad's father and mother."

"What? How do you know?"

Eli put down the soapy sponge and told Daryl his story.

Clay offered Pak Satono the most comfortable seat, the air traffic controller seat, and sat on a high stool. He observed the tension in the man's eyes and decided to try to tell him.

"Pak Satono, please forgive my rudeness to the kepala desa. I am normally not at all that way, but Shaka and I have met before. Twice. And neither time has been friendly."

Taking a deep breath, he summarized the encounter in Jayapura and the one in the village when he first took the injured boy for treatment and ultimate adoption. He took care to avoid accusing Shaka of being responsible for the death of the boy's father and mother, but he alluded to their deaths and the stories he had heard.

Pak Satono listened intently, nodding his head in acknowledgement. "Pak Clay, this is a troubling story. I know very little about Shaka's life before he took the appointment several months ago as head of this region. However, I have to accept him as the regional advisor because his people put him forward and Jakarta commands me to work with the Papuan people."

Clay nodded. "I understand your position. And please accept my apologies to you for being harsh. It was not directed at you."

Satono relaxed and even offered a smile. "I thought you were just being direct like most Americans."

Clay returned his smile. "Well, my wife often accuses me of being too direct, even for an American." Then the missionary became serious. "It is like this. Pak Satono is always welcome here at Sago Lake. I am a guest in your country. But Shaka is not welcome here. He is trouble for all my community."

Pak Satono, apparently not used to such blunt words, sat in quiet thought for a few moments, as if choosing his response carefully.

"Bapak, as I have said, Pak Shaka has the role of kepala desa for this region. I am his supervisor, but some things I cannot change. I cannot promise he will not come here again, but I can promise I will do my best to see he avoids coming here. If you can assist me in what is needed, what we came here for, I will do my best to see that your contact with Pak Shaka is limited."

"Please go on. How may I help you?"

Pak Satono sighed.

"A group of researchers and medical scientists wish to study local plants for their medicinal potential. Others want to study insects, some of which are only found in this area. Basically, they need accommodations and meals. I understand your compound has hosted many guests in the past. Would you be willing to serve these scientists as well?"

Clay raised an eyebrow, and Pak Satono quickly added, "Of course we would pay for the service."

As a community developer, Clay saw the proposition's value immediately. Not only would such visitors provide more service jobs for the locals, but they could also help translators identify needed medicinal plants. They could then include the teaching of the findings in their literacy programs.

"I would need to talk to some of the others, but I am certain they would be agreeable. We would be honored to assist you." Clay bowed slightly, still seated on the stool.

He wanted to invite Pak Satono for dinner at his home but did not want Shaka to accompany him. Clay delicately approached the subject. "Bapak, I do not know of your plans, and I would be failing as a host not to offer you dinner and a place to stay the night, but ..."

Seeing his dilemma, Pak Satono waved and said, "Tidak apa. We have to get back to Jayapura tonight, so we need to be on our way."

"Okay. I will talk to my pilot. At least allow me to send some food along with you." Clay did not wait for an answer. He ushered Satono out the door and beckoned Eli and Daryl inside.

They were curious about the discussion, but Clay told them he would talk later on the topic. He turned to Eli. "I need you to go to my house and ask Ibu Anache to pack a light meal for our two guests. Oh, and maybe a third one for our pilot. I don't want him stealing food from the passengers."

Eli chuckled and looked at Daryl. "Yes, Pak. I will go right now."

Clay called to him as he started off, "Eli, we are burning daylight, so get back as soon as possible. Don't be entertaining Ibu Anache." Eli's grin widened and he nodded before he hurried along.

Clay shook his head and turned to Daryl, but before he had a chance to speak, Daryl voiced his thoughts.

"Slippery, you might as well pack my lunch in navigational maps. I can take a hint. You don't want me around." He pursed his lips in mock dejection.

"Captain, I hate to do this to you. But could you find it in your heart to forgive me and take these cats back to Sentani? The Bupati says he has to get back tonight, and, well, this will not be a good scene if one character stays."

"I understand." Daryl frowned. "Eli somewhat filled me in on who Shaka is and what he did. Besides, I like you owing me favors. Gives me a sense of power." He swelled his chest and stuck his chin out.

Clay looked skyward. "Oh, Lord, what have I done to deserve this?"

Daryl clapped his friend on the back and laughed. "I'll get the bush hopper ready. You do realize I won't be able to return from Sentani today? It will be almost dark when I get there. You need to explain to my bride why I am not sharing the bed with her tonight."

Clay cocked his head to the side. "I will take care of it. She'll be grateful to get one night of rest without having to listen to your snores."

Eli returned with the meals in three small cardboard boxes and three bottles of water. The Papuan met Pak Satono outside of the waiting room where he stood scribbling notes regarding his visit in his agenda book. Eli bowed slightly, offered the meal box with his right hand, placing his left hand on his forearm respectfully. Then he extricated a bottle of water from his string bag and duplicated the formal presentation. Pak Satono graciously accepted the gifts and thanked him.

Eli excused himself and went into the waiting room attached to the hangar where Shaka still sat on the bench, leaning on the wall and dozing. He did not duplicate the polite presentation of the food to Shaka as he had done for the bupati. He merely set the items down on the end of the bench, using his left hand. Shaka glared at the insult, but he did nothing.

Clay stayed with Daryl as he refueled the airplane and finished his servicing. Despite the urgency, there was never room for error in bush flying. Going down in this land promised an unforgiving adventure.

The two men had finished their meal by the time Daryl had the aircraft ready. Pak Satono thanked Clay for his cooperation, and Clay told him he was honored to assist. He said nothing to Shaka.

Eli and Clay stood watching as the little aircraft took off, banking left toward Sentani. They watched the plane until it flew out of sight.

"I hope Shaka is taking all his invisible evil minions with him." Eli murmured.

Clay echoed his friend's sentiment. "And that we will not see the man again."

Deep inside, he knew better.

# CHAPTER 25

Alice sat on the veranda as she worked on the lesson plan for the care of newborns. She labored to make the training as simple and accurate as possible for the village women, using words and concepts they understood while respecting traditions and customs held for a millennium. Distracted by the sounds of her husband and Ben engaged in an energetic game of catch, she looked up from her legal pad and watched them over the top of her reading glasses as they played, oblivious to her presence.

She could not believe how time had flown. The family had taken a long-needed furlough last year to return to the States. Ben had been overjoyed with what he experienced, but not overwhelmed. He met the family and friends of Alice and Clay. She could not have been prouder of him. He was indeed her son. The churches they'd visited welcomed them with open arms.

Ben, at fourteen and becoming a man, had been blessed with strength, health, and a gifted mind. The young man had amazed Steve and Doris Pickman with his rapid grasp of language, math, and critical thinking. He had already caught up with international students his own age, and,

YOU CANNOT GRASP THE RIVER

in many cases, surpassed them. Frequent meetings among the home-schooled students in the community helped to further Ben's progress.

Alice did, however, find herself pondering his spiritual life. Ben had made great strides in education, he spoke Indonesian and English with equal fluency, and he had an understanding she did not have of the way technology worked, but he was still influenced by the spirit world of his ancestors. She knew he had an inclination toward the supernatural that conflicted with the Bible. However, he went to church and read the Bible, seeking answers. He asked probing questions about the Christian faith. She knew he was not there yet, but she also knew her prayers would be answered.

Crouching behind their makeshift home plate, Clay provided the patter of a baseball game in progress. He flashed signs for a fast ball to the pitcher. Ben nodded, grinned, and leaned forward, clutching the ball in his right hand against the small of his back. He paused to spit like he had seen the major leaguers do on the VHS tapes. Then he reared back and delivered a solid fast ball straight into Clay's glove with a satisfying smack.

Clay pulled his hand out of the glove and waved it through the air as though it were on fire. "Smokin'!"

Ben grinned. "Actually, my shoulder is tired, so I am no longer throwing at my usual supersonic speed."

Clay laughed. "All right, all right. Humility has not caught up to your pitching skills. Work on it." He stood up from his catcher's position and removed his glove. "Tell you what. Since you are such a cutup, let's see if you do as well with these projectiles." He strode over to a nearby bench used mainly for resting sports equipment, set his glove on one corner of the bench, and then picked up a cloth-wrapped package.

Ben jogged to the bench while Clay unwrapped the package revealing four gleaming flat throwing knives.

"All right!" The teen's eyes shone.

Alice removed her readers. Although their backs were toward her, she caught a glimpse of the reflected sunlight on the throwing knives.

"Clay!" She called to her husband in a voice that smacked of disapproval.

Her husband turned his head toward the veranda and smiled impishly. "What?"

Alice sighed. "You know we talked about the knives."

"I know, but it's just sport. What's the difference in throwing darts or throwing knives at a target?"

Alice repeated her sigh and accompanied it with a shrug. "I give up."

Clay turned to Ben. "Remember, your mom is uncomfortable around all weapons. She sees knives as weapons."

Ben grinned at his father. "Well, you ought to remove all knives from the kitchen, and we can sit and watch Mom cut up a chicken with a spoon."

Both man and boy broke out laughing at that image.

"I've got good hearing!" Alice called from the veranda. "I can't help it if your son is a joke boy."

Clay and Ben moved to the slab of a cross-cut tree, set up as a target near the bench. Clay had drawn concentric varying circles in white and black paint on the heavy wood with a black bulls-eye in the center. "I'll let you go first, so I'll know how much effort I'll have to expend to beat you."

"Hah!" Ben grinned. "That much effort, you do not have."

The throwing knives were carefully balanced and well cared for. Clay had purchased them while in the military—he had carried two concealed in his boots when he was on patrol in the Vietnamese jungle. Although he'd practiced with them regularly with other men in his group, he'd only enlisted them for use one time during his service. That one time probably saved his life. Now, he just enjoyed target practice for sport.

Clay's experience showed, but Ben, a keen learner, proved himself a worthy adversary.

After the third match between father and son concluded, Ben turned to Clay. "Congratulations! Again! I don't think I will ever win."

"And I hope you maintain that attitude, so I can continue to beat you."

They gathered up the hobby materials while Clay quizzed Ben on baseball knowledge. The boy had an amazing memory for details. They made their way to the veranda and sat down near Alice. Both grabbed for the pitcher of lemonade.

"Got it!" Ben exclaimed. Glancing at the table, he saw only Alice's glass. He frowned and slowly tipped the pitcher up towards his face pantomiming drinking from the container.

Alice lifted her hand. "Hey, stop that! Get a glass."

Ben winked at his mom. "Just goes to show you, you can take the boy out of the jungle, but you can't take the jungle out of the boy." Both Clay and Ben chuckled.

Alice looked at her husband. "Who does he get this from?"

Once in the house, Ben retrieved two glasses. He heard the crackle of the Motorola walkie talkie sitting in its charging cradle on the kitchen counter. Eli's voice emerged above the static.

"Pak Eli, come in. This is Ben. Over."

Eli spoke curtly. "Tell Clay to come to the hangar right away."

Ben carried the two glasses onto the veranda and placed them on the table beside the pitcher, as Alice and Clay discussed her future class in the village.

"Excuse me. Pop, Eli needs you in the hangar right away. He sounds a little upset."

Alice, pouring the lemonade into the two glasses, paused at this news. "Upset?"

Ben nodded, taking one glass and handing the other to Clay.

"Thanks." Clay rose and tossed down almost half of the lemonade. "I better get down there."

Alice remarked, "I will join you. It might be a medical issue."

Ben mimicked Clay's action, then said, "I'll go with you."

"Stay with your mom while she gets her medical kit together. I'm not sure what kind of situation is unfolding, so wait until I contact both of you via radio."

"Aw, Pop!"

Clay was already descending the steps and only answered with a raised hand.

Clay trotted down the path but slowed to a walk when he neared the hanger. He took in the scene. Eli was in an animated conversation with a big Papuan, whose brown uniform and large build were unmistakable. It had been a long time since their last meeting. Shaka had not flown in on their aircraft, but Clay heard he had made several appearances by boat. He even reportedly took a team of researchers into the jungle to search for plants, in exchange for money and gifts. The scientists, out of their element, gladly gave him some rupiahs, ostensibly to pay off some clan chieftains for trespassing, and gave a tape recorder to the government official.

The researchers had reported Shaka's bribery to Clay when they returned to Sago Lake where they stayed, and he had gone to the Bupati's office in Jayapura and reported the incident to Pak Satono. Satono assured him he would investigate the case, and if he found evidence, he would take corrective action.

Clay had also stopped and visited the office of Colonel Imade, a Balinese military man with whom he had developed a rapport through playing golf. They frequently ate lunch together when he made his trips to Jayapura. Often Ben would accompany him. The colonel, who did not have children of his own, had taken a special liking to Ben. He never failed to take him out for ice cream.

Clay had thought it beneficial to invite him along as they visited with Pak Satono. He hoped it would lend some motivation for action on the Bupati.

Evidently, either Pak Satono had not delivered any ultimatums, or the colonel did not have the weight he thought, because Shaka still wore the uniform.

As Eli and Shaka exchanged harsh words, village fishermen stood by with their fresh catch from the lake.

Clay did not recognize the two men flanking Shaka. One had a machete slung on his back. The other did not appear to have a weapon.

"Is there a problem?"

Eli swung around. "I caught him charging the fishermen a tax for catching fish!"

Clay eyed the uneasy fishermen. "Is that true? Is this man trying to collect money from you?"

The men looked fearfully at Shaka without answering. Shaka answered instead. "The clan chiefs insist on a tax if they want to take fish from the lake and send it to the Sentani market. I am here to collect for them."

Clay gestured with his head. "They and their ancestors have been fishing these waters ever since the earthquake formed the lake." He took a step forward. "It is their lake. No one has to pay a tax on the fish they catch."

The two men with Shaka shifted their positions.

"Why don't you both stay put." Clay spoke through clenched teeth.

The men stopped moving as Eli inched within reach of a wrench lying on top of a fuel drum. Only the sound of birdsong broke the silence.

Clay turned back to Shaka. "Do I need to check this tax policy out with your Bupati?"

Shaka flashed two rows of filed teeth. "Do as you wish. I am just following orders."

"Whose orders?" Clay tensed. "I suggest you leave. Next time you show up around here without an invitation, I will see what the military thinks of charging these people."

Shaka stepped within five feet of Clay. At the same time Clay heard rapidly approaching footsteps just as Alice shouted, "Ben!"

Ben raced toward Shaka, fists clenched and hatred and determination darkening his face. Not taking his eyes off the three men, Clay uttered one word, "Eli."

As if rehearsed, Eli covertly snatched up the wrench and placed it into Clay's waiting hand behind his back, then flew toward Ben. In a simulated pincer movement, Eli reached Ben's side and slid his arm through his left arm, while Alice, bounding up from behind, caught his other arm. The boy's strength as he briefly struggled against them surprised her, but she held firm and whispered, "No."

Shaka turned his eye toward the boy. He sneered and touched a thumb to his eyepatch and then thrust the digit toward Ben. The man with the machete reached toward his neck and Clay brought the heavy pipe wrench from behind his back to the front, tapping it on the empty palm of his other hand.

As if realizing there were too many witnesses, Shaka took a step back. "We are going—for now. But remember, this is my land, my people. You are only here by my permission."

"We discussed this before, and things have not changed." Clay tapped the wrench again.

Shaka turned abruptly and headed up the path toward a neighboring village, followed by his henchmen. Over his shoulder he called out, "We will see who stays here."

Clay moved to the three who were clustered together and handed Eli his wrench. "Could you not do better than this? Maybe you could have handed me a machete to match the one they had?"

Eli grinned. "Pak, you need to give me a raise to buy some more tools." He released Ben and patted him on the shoulder. "It is over."

Alice relaxed her hold and put her arms around Ben's shoulders. She smiled at Ben. "Did I tell you today that I love you?"

Ben could not speak, but only nodded.

Clay watched the three men disappear down the path. He whispered to one of the larger fishermen to follow Shaka and his henchmen. "Make certain they leave the area."

The man nodded and took off.

Clay turned to Alice and Ben. "I thought I told you two to wait for my radio call?"

Alice said, "You did, but while I was trying to get my medical kit together, I heard the screen door slam and Ben was on his way. I barely caught up to him."

Ben dipped his eyes to the ground. "Sorry, Pop. I just got worried when you didn't call right away that something was wrong." Ben looked up at Clay. "I am sorry."

All eyes were on the boy. Clay smiled and reached out, grabbing both of Ben's shoulders.

"Okay. You're forgiven, but next time there will be brig time. You have to learn to obey orders like I do when your Mom gives me orders." Clay chuckled and glanced at a frowning Alice. "Well, that kind of puts a damper on things. How can we change this mood?" He pondered for a moment, then gave Eli a wink. "Hey, we were going to celebrate Ben's birthday tomorrow. Seems like we should push it up a bit."

Eli grinned and disappeared into the hangar. He returned, pushing a 125 cc Suzuki dirt bike. Ben's eyes widened, and for a moment he forgot what he had just been through. He looked at Clay and Alice. "For me? Is it really my birthday gift?"

They both nodded.

"Just one stipulation. You will wear a helmet when you are on it," Alice warned.

Clay added, "And your Pop gets to ride it whenever he wants to."

Ben ran up to the bike and caressed the handlebars. "That's a deal!"

Clay had been waiting for the motorcycle to be delivered from Jakarta, and then for a time when Daryl had a light load so it could be flown from Sentani to the lake. Eli had set it up and ensured it ran like a dream. The rest of the afternoon until darkness overtook them, Clay taught Ben how to ride and shift through the gears. He showed a natural aptitude for riding.

The next morning, Ben woke his parents by tapping on their bedroom door and asking for permission to ride his bike. Clay looked at the worried expression on Alice's face and said, "He will do fine."

Alice called out, "All right, but be back by breakfast time."

At lunch time, they surprised Ben with a birthday party. Alice sent him on a fictitious errand, and when he returned, all his friends who still lived on the compound and were not on furlough leaped from their hiding places, shouting and blowing horns.

"Happy birthday, big boy," Fina said softly, then Robert clapped him on the back and pulled him toward his friends. The young adults spent the next hours playing games and thoroughly enjoying each other's company.

Later, as Alice and Clay sliced and plated cake in the kitchen, she said, "I thought the looks Fina and Ben exchanged today were priceless."

Clay halted his knife in mid-air. "What do you mean? What kind of looks?"

Alice sighed. "You can spot a cross-eyed ant fifty feet away in the jungle, but you don't notice the looks they share?"

Clay stared at an imaginary movie screen, trying to recall their exchanges. Exasperated, Alice spelled it out for him. "They have a thing for each other. Maybe it's just puppy love, but they are growing close. No more competing and trading insults, or at least they are lessening."

"Oh, oh. I gotcha," Clay said. Alice rolled her eyes and shook her head.

After the guests left, Alice and Clay sat on the veranda, watching the sun sinking in the west into a short-lived tropical twilight. Ben came out to join them.

"Pop, Mom, I want to thank you for the best day of my life. No, the best day was when you adopted me." Ben hesitated, then grew serious. "I am sorry for going after Shaka in front of you. I realize I put you on the spot as missionaries."

Clay cleared his throat. "So, what were your plans if you had reached Shaka?"

"I am not sure. I just want him to pay for my mother and father. I want him dead." Ben looked away.

The evening insects were tuning up for their nightly orchestra. In the darkening papaya grove, the deep "whoop" of giant fruit bat wings joined the percussion section as the nocturnal creatures searched for the choicest fruit.

Benjad sighed deeply, then spoke in a soft, measured voice. "Pop, you were a military man, like a warrior in Papuan culture. You once shared with me that you joined the fight after the death of your best friend. What is the difference in what you were doing, killing in the name of country to avenge your friend, and my desire to avenge my blood parents?"

Clay responded gently. "Ben, I have not been through what you have been through, but I have lost people close to me too. I also wanted revenge, but revenge is a slow poison. When I realized the Lord could not live in my heart beside my vengeance, I had to make a choice. And now I know I made the right choice."

The boy leaned on the rail, staring upward as the first stars appeared on the horizon. "Remember when I told you my father said, 'you cannot grasp the river'?"

Clay nodded. The young man continued, "Well, I guess it is true that no matter what you do, some things you cannot control. They slip through your fingers. It seems like I have never been able to control my life."

Clay leaned forward. "Listen to me carefully. Your father was a wise man, and I hear he was also kind and brave. He taught you special things. Now that he is gone, I believe God has provided Mom and me to continue your education. Do you believe that is possible?"

It was Ben's turn to nod.

"So, he left you with a saying that challenged you to find the true significance of what it means to try to grasp the river."

Ben studied his adopted father's face as Clay continued to speak. "I believe God has called me to provide the answer to the idea your father planted in your mind. Water is necessary for life, and Jesus is called the Living Waters. Could it be the water your father spoke about would be revealed to you in the future as the Living Waters?"

Ben knitted his brows. "I ... I'm not understanding."

Clay reached for the glass of water on the table beside him. He poured a little stream out, opening and closing his hand as it filtered through his fingers. "Just like the river, if you try to grasp it, you fail. However, if you use the river's flow to carry you along, you can go places, as we did when the river carried us here a long time ago. In the same way, the Lord is in control of all, and he wants us to surrender to him and allow him to control our lives. Sure, there will be rocks along the way, but he will carry us around the rocks and through the rapids and eddies. The river can be the journey, or it can be a frustrating force you try to control. Let the river take you and awaken you to new things. Let God float you along to his purpose under his protection."

Ben's face shone in the rising moonlight as he pondered the concept. Clay knew Ben would need time to unravel the feelings in his mind, but that was okay. He had two people who deeply cared for him, friends who surrounded him, and a new life before him. Clay prayed the boy would come to see the water as essential for his journey and learn to trust God to take him to the planned destination.

"Son, we cannot control all the things in life, but as long as we journey with God, then he will care for us. Your father described a problem, and perhaps the God I share with you is the solution."

# CHAPTER 26

The high-pitched whine echoed throughout the hills as the two-stroke Suzuki engine powered Ben and his bike up the mountain trail. Ben could see the villagers watching from below as he dashed up the nearly impossible slopes, his rear knobby tires spewing out reddish clay. Perhaps they found it entertaining to see a Papuan succeeding in the orang barat world. Two Papuan women stepped off the trail and cheered him on as he raced past, giving a quick smile and a nod of his helmet.

Ben had always been friendly, and he talked freely with the tribal people, spending equal time with them as with the foreigners. He hunted with his Papuan friends and developed excellent tracking skills. He'd also learned from his family to be quick to share food or to help those who needed it.

Today, Ben was taking his last bike ride until Christmas. Although he would miss this daily trek on his machine, he felt blessed. Soon he would park his bike in the hangar and join Fina and Robert on a flight to Sentani to attend the International School.

# You Cannot Grasp the River

He halted the bike and turned off the ignition on the side of the mountain overlooking Sago Lake to the west. To the east, he could see the tiny community of the expats, as well as the airstrip and hangar. He enjoyed watching aircraft take off and land, often pretending to be in an aircraft himself circling the airstrip, waiting for his turn to land.

Daryl had launched this love for aviation by explaining the mystery of flight in his own animated way. He often allowed Ben to ride with him when he transported a light load. Sometimes he even allowed Ben to take over the duplicate flight controls. To Ben, nothing compared to the feel of the yoke and pedals under his feet.

Now Ben just wanted to reminisce about his life since arriving at Sago Lake. The change he faced today would have similar impact as those changes he'd faced when Pop rescued him. His education had prepared him for high school, and the International School would take him further. Robert's sister, Cora, already a year ahead of them in her sophomore year, had given them a good idea of what to expect.

Ben wavered between excitement and apprehension. He would be among new international students, mostly children of missionaries. In some ways, he would have preferred to remain at Sago Lake, working on airplanes, riding his motorcycle, playing catch with Pop, reading, and having fun with friends. He had found peace and love here.

Ben's happy childhood with his new parents made him feel guilty sometimes. He tried to avoid his thoughts about Shaka, not only because they depressed him, but also because his Christian parents expected him to put events behind him.

But his parents' killer still lived. If he had never met Shaka or known that he still lived, maybe he could have gone on with his life untouched by the tradition of vengeance passed down through his father. In his new world, revenge did not have approval. He struggled with that. He knew Jesus, and believed he was the Son of God, but even God condoned punishing evil people. How could a kind and loving God not allow good men to kill the evil ones?

He brushed aside these thoughts to focus on the here and now and the joy and excitement of a new experience.

He'd better get back to the hangar for his flight.

What would it be like, living in a dormitory with other boys? Ben took a deep breath, replaced his helmet on his head, and kicked the engine over. This would be his last descent from the mountain for a while. He would make the most of it.

Alice stood in front of the hangar talking with Robert's and Fina's parents while Clay checked off names from a list of missionaries in the villages as they radioed in to report their status. Their isolation made it imperative that each couple or individual check in on the radio with the compound each morning.

Parents and children were demonstrating a range of emotions as the time neared for the teens to board the plane. Alice joined other adults in the bittersweet lament over children who would not be the same when they returned. The teenagers seemed generally eager for the adventure that lay ahead, but she could still detect a bit of worry and onset of homesickness on their faces.

"Have you seen Ben this morning?" Alice stopped Robert and Fina, who were nervously laughing as they chatted about life at the International School.

Robert looked around. "Yes, ma'am. He came by my house while I was getting ready. I think he's out for a last bike ride before the flight."

"Aunt Alice, I am sure he is okay." Fina smiled. "I have to admit, he rides well."

"Well, I know he wanted to take a last ride, but a short one—he knows the flight departure time."

Alice went to stand with the other parents, but her mind strayed. She scanned the tree line for Ben. She should have set a time for him to return. If that boy returned with his clothes in disarray or dirtied ...

The faint sound of a high, whining, two-stroke motorcycle engine broke into her thoughts. She squinted into the jungle, seeking a glimpse of rider and bike. The other parents fell silent, watching Alice's worried face. Robert grinned at Fina, who shook her head and rolled her eyes. Daryl looked toward the group and half-smiled. Alice did not smile back.

Clay emerged from the radio shack where the waiting group stood watching the narrow trail as the intense sound of the motorcycle increased.

Alice gave Clay her tight-lipped grimace. Clay shrugged his shoulders.

The descent exhilarated him. Ben would beat his personal best time from mountaintop to hangar. He wanted to look at the stopwatch on his wrist, but he dared not take his eyes off the trail. The bike and its rider sailed into the air as it cleared the last berm and broke out onto the airfield. He slid to a halt in front of the hangar and quickly pressed the button on his chronograph. He studied the marked time.

A new record!

He lifted his arms in a triumphant celebration and imitated a roaring unseen fan club. "Yahhhhh!"

Not until he removed his helmet and turned his head did he see his real audience standing there. Robert grinned, and Fina stared blankly. Pop and Daryl just looked at Alice, who had her hands on her hips. A bad sign, hands on the hips.

"Ooh, am I running late? Sorry."

Alice must have been holding a lot in, because she marched right to him. He swallowed a smirk when he realized she had to stand on her toes to look him in the eyes.

"Put that bike up, clean yourself up, and get your things together."

"Yes, ma'am." His moment of bravado deflated like a leaky balloon. Ben pushed his bike toward the hangar, where he met Eli securing the cargo inside the airplane.

"I will take care of that, Wild One." Eli grinned as he grasped the handlebars.

"Can you make sure it is serviced until I get back, Eli?"

"I will take care of it. You have a good trip and study hard." Eli leaned the bike against his leg, clutched the boy's hand, and shook it. Ben nodded.

Ben ran into the hangar and directly to the deep-well sink where aircraft parts were cleaned. He turned on the water and briskly rubbed his hands and face. He looked for a towel and spotted a greasy one, but chose instead to flap his hands to air dry them.

He returned to the group and faced his mother. She softened immediately, smiled at him, straightened the collar of his shirt, and said, "I hope you don't do things like that when you get to school."

"No, Mom. I only do things like that here."

Alice halted her rearranging of his shirt and frowned at him.

"Just kidding." Ben grinned.

Alice leaned in and spoke quietly. "And lest you go into a panic when you check your luggage and find something missing, I removed them. The throwing knives are not something that should be in a dorm."

"Ahh, Mom, I gotta stay in practice. Pop will keep in practice with them while I am gone, and I will never win our contests!"

"I will hide them from him, so when you get back, no one will have any advantage. Now, you concentrate on your studies and having fun. But not too much fun." She kissed his forehead.

Ben smiled. "Bye ... love ya." Then he sheepishly looked around to see if his friends were observing the exchange.

Clay approached them. "Well, Steve McQueen, your bike is going to have a rest. It and I expect you to concentrate on your studies while you are gone. Understand?"

"I understand you both," Ben replied.

Clay shook Ben's hand, then pulled him close and gave him a brief hug.

As Daryl loaded the passengers into the craft, Ben noted the misty eyes of the mothers and Fina. He caught Robert's eyes and shrugged. If Robert wouldn't show emotion, he wouldn't either.

Soon they were airborne, and Ben watched his family members become miniaturized as the aircraft gained altitude, certain his friends were doing the same. Were they a little homesick already too? The roar of the engine made conversation impossible, which he considered a good thing.

Two hours later, compliments of a steady tailwind, the little aircraft landed. Ben climbed out of the plane. The cargo handlers already had the door to the aircraft storage open. Ben reached in and grabbed his backpack from behind the passenger seats. An afternoon shower had left warm puddles all over the tarmac and the blazing sun that followed created intense humidity. He walked with the others into the waiting room, his pack slung over his shoulder. Their hostel parents would arrive any minute to transport them to their new home away from home. As the freight workers unloaded their belongings from the craft, Ben plopped down onto a bench, swinging the pack between his legs.

Fina took a seat opposite him. She stared into his eyes. "Birdbrain."

Ben sat up, surprised. "What is your problem?"

"It takes a birdbrain to take off on a motorcycle wearing good clothes and make like Evel Knievel when you're about to leave your family."

Robert, sitting beside Ben, placed his hands behind his head and rocked back on the bench, grinning. "I thought it was cool."

"If I wanted your opinion, I would have given it to you," snapped Fina.

Robert looked up at the ceiling, still smiling, but with a puzzled look as well.

"Yes, that was an insult," Ben said, then cocked his head toward Fina. "You have no appreciation for the finer aspects of my character."

"The only character you have shown is not having good sense," retorted Fina. "Honestly, you are constantly taking chances and do not consider the feelings of others."

Ben feigned hurt. "Oh, you cut me to the quick!" Then he grinned and slyly said, "Are you trying to say you care?"

Fina gave him a flustered glance and fumbled for words.

"Guys, our keepers are coming!" Robert stood.

Lloyd and Nola Christian, houseparents for the school, entered the waiting room, smiling. They were in their late thirties. Mom had told Ben they had a three-year-old girl of their own, and they were both former counselors in public schools.

The kids already knew the houseparents from trips to Sentani, when they and their parents had visited to observe life at the hostel. The pair greeted them enthusiastically.

Ben found Nola's lilting voice soothing. "I know I met you three last year on your visit," she said, "but I would like to know what each of you would like to be called?" She pointed at each child, "It is Fina, Robert, and Ben, right?"

"Birdbrain!" Fina corrected in a barely audible annoyed whisper.

"Sorry?" Nola looked confused.

"She often says things that don't make sense, Mrs. Christian," Ben offered politely.

"Oh. Okay. And it's Aunt Nola and Uncle Lloyd here. Let's grab your stuff and head for the ranch. We have more kids to meet there, and pizzas are waiting for us."

When the houseparents turned and walked toward the waiting van, Ben raised his arms and waddled like a pigeon out the door behind them for Fina's benefit.

Fina had lost this round. He grinned at her as she dispassionately brought up the rear.

The school and hostel were perched on a high steep hill with mountains in the background and were surrounded by cyclone fencing. An open gate with a guard shack greeted the van. Three Papuans leaned against the concrete block structure. Lloyd raised his hand to the guards, but only slightly slowed as he passed them and crossed into the inner compound of the school.

As he rode, Ben admired the facilities and the immaculately landscaped campus covering about thirty acres. Approximately three hundred yards from the actual school sat a long building he would call home for the next four years. He elbowed Robert and pointed out the window. "There is our prison until we are paroled at age eighteen."

Robert laughed. "Yeah. I wonder if the other inmates will accept us?"

"They have probably heard about the Sago Lake Lunatics and will not mess with us," Ben said.

Fina half turned in her seat in front of the boys. She rolled her eyes at Ben. "You are still a birdbrain."

"Well, then, if I decide not to stay here, I will simply fly away, but you will be stuck."

She rolled her eyes upward and turned back to face forward.

The van halted in front of the hostel's extra-wide door. Out rushed three girls and two boys, with hands extended in greeting. They exchanged names and asked routine missionary-kid questions—Where is home? What mission are you with? How long before your furlough?

Ben and his Sago Lake pals entered the hostel, passing through a small lobby/greeting room and into a large room with overstuffed couches and chairs. There were bean bag chairs and several soft rugs on a cool tile floor. On one wall, a huge screen hung over bookshelves jammed with VHS tapes. Ben crouched to read the names on their sides. Some were Hollywood movies, but most were just home recordings of television shows, sports, and National Geographic documentaries.

On a low table in the corner, two girls and two boys played a fast-moving game of Dutch Blitz, while in an adjoining room, two significantly older boys had a ping pong ball bouncing back and forth. They halted their game and greeted the group.

"Hey, David." Lloyd addressed one of the senior boys who had been engaged in the ping pong game. "Would you show Ben and Robert to the room they will be sharing?"

The big redheaded boy smiled and headed toward them.

"Sure. Walk this way." He proceeded to hunch over, drag one foot behind the other, and head toward a long hallway.

Robert leaned over and imitated David's walk. Ben followed, chuckling. David glanced back and caught the last seconds of Robert's antics. "That's it. You saw the same movie!"

Robert reddened and straightened, "Ah, yeah. Great flick, wasn't it?"

David stopped in the hallway at the door to their room, turned and gave an exaggerated bow with a full sweeping arm gesture into the room. "Gentlemen, your humble abode for the coming year."

Ben stepped into the austere room containing two single beds separated by a window. Through an open door they could see a shower, toilet and sink.

"Home away from home," Ben quipped.

David grinned, leaning against the door jam. "It's all in the mind. It pays to have a vivid imagination."

Their host gave them a rundown on the particulars of the room and policy requirements, such as where they should take their trash baskets when they were full, expectations for cleanliness, and lights-off curfews. He also warned them of impromptu inspections.

Looking at his watch, David headed out the door. "It's time for pizza. You snooze, you lose. Come on."

Ben and Robert tossed their bags on the beds and followed their new acquaintance to the dining room. He kept chatting as they walked. "I think your suitemates just got in from a swim. You can meet them over the pizza. Hopefully, Bernie will be too busy eating to interrogate you to death."

The new students spent the rest of the evening eating and getting to know the hostel members. For Ben, the experience resembled coming to Sago Lake for the first time—except he now knew the language, and the culture shock was less.

That night Ben slept lightly, waking several times. There was so much to get used to—sharing a room and being with lots of kids from places he had only heard of, and the kids were all so different in their talk and personality.

Ben looked at the clock that had been his nemesis when he first arrived at Sago Lake. The clock's hidden demons had disappeared, and, though old, it kept good time and had become his friend. Ben smiled at the glowing face. He yawned as 12:30 a.m. blinked to 12:31. The boy closed his eyes one last time for the night.

He looked forward to a great time here.

# CHAPTER 27

The years passed quickly, and although Ben thrived in school, he enjoyed his Christmas and summer breaks at Sago Lake. Graduation was bittersweet.

Ben spent much of his time off in the hangar, helping Daryl maintain the plane and working with Eli. He sat in the hangar one afternoon cleaning his bike's carburetor in a pan of airplane fuel when the Australian pilot entered the hangar. Ben gave him a nod.

"I haven't seen much of Eli on this visit." Ben set the clean carburetor on a work bench. "Will he be by today? I wanted to return some tools he loaned me."

"He'll be here soon," Daryl said. "He and Anache made a little house out of that storage building down by the lake. Married life seems to agree with him—he's no longer here around the clock."

Ben smiled. "That was a great wedding. I'm glad they waited until Christmas so I could be home."

Daryl dropped some paperwork and a catalog on the table near Ben. "Here, my little friend. Something for you to look over."

"What's this?" Ben wiped his oily hands on a rag.

"Now, I was counting on the outside chance you could read. Or do I have to read it to you?" The Aussie smirked.

Ben nodded. "Point taken, sir. I will peruse it with great care."

Daryl grinned and tipped his Aussie hat, then shuffled off along the path.

Ben watched his mentor disappear down the trail, then sat down on a well-worn stool beside the workstation with the literature in hand. A slight breeze stirred, sending welcome relief from the heat through the hangar. Rubbing his hands briskly, he picked up the catalog.

Ben read aloud, "LeTourneau University, Longview, Texas."

He had heard of this school, an aviation and engineering institute with a Christian base. Many missionary pilots and mechanics had graduated from there. Ben turned the pages in awe, his heart pounding more forcefully with each sentence he read. Was this his future? Could he really fulfill his dream of flying?

Ben finished reading the catalog and then reread it before he opened the envelope. He pulled out an application form from the school and a letter of recommendation from Daryl. Warmth spread through his chest as he read the glowing remarks about his interest, skills, basic knowledge of a flight program, and praise for his Christian walk.

Ben held a death grip on the letter and catalog as he stared at the Helio Courier squatting outside the hangar.

"Yes, yes! This is what I want. This is what I was made to do!" Ben leaped to his feet and let out a whoop of joy, startling Eli, who was walking in.

"Yaaa, Wild One!" Eli exclaimed. "What is going on? I almost ran back to my house to get my bow and arrows and defend myself."

"Eli, I found where I want to be. I want to be in the sky!" Ben grabbed the older Papuan's shoulders.

Puzzlement clouded Eli's face. "Plenty of time for that when you die."

"No, no. I want to be a pilot like Pak Daryl!"

"Oh, that is good. But don't wear the crazy hat and tease old Eli, yeah?"

Ben laughed. "I promise. Gotta go. I'll talk with you later." He raced out the door, catalog and letter in hand.

Alice watched Ben race up the hill toward their house and launch his tall frame over the steps and onto the porch. At first, she feared something bad had happened, but the smile pasted on his face eased her mind. He threw open the screen door and darted into the house, but halted when she blocked him, hands on her hips. He spun around and caught the screen door before it could slam shut, then closed it with exaggerated slowness and gave her that crooked grin she loved so much.

Alice nodded and smiled. "What's going on?"

Ben adopted a serious expression. "Where's Pop? I am officially calling a family meeting."

"He is in his study. Let's see if he is free."

Ben followed Alice down the hall where they paused while Alice tapped on the door. "Honey, can we talk?"

From behind the closed door, a gruff voice answered, "Only if you have President Suharto, Billy Graham, or Ben with you." Alice smiled at Ben and opened the door. Clay sat behind the heavy desk, leaning back in a creaky wooden office chair. He tossed the papers he'd been working on aside, then leaned forward and said, "Okay. Which of the three are you?"

"I am the president—in disguise." Ben smiled.

Ben set the university catalog on the desk in front of Clay, who glanced at it. "What's this?"

"Now, I was counting on the outside chance you could read. Or do I have to read it for you?" Ben's Australian accent made Clay raise his eyebrows.

"Sorry, that's what Uncle Daryl said to me when I asked the same question."

Clay lowered his eyes back to the catalog. "Hmmm." After reading the cover and thumbing through the book, he took a deep breath. "So, is it a romance, adventure, or mystery?"

Ben sat on the corner of Clay's desk. "What? Pop, I want to attend this school and get a degree from there. Uncle Daryl already wrote me a letter of recommendation." Ben waved the letter in front of him.

"You would have thought the flyboy would have the courtesy to speak to me before giving you all this information and encouragement." Clay took the letter with a solemn air.

Ben's smile faded, and confusion replaced it. He looked at Alice, who leaned against the door jamb with a slight smile and folded arms.

"Don't torture the boy! Can't you see he's on the verge of imploding?"

Clay smiled and popped his lips in his thoughtful manner. "We knew what your Uncle Daryl had planned. And we are one hundred percent behind this idea. We just want you to want it with no reservations."

"Yes, I want to do this. I love flying. Most of all, I feel one day I can be of help to my people and share the Lord with them in the process." Ben's face glowed. Neither Alice nor Clay spoke as he continued. "I believe the Lord has been showing me things I never understood before. Great things."

Clay flipped through the catalog and nodded. "I want to ask one question." His eyes became serious. "How do you look at vengeance for the death of your parents in this process now?"

Alice could see his blunt question took Ben by surprise, and for a few seconds, he sat quietly.

"I don't know. I mean, I know how I feel. I cannot forget my anger and hatred that easily. Most of all, I still feel that if I don't avenge my parents, then I am one who has forgotten honor."

Alice sighed. His answer fell short of the one Clay wanted, but at least he spoke the truth.

Clay showed neither anger nor sadness. He folded his hands and placed two index fingers on his lips. He swiveled his chair around and pointed out the window, where the white cockatoo sat on the branch of a giant tree. She walked sideways until she was poised over a cavity between trunk and limb. Only then could Ben see the necks stretching out from a hidden nest to hungrily devour the food their mother had brought.

"Do you remember a couple of years ago that same cockatoo had a nest of young ones in the same tree? What happened to her chicks?"

Ben, puzzled at the change of topic, answered anyway.

"Well, a snake seized them, killing every one of them—all the while the mother had a fit, screaming her lungs out."

"She grieved the loss of her young, yet she chose to raise another family in the same tree. Do you think she is still dejected or plotting to get even with the snake?" Clay looked directly into the boy's eyes.

Ben returned the gaze. "No. I guess she accepted it and moved on. She has another purpose to her life."

"And now you have another purpose to your life." They watched the mama bird. No one spoke until she flew away in search for more food for her chicks.

Clay broke the silence. "I want you to have the freedom to pursue your purpose, but you have to trust that God will take care of Shaka."

Alice put her hands on Ben's shoulders.

"Ben, anger is like a chain tying you to Shaka. That chain can keep you from accomplishing God's plan for you. By giving this over to God, you will be setting yourself free. The school is not only aeronautics—it is also preparing pilots for mission work. Holding hatred is not compatible with the purpose of this institute."

"I never considered that before. I will spend some time thinking about this. I promise."

Clay patted his back. "Son, that's all I could ask for." He slapped the papers on his knee. "Now that you have decided your future occupation in the world, what do you need to accomplish your goal?"

Ben's excitement returned. "Money! I guess money to pay for it, right?"

"Talk to your Mom. She stole all my money when we married. Now she keeps me captive by not allowing me to have more than five dollars at a time." Clay made a dejected face.

"Oh, stop it! Your pop is pathetic." Alice grinned, then lifted his chin to look him in the eye. "If you are sure that is where you want to go, we will help you get there. Of course, you already have a scholarship for your grade point average."

Ben smiled. "I will start the application today."

The family moved into the living room and sat around the rattan coffee table, studying the catalog. After the three thoroughly digested the information, Clay stood and held out a hand to Alice, helping her from her chair.

"Your mom and I need to make some medical rounds. We should only be an hour or so."

"That's okay. I want to share my plans with Fina—I mean, my friends." Ben cringed.

"No, you meant Fina. Friends are low on your priority list," Clay teased.

"Okay, okay, so she rates." Ben's sheepish smile lasted only a moment before his face lit up. "Wait a minute! It just dawned on me that Fina is going to Houston to study nursing. We will be close!"

"Well, not within walking distance." Clay offered.

Alice smoothed his hair, then gave him a kiss on the forehead before shooing him toward the door. "If it's meant to be, things will work out for the two of you."

"Yes, yes. Gotta go!"

She watched Ben's face light up as he raced out the door. Such a man already. Where had her little boy gone?

Ben practically danced down the trail to Fina's house, replaying the events of the past hour in his mind. This would come as a surprise to Fina. He had thought he would stay working here for another year. She had thought the same thing.

Now he could share the good news. He had a sobering thought. What if I am not accepted at the school? It's late to be applying. I have to be accepted. They will accept me.

He turned his thoughts to more pleasant ruminations. Not until a couple of weeks ago had he discovered she had the same feelings for him as he did for her.

They had talked about her plans to leave the next month for nurses' training as they walked to the lookout point above the airstrip. He wanted to tell her about his feelings but did not know how. She turned to him on a secluded part of the path and said, "I will miss you. I hope you will miss me."

Her candor took Ben off guard. "Certainly. More than you will ever know."

He found it difficult not to stare. She wore faded jeans and an oversized black, batik-print shirt, but her trim, athletic figure was outlined. Her smooth skin and classic features made him smile, but her eyes were what caught his attention, as they always did. Like deep brown pools of laughter.

Fina raised up on her toes and lightly kissed him, sending ripples of electricity through his body. "I love you."

The memory warmed Ben. Now he was at her door knocking. Fina opened the door and glanced behind her, where her mother was busy writing a newsletter.

She stepped out onto the porch and quietly closed the door, smiling into Ben's face all the while. Her smooth brown complexion was framed by long raven hair. The scent of lavender heated by her warm skin lingered in the warm air. He took her hand and led her to the swing.

"Sit down. I have some news to share with you. It's good news for me, and I hope you will feel the same." Ben seated himself on the swing as he pulled her beside him.

Clay held Alice's hand as they walked the path to the perimeter village. Alice carried a well-worn canvas satchel containing her miscellaneous medical gear. They were heading to change some bandages on a young woman who had sliced her foot with a machete while splitting open a coconut.

While she worked, he planned to pay the fishermen on the list Daryl had given him. Clay was especially proud of the fish project he had managed to set up, as well as the income it generated for the villagers. The successful fishermen would bring their fresh night catch on a prescribed day of the week to the hanger. Daryl would weigh each fisherman's catch and list their name and the kilos, then fly them to the Sentani market. Others would negotiate a price for the fish and exchange it for national currency.

As Alice and Clay made their way to the village, they chatted about Ben's decision for college.

"Of course, I'm happy for him," Alice murmured. "I'm just a bit concerned over how we'll cover the cost."

"I'm sure his 4.0 grade point average will help him get a scholarship."

Alice agreed. "I am sure he will qualify. Also, my family inheritance could supplement the costs."

Clay suddenly slowed his walk, and Alice followed suit.

"Keep walking," he hissed, moving close to her side.

He had caught a slight flash of light out of the corner of his eyes, high above their path—just a brief flash, but he recognized it immediately. A reflection off some sort of mirror or lens. Binoculars. They were being glassed!

Clay focused on Alice and affected a smile. "Don't look up. Keep looking at me. We are being watched."

Alice stiffened, but did as commanded. "Who is watching us? And why?"

Clay said, "I have no idea, but keep walking until we make those trees. Don't let on you are aware of anything."

Clay knew Alice trusted his military training and wartime experience. It had given him a sixth sense that rarely proved wrong. They moved into the dense foliage of the trees overhead, and only then did they stop. Clay took Alice by both arms and directed her to stand with her back to a large tree. He then moved toward the source of the suspicious glimmer, keeping hidden under the thick canopy. He leaned against a twisted, lightning-struck mango tree and systematically searched the distant area for clues.

The light did not repeat itself. He knew someone sat watching high above the landing strip. The local villagers did not own binoculars, and the people in the community who did were away. Clay debated climbing the jungle mountain to investigate, but he couldn't leave Alice alone. He retreated to where Alice waited, and they resumed their walk to the village.

While hidden high up on the mountainside, Shaka had quickly lowered the field glasses to his chest when the missionary abruptly slowed his pace. Burris could not have detected him. Still, this unusual westerner was skilled in the ways of the jungle. He'd known this from the first time he had seen him after he had killed Drako's woman many years ago.

300

The couple reappeared on the path after being out of sight for a short time.

Why did they stop? Maybe to pick some fruit from the mango tree near the path. He would not take a chance. Not now.

He turned to Sim, his assistant, who squatted nearby, gnawing on his fingernails. The moment Shaka made eye contact, the man showed his nervousness.

"Pak, I am worried about being seen here. You know Bapak Satono said we should avoid coming here," the man pointed down the hill. "The orang barat does not want us here, either."

Shaka seized him by the shirt and swung him backwards on the ground from his squatting position. "This is my land. These people are intruders. I will be here when they are long gone. Then the whole Lake Sago will be mine!"

Sim sprawled on the ground cringing. "Yes, Bapak."

That was more like it. Shaka suspected Sim feared him more than Satono or the orang barat, and he wanted to keep it that way. Besides, as long as the money kept coming, Sim would be satisfied to collect his salary and ignore Shaka's indiscretions.

Shaka turned back to his surveillance, but the Burris couple had disappeared down the trail. He prepared to head back to the canoe to move out of the area before anyone spotted him. One day this land would be his, along with the wealth of fish, crocodile hides, and the profitable payments by outside researchers. He would be chief of all.

"Now, I am ready to go. Tell no one we were here."

The two men moved down the mountain toward the lake, creeping from tree to tree. The canoe was concealed in the lakeside foliage away from prying eyes. They were careful to avoid meeting with any local inhabitants. Shaka murmured to himself, "I will be back here for good—and soon."

Shaka and his accomplice stayed on the path for about half a mile. Then they broke from the trail and descended through swampy growth until they located their hidden canoe with its new Johnson motor. Shaka had acquired the boat motor from a Jayapura dealer after hearing the ethnic Chinese dealer express his fear of traveling to remote areas to sell and repair motors. Shaka offered guaranteed safe passage to outlying lumber camps and remote camps for geologists, mining experts, and botanist researchers. The boat motor was given for protection.

Shaka and Sim paddled the canoe out into the lake, maintaining stealth until they were well offshore, then started the motor for the journey home. They would not be seen. They traveled down a tributary to the Mamberamo, then downriver to the government vehicle and driver waiting to take them back to Jayapura.

As he powered the rough dugout downstream throughout the lengthy trip, Shaka had plenty of time to construct his plot. As long as the westerners controlled Sago Lake, especially with Burris at the head of the community, there would be little he could do to exploit the profits of that resource. There was money to be made, and money was power. He had learned well from the outside world.

Mulling over how he could get the government to make these people leave, Shaka sensed Sim staring at him and sent him a glare. Sim quickly dropped his eyes and looked forward. Shaka let a slow smile creep across his face, exposing his sharp canines to a worried-looking Sim.

He had formulated a solution to the problem.

The westerners were guests in the country. The last thing the government would want to happen would be to have a guest killed. Governing officials would lose face — something they had to avoid at all cost.

He considered the infamous Papuan Separatists. They were more a nuisance than a danger, but they were gathering in increasing numbers, and there had been some violent clashes. If government officials could be convinced this rebel movement presented a real and credible threat to westerners, they would quickly evacuate westerners from Sago Lake.

Mere rumors would not be enough. However, a death attributed to the Papuan rebels could concern the government, and they would order westerners out of the area for their safety.

He needed a modern weapon, a weapon that only the military or police were authorized to possess. The rebels were known for obtaining contraband such as guns. It would be compelling evidence of the work of the nefarious resistance movement if a gun were used in the death of an expatriate. Shaka knew exactly who he wanted to be the martyrs for his cause—Burris and his adopted Papuan son. Benjad had cost him his eye. Burris had humiliated him in their physical encounters and stood in the way of his quest for power. They both deserved to die, and their deaths would clear the way for him to take over the area of Sago Lake.

Shaka laughed out loud above the noise of the outboard motor, startling Sim. The underling stared at Shaka. The shaman leaned forward and reduced the motor speed to idle.

"I have a plan, and you will help me to carry it out. Again, tell no one we were here. If you do what I tell you, you will be rewarded."

Sim licked his lips and nodded. Shaka let the canoe drift with the current and specified what he wanted Sim to do when they returned to Jayapura. After he finished laying out the plan, Shaka leaned back, twisted the throttle and resumed their journey.

He tilted his head, embracing the feel of wind and spray on his face. He would destroy the man and the boy. He might even have to taste their flesh, something he had not done since he was a young man. Imagine the power he could acquire by devouring them.

Waiting would be the hardest part.

# CHAPTER 28

Pak Satono's heart raced as he waited outside Colonel Imade's office for the man to acknowledge his presence. The two met infrequently. However, today Satono had requested a confidential meeting. He hated reporting anything but good news to his senior.

The colonel finished his task and looked up, inviting him to enter. After he had been seated in the military leader's office and they had exchanged pleasantries, Satono said, "Colonel, I have been hearing the Papuan Separatists have been active around the Sago Lake region. I have heard of nothing they have done, but it makes me uneasy."

Imade tilted his chair back and squinted at the government official, taking a few seconds before he replied. "That is interesting. May I ask who your source is and if they are reliable?"

The question made the Bupati squirm. He did not want to name names in case the military called the source in to be interviewed. "It came from one of my workers from the area."

Imade waited. He kept his face expressionless.

Satono knew he had committed himself, and nothing short of the source would be acceptable. "Sir, it is someone familiar to both of us, the kepala desa, Shaka. He has been warning me about the danger to the western community working in Sago Lake. I am just relaying this information."

The colonel stood up and turned to the window in his office. He remained silent for a few seconds and then turned to the concerned Bupati. "Pak, do you believe this man Shaka?"

"I don't know. I don't trust him, but what reason would he have to make up the story?"

"Well, for one thing he hates Bapak Clay, the director of the community. Secondly, he would like to have access for enriching himself by extorting the scientists who are studying in the area."

Imade leaned his knuckles on the desk and looked directly at Satono. "I have known Pak Clay and his wife Ibu Alice for many years. I know him to be a man of his word, and he is my friend. What he tells me about Shaka, I believe, including his claim that this man killed his adopted son's mother and father. I know the boy, Ben, and he fully remembers Shaka took his parents' life. Seems there is no proof, but if Pak Clay says that it is true, then it is true."

In the ensuing silence, Satono's breathing slowed with the realization the man shared his concerns regarding Shaka. Now he could be candid also.

Satono sighed, nodded, and said, "I believe the merit of your words, Colonel. Regrettably, I have no evidence against Shaka for his intentions or his crimes. No one will dare testify against the shaman." Satono leaned forward in his chair. "What do you think we, or I, should do? I will say, Shaka gives me chills. He is evil."

The two paused their conversation while a sergeant entered with some customary tea and fried bananas.

306

Colonel Imade took his time adding cream to his tea and taking a slow sip before responding.

"Sooner or later Shaka is going to make a mistake, and I will be there. If you would watch him carefully and report any suspicious activity to me, I would be very grateful."

"I will definitely keep you posted." Satono held up his cup in salute and the two men settled into small talk while they enjoyed their tea and rice. Then Satono stood.

"Permisi, I need to return to my office," Satono gave a shallow bow followed by a handshake with his left hand over his right forearm as a gesture of respect.

He paused at the door. "Oh, Colonel, there is something I should tell you. It may be nothing."

Colonel Imade tilted his head.

"Shaka wants to borrow our vehicle from the carpool to deliver some medical products to the villages north of Sentani. I find it strange because he has never shown concern for the Papuan people, especially people of another clan. He is making his trip tomorrow."

Imade nodded. "Keep me posted. Just monitor him. Probably it will be best that we keep this meeting to ourselves."

"Be assured, I will do that. I agree that we need to keep this confidential." Satano bowed again and left the colonel's office, stepping out onto the bustling Jayapura street.

Pak Satono kept his head down as he walked toward his own office. He had traveled no more than a few yards when he looked up into the eyes of Shaka, who stood in front of a store holding a white plastic bag. The abrupt meeting startled him. Had Shaka seen him exit the colonel's building?

He forced himself to remain calm.

"Oh, Pak Shaka, I thought you were coming tomorrow."

Shaka's face was devoid of expression. "I decided to leave today to deliver the medicines. There is a great need for them. Of course, I need a vehicle. Sim will be driving."

"Yes, yes. I think the vehicle is available." Satono searched the man's face for a sign that he had been found out.

"Good, then I will head over to the motor pool."

Satono, eager to be done with this encounter, edged backward. "Yes. Well, I have a meeting with the director of agriculture. Please, allow me to be on my way."

He inched by Shaka and fought the urge to run. He race-walked all the way to the street corner without looking back.

Shaka watched until Satono disappeared around the corner.

"I need to be careful," he muttered, then turned and entered the store where Sim hunkered behind a tobacco display.

Shaka motioned for Sim to come. "He is gone. Let's get the vehicle."

Two hours later, he and Sim were north of Jayapura, Sim clutching the wheel of the Mitsubishi van. In the passenger seat, Shaka kept looking out the window behind them. They had dodged some heavy traffic in the small towns linking Jayapura and Sentani, making it difficult to determine whether anyone followed them. Now that they were moving past Sentani, where the road transitioned to gravel and dirt, any surveillance would be obvious.

Shaka finally relaxed. They had not been followed. Even with no reason to suspect someone surveilled them, he would remain vigilant. Satono might be too fearful and stupid to monitor him, but he could have said something to others who were bolder.

"Turn here!"

The van bounced violently as Sim obeyed his leader, forcing the vehicle over deep, rain-washed gullies of what had once been a road. They lurched about two hundred more yards, and then Shaka commanded, "Stop!"

Shaka motioned for Sim to shut off the motor. He rolled down the window and listened, peering intently at the terrain around them. After a few minutes he stepped from the vehicle and nodded at his companion. Sim, ever the obedient servant, followed suit.

The men approached the rear of the van and opened the tailgate. Shaka moved aside a pile of nokens to uncover an item wrapped in coffee bean sacks and tied with string. After a final glance around, Shaka untied the strings and pulled off the sacks to reveal a military M16, along with two magazines, each fully loaded with twenty rounds. He picked up the rifle gingerly, and a warm sense of satisfaction flooded over him.

Without looking at Sim, Shaka asked, "Have you heard anyone talking about the weapon being missing?"

Sim thumped his chest and gave a smug grin. "No. The base has not missed it. There have been no reports from the armory, and the soldier who smuggled the gun out was very happy to get the money. If it is found out he is the one who stole the gun and sold it, he could be executed. He will not say a word to anyone."

Sim turned to the rear of the vehicle, opened a cardboard box, removed a military can, and flipped the latch and lid up to expose more ammunition to view.

"I believe Bapak Shaka will need these to practice," said Sim.

Shaka nodded, admiring the M16 that had been used by US Marines and other soldiers during Vietnam. "Good. I do not want any ties to me."

The shaman plunged his hand into the ammo container and pocketed some shells, picked up the rifle and the two magazines. He started walking through high grass up the hill adjacent to the rutted road, calling over his shoulder, "Bring that empty box and follow me."

Sim snatched the cardboard box from the cargo space and slammed the tailgate shut, pausing to lock the vehicle before starting up the hill. On the other side of the hill, the area was uninhabited. Shaka told Sim to go down the hill until he called for him to stop.

Sim descended the steep hill with the box, glancing back at Shaka until he shouted at him to stop. He motioned for him to set the target about seventy yards from where Shaka stood. Sim could not help but be a little anxious. He had to turn his back to Shaka in order to position the target, and Shaka had the gun. Trust was not something that this shaman elicited from most people. He consoled himself with the fact that Shaka needed him for his plots. Sim had considered turning him in to the authorities, but then he would have to admit his part in criminal activities in the process.

Sim had not been told the details of Shaka's plan. He assumed that the gun played a role in the scheme, but he did not want to be a part of its destined use. He was satisfied with obtaining the weapon.

At any rate, Shaka needed him, at least for now. He placed the target and trotted back to Shaka's position, assuming a position behind the shooter.

Shaka slotted one of the twenty-round magazines into the weapon. He knew the ritual began with a solid smack to seat the magazine into the receiver.

Although Shaka had never fired a weapon or even handled one until two months ago, he made up for his unfamiliarity by dedicating himself to practicing at least once a week. He had become as proficient with the rifle as the bow.

Shaka lifted the rifle to his shoulder and took aim. He checked his rifleman stance. Not militarily perfect, but it would do. Shaka fired. After emptying the magazine, he lowered the weapon and spoke to Sim. "Go get the box."

Sim jumped up and ran to retrieve the box. He returned grinning, "Pak, you have all the holes in the box. All 20 holes. How did you know how to shoot so well?"

"Remember when you dropped me off at the base every Saturday for the last two months? I knew a sergeant who let me watch them practice. When no one was around, he would let me practice some."

A light went on in Sim's eyes. "Oh, Sergeant Petrus. Yes, yes. The one you gave cigarettes and beer to."

Shaka stood silent as Sim processed this information.

"Ahh, I thought you were doing business for the office. You were exchanging what he wanted for what you wanted."

"Everybody wants something. The only difference between him and me is that I know what he wanted and why. He knows what I wanted but does not know why. He thought I was a poor ignorant civil servant who only wanted to play army." Shaka sneered.

"But why did you want to learn to shoot, and why do you want this weapon? You know you can never legally possess one, let alone shoot it." Sim's expression was serious now.

Shaka showed his teeth. "Now, we are ready. I will take the next step in my plan."

Shaka carefully wrapped up the M16 into the coffee bags and retied them tightly. "Let's go."

When they were again in the van, Shaka said, "Take me to the village where my boat is kept. I want you to drop me off there and return tomorrow before evening. My clansmen will join us then and we will leave early the following morning."

"Leave for where?" Sim held his breath.

"For Sago Lake."

Sim squirmed. "Why Sago Lake? They don't want us there. The orang barat made that clear, and Pak Satono also said not to go there."

Shaka's fist struck the side of his head, driving him into the closed driver-side window. He gasped and slurred, "Ohhhhh, sir!"

But Shaka ignored him. "It is my land! They are trespassers. The westerner will surely die for insulting me, and the Papuan boy will join him if I get the opportunity."

The focus had returned to his driver's eyes, but the man kept his head pressed against the window, cringing as if he expected further blows.

"Maaf, maaf!" wailed Sim. "Please, I did not mean to offend you."

Shaka forced an almost trancelike, peaceful expression over his face. He narrowed his eyes and relaxed his fist, which had been primed for another blow. Instead he gently patted Sim on the shoulder.

"There. You have made me angry. It is not wise to question my plans." Shaka lowered his voice. "Besides, you want to be a rich man, right?"

Sim nodded, still cowering. "Ya, ya. Tell me what you want me to do."

Shaka straightened in his seat. He spoke slowly and deliberately. "Take me to the boat. Go back to Jayapura and turn in the vehicle. If anyone asks, you took me to Abepura, where I stayed with my cousin. Then you go home and pick up some food for the journey. Also, bring a machete. I want you to take a taxi to the village of Tempi. Don't come to the boat village. You can walk the rest of the way—it is not far. Be there by nightfall tomorrow. No sooner, and no later. Do you understand?"

Sim raised a trembling hand toward the knot rising on the side of his head, but Shaka glared at him and he halted abruptly. The servant nodded vigorously, "Yes, Pak Shaka, I will do that."

Shaka sneered.

"Sim, Sim. I will own Sago Lake and you will have a part in the riches that flow into our pot. Don't you want to be a big man? Just do what I say, and I will take care of you."

This time the nod was barely perceptible, yet pain filled the man's eyes. "For certain, it is as you wish."

The village where Shaka kept his boat lay only about a twenty-minute drive from Shaka's target practice range, but to Sim it seemed hours before they arrived. His head throbbed. He'd never experienced such shock and pain before. The blow had elicited a light show like firecrackers before his eyes, and now he fought to stay alert. Any swerve could bring another blow.

As soon as they stopped, Shaka yanked the keys from the ignition and jumped from the vehicle. He opened the back and retrieved the rifle and ammo box. Walking to the driver's side, he tossed the keys into his assistant's lap, then leaned in, putting his face close to Sim's face.

"Remember, tomorrow by nightfall, and speak of this to no one."

"Yes, sir." Sim wanted to be out of Shaka's company, but he knew better than to speed away and reveal his fear to the Papuan. He forced himself to drive slowly, but kept eyes trained on the rear-view mirror.

When he could no longer see Shaka, he pulled over and let out a series of gasping sobs. He gingerly reached his hand up to check the knot on his head. Stealing and tricking people he could understand, but killing was not part of his set of skills.

He put the van in drive and continued on his way. This had to end. But what could he do?

Shaka watched the van disappear. The fear he had instilled in Sim should keep the man's cooperation. When he had served his purpose, then he, too, would die. Right now, though, Shaka needed him.

The shaman looked forward to meeting his two clansmen, who should arrive tomorrow. They had been with him on war parties and shared in his killings and spoils many years ago. They had remained in the jungle, which is why he chose them. They had no real contacts with the outside world and had proven to him their capability for brutality.

Shaka placed the wrapped weapon on his shoulder and smiled in anticipation of the fruits of his plan. He hoped the henchmen would arrive on time. He turned and strolled into the village. One of his wives awaited him, albeit, he suspected, a little reluctantly.

The next day dawned without the usual overcast. Shortly before noon, Shaka's two accomplices arrived. Dima, a tall, angular man only a few years younger than Shaka, had participated in several brutal battles with Shaka. The younger one, Pata, was short, stocky, and too stupid to be afraid of anyone. They both had excellent tracking skills. In addition to their isolated jungle background, Shaka chose these men because they were not given to boasting and had already kept some dark secrets.

Additionally, they respected Shaka for his supernatural powers.

After Shaka's wife fed them, Shaka took them aside to the shade of a mango tree and began to ask questions about their monitoring of Sago Lake. Particularly, he wanted to know all about Burris's day-to-day schedule, asking probing questions. He had long since realized men were creatures of habit, and he had learned to exploit that weakness.

The two clansmen reported all they could recall.

"Every Wednesday, Burris walks to the Korsi village and pays the fishermen with money his pilot brings back from the Sentani market." At Shaka's raised eyebrow, Dima quickly explained, "We overheard a fisherman who walked past our hiding place after he'd been paid."

Shaka paced as he processed the information. Pata drew in the sand with a stick. The drawing coincidentally took the shape of a woman and Pata, with renewed interest, made some anatomical additions. He fixed his attention on his drawing and smiled at his artistic ability. He nudged Dima, who glared at him and down at his drawing, then elbowed him back with an angry whisper. "Stupid!"

With a hurt expression, Pata dropped his stick and sat quietly by his comrade while Shaka continued to pace back and forth. Finally, his pacing slowed as he raised his head.

"Here is what we will do." Shaka laid out the plan of action. "We will wait for Sim to join us this evening. Then after a night's rest we will travel by boat to the lake and camp overnight on the opposite side of the community. The next day will be Wednesday. The day when the man travels to pay the fishermen."

He repeatedly cautioned the two men that they were to remain hidden. "Early the next morning before light, we will cross the lake and take up positions near the hangar along the path Burris takes."

Shaka squatted and grabbed the stick Pata had been using for his drawing. He obliterated Pata's intimate illustration of the female form and proceeded to draw a map of Sago Lake.

"Here is the hangar, the place where they keep the airplane."

Both men nodded.

"Here is the path that the westerner takes to the Korsi village." Shaka paused and then continued after ensuring the men were paying attention. Then he drew a square connected to the hangar. "Here is the radio shack. We need to destroy the radio so no one can call for help. It will also give us time to get out of the area unseen. There should not be anyone in the radio shack that early in the morning. But if there is, kill them. Quietly."

Shaka stared deeply at the men as he spoke. They did not show any signs of surprise or shock. "When the white man comes down the trail, we will wait for him to go a short distance. I will shoot him, maybe many times. If anyone hears the gunfire, they will think it is children playing with fireworks."

He again paused to impress upon his cohorts that he would deal the death card to Burris. "Once he is down, I want you to use your machetes to cut him up. I want anyone who sees his body to be struck with fear. Furthermore, the money for paying the fishermen, and there should be plenty of it, belongs to both of you. You can take it all."

Dima and Pata looked at each other and smiled. Shaka did not know whether they were more pleased at the thought of mutilating the body or at the promise of money.

"One thing is very important," Shaka added. "It has to look like the work of the Papuan Separatists. That is why you are not to be seen."

Both men nodded. Shaka scratched out the map of Sago Lake and stood up. "Sim should be here tonight. Get some rest, and no palm wine. I want you fresh to leave early tomorrow morning."

Shaka returned to the hut he shared with his woman and uncovered the rifle hidden under the blanket in the corner. Satisfied, he caressed the wrapped weapon, laid down on a thin mat and fell asleep, gleefully anticipating his future riches and the death of his enemy.

# CHAPTER 29

Darkness had blanketed the valley when the three assassins made camp lakeside. Shaka could make out the structures of the little community. In his isolated camp, he felt safe to build a small campfire. Sim had not shown up to join the group the night before as planned. The shaman's good eye darkened, reflecting his thoughts about Sim's cowardice, but he had no time for this now ... he would deal with him when he returned. Sim's fear of him should have made the man more submissive.

He would pay for his disobedience.

Shaka didn't fear discovery, even with the fire. No one traveled in this secluded area after dark. There were too many nocturnal creatures such as snakes one could stumble across. Also, the spirits moved freely about at night. Besides, twinkling campfires around the lake were common when hunters and fishermen failed to make it back to their villages by nightfall. The men made themselves as comfortable as they could in blankets. Shaka dressed like his cohorts, in cargo shorts and a dark brown, well-worn T-shirt. His feet stretched a pair of dirty black plastic sandals to their breaking point. Soon, all three were snoring.

"Get up!" Shaka's husky voice hissed as he kicked the leg of the sleeping Pata. Dima had already sat up. The small gray fire emitted only glowing embers.

In the predawn darkness, the three launched the canoe and headed across the lake. Shaka tilted the motor out of the water and the men paddled the canoe silently toward the far shore. The sound of dripping paddles that carried over the surface of the water could not be helped, but nobody would notice. Everyone would still be asleep.

They lifted their oars and coasted into the shore about twenty feet from the bank. Dima leapt from the canoe onto solid ground. He turned and pulled the prow of the canoe onto the shore. The other two also stepped out, and then proceeded to cover the dugout with hyacinths and bamboo that grew nearby. When satisfied that they'd concealed the boat well enough from all but the most serious searcher, Shaka picked up the now-unwrapped M16, leaving the coffee sacks in the watercraft.

With a tilt of his head, Shaka beckoned the two men to follow him up the steep hill overgrown with grass. Once they made it to the tree line, they used the trees for cover, darting from one to another. Shaka paused and listened for sounds on the path before him. He heard nothing except the predawn bird calls. Shaka entered the path and jogged down it toward the Sago Lake community with his comrades in tow. They presented a formidable group with the leader carrying the rifle and the others clutching their machetes.

When Shaka neared the clearing to the community, he veered off the path, climbing up the steep hill into the jungle. He then traveled parallel to the path until he neared the opening to the hangar and grass airstrip. Shaka signaled Pata to stay there and watch the trail through the trees. He touched Dima on the arm and indicated that he was to accompany him. Both men made their way to the rear of the hangar. They crept down the side, alert for any activity. They saw no one.

Shaka approached the radio shack attached to the hangar. He tried the door and found it locked. The lock itself presented no obstacle. It probably served merely as a precaution to keep out curious youngsters or those who had a need to "borrow" things they thought interesting. Shaka pointed at the door lock and Dima's machete and in answer to his gesture, Dima slid the machete blade between the door jamb and the locking mechanism. He pried the door, and it complained in squeaks. Shaka signaled to be quieter. Dima nodded and applied pressure in a slower manner. The door gave way and swung open.

They entered and closed the door behind them. Shaka immediately spotted his objective. He moved to the desk with the Motorola radio sitting on the stained wood table. He flipped the radio on its face and exposed the back for access. The shaman used a large screwdriver from a shelf to pry the back off the radio. He stabbed the circuit boards until they were useless, then ripped out all wiring and threw it across the room.

Shaka and Dima exited the radio shack and returned to where Pata stood watch.

"We are all set." Shaka hissed. "Dima, you take a position a little way up the path. Stay level with me."

Shaka turned to Pata. "You go stand near the beginning of the path. When you see Burris coming, let me know."

They both went to their assigned positions while Shaka moved down a little lower on the slope until satisfied he had a clear shot toward the path. Dawn peeked out over the valley. Soon people would be stirring. He sat down on an outcropping of rock and cradled the M16. Today he would avenge his humiliation.

Ben woke early. He put his hands under his head as he looked around the familiar bedroom. Photos on the wall showed him and his baseball and soccer teams holding up ribbons they had won. On the chest stood many trophies and plaques for sports and academics. He loved his room, even the alarm clock. He grinned at it before turning his head to look at the picture of Fina on his nightstand.

Inside him, elation over college and flight training warred with the heartache of leaving family and friends. My life will never be the same. But the future, the future is there.

"God has really blessed me," Ben said aloud.

Outside, the community began to awaken. Many families were still away on furlough to their own countries while their children were out of school for the summer vacation. Some couples without children were back in their remote village assignments, studying the local languages, developing an orthography and learning customs and cultures.

Fina and Ben had been enjoying their last days before college. Fina's parents had gone to another translator's village to assist in checking their translation work, so she grudgingly agreed to stay with Ibu Anache and Eli at night. She did not enjoy being treated like a child, but the other option was to spend a few boring days in the village where her parents intended to work.

Ben languished in his bed, counting his blessings.

He had been taken in by Mom and Pop. He was surrounded by kind, well-meaning adult friends, and he had made many friends in his school. No longer the superstitious, backward child of the jungle, he'd become an educated man with a future as a pilot. Ben picked up the well-worn aviation school catalog.

A touch of sadness at the thought of leaving here and going to a new environment stirred his emotions, but the thought of parting with Fina nearly overwhelmed him. They'd grown up together, and although they had their spats, they cared deeply for each other. However, the separation should be temporary. And Longview and Houston were not like they would be on different continents. He wondered if they would be able to visit each other.

What if she found someone else in college?

Ben shook off the feelings and bounded out of bed. He determined to make the best of the time they had left together.

Clay counted out the money earned from the market and set it aside to pay the fisherman. He liked taking this little jaunt once a week to give them their earnings, and to surreptitiously observe life in their village. He had learned a great deal about the culture of the people simply by spending time in their environment.

"Wah! Brrrr!" A squeal and a splash from the other room told him Ben had just jumped into the cold-water shower.

Clay chuckled. The boy had been willing to brave the water before the solar drums had a chance to heat up from the sun's rays because he had plans to meet Fina. Clay shouted across the hallway to the closed door. "That's right, son, suffer for the sake of love. That's just the beginning— get used to it." He winked at Alice as she paused by his office door.

"Clay! Leave the boy alone. And you don't know what suffering is with me. You never had it so good." Alice flipped her hair as she continued to the kitchen.

Ibu Anache, already at work preparing breakfast, flashed her a shy grin. Soon Clay and Ben joined them. While they enjoyed the meal, they shared their plans for the day.

Alice looked at Ben. "Are you going to deliver the meds to the health worker in the South village this morning?"

"Yes, indeed!"

"Well, stay on the path with your bike. Don't go playing Evel Knievel."

"I can't, because I am walking, and Fina is coming with me," Ben responded.

"Well, still, stay on the path." Clay looked up from his granola with a grin.

"I am lending my motorcycle to you, Pop." Ben straightened in his chair. "Make sure you leave it with gas, without scratches ... and be home by dark."

"Yes sir! Do you want me to wash and wax it too?"

At Alice's raised eyebrow, Clay explained, "I need to go to the Porters' village while they're away on furlough and replace a radio we just received. Even with Ben's bike it's about an hour-long trip. He's more than happy to hang with Fina while I put his cycle to productive use."

As if on cue, Fina appeared on the front porch and lightly tapped on the screen door. Alice looked up. "Oh, Fina, come on in."

Ben's spoon halted on its way to his mouth as his eyes followed her entrance.

Clay hid a smile as he watched his son give Fina his rapt attention. She joined them at the table.

"Ben, wipe the boiled egg off of your chin." At Alice's voice, Ben snapped out of his reverie.

"Oh, sorry." He quickly wiped a napkin over his chin to cover up his embarrassment.

"Top of the morning to you, Miss Fine," he said, deliberately misspeaking her name.

"Well, Benny boy, I am fine, but you should know how to pronounce my name after all these years."

"Smack him. I'll turn my head." Clay grinned.

After some small talk about schools, the breakfast party broke up. Ben and Fina started their trek to the nearby village, and Clay returned to his office to finish the payroll. With all money accounted for, he picked up his backpack. He placed the new radio in the bottom, and then added the individual packets of money with the names of the fishermen on them, bound up with rubber bands. Clay gave Alice a quick kiss and started out the door to the hangar where Ben had parked his bike.

Alice called from the doorway, "Ahh, aren't you forgetting something?"

Clay turned and scrunched his face, acting like a deep thinker. "Hmmm? Well, I did kiss you, but it must not have been impressive enough if you've already forgotten."

Alice shook her head and then patted the top of it. Clay said, "Oh, that's a little unusual, but if you want a kiss on top of your head, I'll comply. Anything for matrimonial harmony."

"No, you goof. Wear Ben's helmet."

Clay spun around and swept the helmet up out of the corner behind the door. He put it on backwards and said, "How do I look?"

She shook her head. "Just be careful."

Clay waved and took off toward the path. He found Eli muttering in the hangar over a carburetor from an ancient push mower. "What's up?"

Eli held up the mechanical piece. "These lawn boys keep tearing things up. I think this time they thought water would work as well as gas."

Clay shrugged and gathered some tools from the workbench and then placed them in his backpack. "You going to need this?" He held up a can of wasp spray from the shelf.

"No! I am too ugly for bees and hornets to bother me."

Chuckling, Clay said, "Last time I worked on the Porter radio system, hornets held a welcoming celebration for me. They also held a farewell party. Hey, Eli, would you cover my radio schedule this morning while I am gone? I'm running late and haven't even checked in at the radio shack."

"Will do, Pak."

Eli noted the helmet in Clay's hand. "Does Ben know you are stealing his sepeda motor?"

Clay looked around furtively. "Shhh! I'll make a clean getaway. Besides, he'll never take me alive." He donned the backpack and wheeled the cycle out of the hangar. Eli called after him, "Be careful."

"You're the second person who's said that to me today."
The big man swung his leg astride the bike and kicked it
over three times before it roared to life. He headed across
the open field and entered the jungle path.

High on the hill, Pata fought sleep as he watched the
hangar. He had seen Eli enter the building and heard faint
sounds of metal against metal. Then he saw Burris walk
toward the path, but before he could leave to tell Shaka,
Burris swerved and headed toward the hangar. Afraid
he'd miss Burris' departure, he delayed his report. Then,
suddenly, the roar of a motorcycle engine filled the air and
the westerner came into sight, heading for the path.

Pata ran up the mountainside to where Shaka waited.
Breathlessly, he shouted, "The westerner, he is coming,
but he is riding a sepeda motor!"

Shaka leapt to his feet at the sound of the motor. He
had not counted on this. He ran, slipped forward down the
slope, and regained his balance. The drone grew louder. He
placed the rifle on his shoulder and looked down the open
sights. As the bike approached, Shaka fought to control his
breathing to hold the gun steady. The motorcycle and rider
burst into view.

Shaka tried to follow the moving image in the gun
sights, but he had never shot at a moving target and did
not know how to lead. He pulled the trigger and the M16
exploded in rapid bursts. He had not realized he'd selected
fully automatic on the weapon. The projectiles tore through
the jungle foliage and he saw the rider snap backwards.
The bike and rider ran off the path and hit a stump, which

sent the motorcycle screaming into the air and the rider somersaulting down the slope.

Got him!

Pata stood frozen with machete in hand. Dima leapt up and began making his way down the slope to the fallen rider. Shaka hissed. "Go. Do what I told you to do. Chop him like a pig!" He shoved Pata, almost pushing him down. Pata joined a race against Dima to the still body of the rider to strike the first blow. Shaka almost casually walked down the slope glancing up and down the path to see whether anyone appeared.

The westerner had finally fallen.

Clay had no warning, no sound, until something hit the top of the gas tank on the bike and he heard the ping. Clay looked down. A hole had appeared in the tank. A burning pain seared through the side of his chest under his arm. He was taking fire!

The pain enveloped his chest and his lungs as he fought for air. Another bullet struck his forearm and he lost control of the throttle, rocking back on the seat. The cycle left the path, hit a stump, and both rider and bike took flight.

Time slowed as Clay flew through the air. He hit hard, pain erupting in his chest. The jolt knocked the wind out of Clay's already damaged lung. Even his helmet did not prevent the impact on the ground from scrambling his thinking.

As he struggled to assess the damage, he heard footsteps coming down the mountainside. He painfully turned his head. His vision focused. Two Papuans were racing toward him with machetes.

His Special Forces training kicked into gear.

Adapt, Improvise, and Overcome.

With the Papuans closing in, Clay rolled on his side, wincing and coughing. He managed to slip his arms out of the backpack and pull it in front of his chest. Clay lay his wounded hand on the pack and unzipped it with his good hand. He searched quickly and found what he wanted. He pulled out the can of wasp spray, then directed his attention to the younger man, who had almost reached him. I remember him—Shaka's sidekick!

He halted about five feet from Clay and raised the machete. Clay squirted a thick, foamy stream of wasp spray directly into his face and eyes. As the howling man dropped to the ground, Clay said one word.

"Improvise."

Pata dropped his machete and writhed, rubbing his eyes and groaning. Clay turned to Shaka's other crony, who had leapt to within a few feet of him and already started a slashing move with his machete. Clay fired the wasp spray, but the can was almost depleted, and the stream only hit the lower part of his face. Still, it was enough to slow his slashing movement. Clay delivered a side kick from the ground, targeting the outside of Dima's kneecap. The blow dropped the assailant screaming in pain to the ground. Two threats neutralized.

"Overcome."

As Clay thought over his options, he heard a third man approach. Looking up, he saw Shaka about twenty yards away, rifle in hand, already aiming. A single explosion roared across the land, but Clay never heard it.

# CHAPTER 30

Back in the hangar, Eli had been absorbed in fixing the lawn mower when he heard the rapid pops of what sounded like fireworks, followed by the high-pitched scream of the bike engine.

Something's wrong.

Eli swiped his hands on a rag and raced from the hangar and down the path Clay had taken. Then he heard another pop, but not so distant.

At first, he only saw two men on the ground. One was sitting--vigorously rubbing his face. The other was lying on his back clutching one knee and groaning.

It was then he saw a lifeless form lying near the path. Clay!

They have killed him.

Eli started to run.

He halted when a third man appeared from the opposite side of the path from Clay. The man was carrying a rifle.

Shaka!

The man on the ground stopped rubbing his face and gingerly stood up. Now Eli could see his face. He recognized him as a friend of Shaka's.

This was no accident! Shaka has killed my friend!

The killers had not seen him yet. He was certain of that. He stepped behind a tree to plan his next move.

Eli heard voices further down the trail. Voices of a man and woman drifted into the hearing zone of both Eli and the three assailants. The owners of the voices were still out of sight.

Shaka looked toward the approaching voices in the opposite direction. He spotted Eli when he peeked out from behind the tree. Shaka and the standing man seized the injured man on the ground by his arms and dragged him up the slope. The three men struggled up the side of the mountain.

Eli could wait no longer. He rushed to Clay's prone body and knelt beside him. He glanced up at the retreating figures as Shaka turned around to look back at the scene of the crime.

Eli's blood ran cold. Shaka turned quickly when he saw Eli looking up at him, he stopped, raised his weapon toward Eli, but did not fire. He turned toward the approaching voices then whirled to join the two men struggling up the mountainside.

Eli sighed and turned back to Clay and knelt by him. Clay's eyes were closed as blood ran out from under his helmet. Eli leaned forward placing his hand under Clay's neck. Clay groaned.

He's alive!

Tears crowded his eyes as the voices grew louder and the people speaking rounded a bend and came into view. It was Kimis, one of the grass cutters from the Korsi village, and his wife, Olna. They stopped, eyes wide in horror. Eli knew he should not move Clay because of his injuries, but he could not leave him there. What if Shaka returned? He turned toward the couple. "It is Pak Clay. Help me carry him to his home. He is hurt bad."

The man quickly sprang into action and helped Eli pick Clay up and move him to the footpath, grunting at the big man's weight. At first, Eli had no idea how he'd get Clay to safety, then he noticed Olna carried two large empty nokens, likely to fill at the market. Eli took the string bags and tied them together. Then, with the assistance of the villagers, he placed the bags under Clay's head and body. The three of them then lifted Clay's unconscious body, Kimis on one side and Eli on the other. The wife seized Clay's legs, facing away from him, and together they carried him into the community.

"Ibu Alice will be there to care for his injuries." Eli fought to keep his voice even. He whispered under his breath, "My friend, please do not die."

The three of them carried Clay down the path past the hangar to his house. They climbed the steps and gently laid him on the porch.

Alice had seen the trio through her bedroom window, carrying her husband. She flew down the hallway and burst onto the porch. "What happened, Eli?"

"Pak Clay has been shot. They ran off when they saw us coming, but I recognized Shaka. I think there are three of them, and all of them are still here, somewhere." Eli squinted, scouring the area.

Shock pulsated through Alice's body. She prayed. "Heavenly Father, I know you are with us. Please help me focus and not panic. Please don't let my husband—oh, Lord, please save him."

Brushing tears aside, she set about determining the extent of his injuries. Ibu Anache stood frozen in the doorway watching as Alice removed his helmet and examined the bullet fragments in his blood-matted hair.

Praise God, no entry wounds in his head.

"Anache, please bring my medical kit and some clean towels."

He has a concussion, for sure. She worried more about his breathing. It sounded like a collapsed lung.

She located the bullet wound in the side of his chest. Upon seeing the exit wound in his back, she thanked the Lord, grateful that the bullet had missed his spine.

She had to re-inflate the lung.

Out of the corner of her eye she saw Eli run to the corner of the verandah and retrieve a machete left by a groundskeeper and return to her side as she worked on Clay. Then Ben and Fina came around the corner, returning from their errand to the village.

"Ben is coming!" Eli said.

Alice steeled herself for the moments to come. She could tend to Clay, but who would keep Ben from racing off into danger?

Ben had already seen Alice kneeling over Clay and assumed the worst. Surely Pop had crashed the cycle and must be hurt. He was too tough a man to be lying on a porch unless something serious had happened. Ben broke into a run.

Fina ran, but for once, she could not keep up with Ben. He bounded up the steps and then knelt over Clay's unconscious form. Alice looked up from her attempts to stop the bleeding. Ben searched her face.

"He will be all right, won't he?"

"I'm trying," Alice snapped

Ben turned to Eli. "What happened?"

Eli told him the story.

Ben's jaw clenched, and his eyes darkened. He assessed the surrounding area.

"Mom, we have to get Pop out of here. They'll come for him. His home is on their radar—no one is safe here. Shaka knows he has been recognized. He cannot afford to leave witnesses."

"We shouldn't move him until his lung is inflated." Alice trembled. Ben knew two equally frightening decisions tore at her heart.

He took her by the shoulders. "We have to take defensive action. We are sitting ducks here. Shaka will come. I know him."

He watched her face. She had to trust him. He breathed a quick sigh of relief when Alice gave a curt nod and began gathering her medical items.

Ben turned to Eli. "Let's carry him to the generator shack. That will be the last place they will think to look." Ben did not wait for agreement—he stooped to pick up Pop. Immediately Eli and the Kimis jumped in to assist.

They placed Clay on blankets behind the massive generator. Anache and Alice knelt beside him. Ben knew he couldn't be in better hands.

"What do you need to treat him?"

Alice hastily inventoried her kit. "I think I have everything I need. I have a syringe and a chest tube."

Ben turned to Eli. "Can you go to the Korsi village without being seen?"

"I think so."

"Bring back some men with bows who are not afraid to fight."

Eli handed the machete to Ben. "Here, you may need this."

"No. You take it. You don't know what you'll run into."

Eli sped out the door, looking furtively in each direction before trotting into the cover of the jungle. Ben pulled Fina aside and lowered his voice.

"Fina, I need you to stay here and help Mom."

She nodded through tears and squeezed his hand. "I'll do as much as I can. You be careful."

He posted Kimis and Olna on guard duty at each side of the machinery to watch through the gaps in the wood for Shaka and his sidekicks.

"No one comes in but Eli or me."

Fortunately, Clay had shut the generator off to save fuel with so few residents in the community over the break. On a typical day, the generator's noise and heat would have been unbearable.

As Ben headed for the door, Alice looked up from her patient. "Where are you going?"

"I am going to find Shaka before he finds us. He will not expect me to hunt him."

"No, Ben, you don't have a weapon. Stay here with us. There is safety in numbers," Alice pleaded.

"You don't understand. He is looking for us. I will get my bow. That is the only chance we have."

He softened his tone when he saw the worry in her eyes. "Mom, I will be back. I have lost one set of parents. I refuse to lose another."

Fina jumped up and hugged and kissed him on his cheek. She trembled but stood up straight. "We'll be okay."

Ben managed a sorrowful smile and then turned and raced out the door. He sped home in a crouching run. He wanted his bow and arrows. Perhaps he would be able to even the odds.

# CHAPTER 31

Shaka led his wounded comrades to the safety of the trees above the landing strip. Pata washed the stinging wasp spray from his eyes with rainwater from a stagnant pool in the forest floor. He blinked rapidly, his swollen face forcing his eyes shut.

Shaken by the turn of events, Shaka raced through his options.

Burris may still be alive—in which case he can identify me. The old man, Eli, saw me too.

Since his injured accomplices might not be up to the job, he assessed his two choices. They could flee the area and take a chance there would be no repercussions. Or they could find Burris and make certain he was dead, and then find Eli and kill him. That might involve the need to kill more people in the area to ensure no one talked.

Shaka spun around and addressed his comrades.

"You stupid dogs! You could not even finish off a dying man. Now our identities are known by all of Sago Lake. We are doomed, unless ..." Shaka had their attention. "We must kill all those living in the community. Then there will be no witnesses. Any investigation will point to the Papuan

Separatists. They will be blamed, and eventually we will be in control of this entire place."

Shaka continued to lay out his solution. "There are, at most, two or three westerners and three Papuans here. It will be easy."

The men nursed their wounds as Shaka continued. "If we leave only one witness alive to identify us, then we will be brought up on charges. We must leave no witnesses—then we can assure future riches to pour into our hands."

"What next?" Dima rubbed his wounded knee.

Shaka cursed inwardly at the inept men. He needed them now, but they would not be needed in the future. "We will search the westerners' houses and kill anyone we find." He spoke in icy tones. "First, we will check Burris's home. If he is not dead, he at least needs care. Either way, he will probably be in his home."

The trio took the back trails toward the Burris home, slipping from bush to bush and from tree to tree. Once at the house, Shaka signaled Dima and Pata to cover the back door while he went to the front. As he climbed over the side railing, he immediately saw the fresh blood on the porch. Shaka checked to ensure his weapon had the safety off as he slipped through the screen door. His accomplices were entering through the back door. The three slithered down the hallway, checking every room along the way.

Empty.

They'd moved Burris to another location.

"Come!" Shaka stormed from the house. He stopped on the porch and looked down at the steps. One trail of blood led up the steps and minor drops traveled from the steps on the grass in a different direction and stopped.

Someone had evidently prevented more blood loss and taken Burris to conceal him.

Shaka turned to his men. "Go from house to house and search for Burris. If you find anyone, kill them. No exceptions. I will search the buildings by the lake." The shaman went down the hill and, bending low, ran to the carpentry shop. The other two men went back through the house exiting from the back door.

Ben crouched in the bushes, plastered against the library building. He watched two men race off to one of the linguist's homes. The owners were on furlough. In fact, the only remaining residents of the community were hiding in the generator shack.

They had only a matter of time before the attackers cleared the homes and checked other buildings, including the generator shack. But where was Shaka? He had the gun.

If he could get to his bow, he'd have a chance.

It's now or never.

Ben crept toward the door, then hesitated.

Maybe this was a trap.

Shaka could be waiting for someone to return to the house while he sent his two men to flush out the rest of the residents.

Ben looked down at the carpentry shop by the lake. He decided not to take a chance, but instead look for a weapon in the shop. Sometimes workers would bring their bows to take advantage of the sanders to smooth them. Even if there were no bows, there were all kinds of tools that could make improvised weapons.

Ben started toward the carpentry shop, all the while watching his home for the possible appearance of Shaka.

He was about twenty feet from the shop when the door opened and Shaka emerged, clutching the M16.

Shaka recovered from the surprise and yanked the rifle up to his shoulder, not taking the time to aim, but squeezing off two rounds.

Ben launched into action, zigzagging toward the gunman as bullets whistled near his head. He heard a growl from his own throat as he closed in on Shaka.

Ben drove his shoulder into Shaka's abdomen, knocking the wind out of him and sending the M16 flying. They landed heavily on the ground and Shaka rolled to his feet as Ben sought to pull him down by his leg. Shaka freed himself and regained his weapon. He raised the rifle and fired at point-blank range.

Nothing.

Empty!

Shaka frantically released the spent magazine and had just reached in his cargo pocket for another when Ben's fist walloped him on the chin. He fell and the weapon hit the ground a few feet away. Ben kicked the M16 toward the lake and pounced on the shaman. His fists rained blow after blow on Shaka's face.

Shaka grabbed the amulet around Ben's neck and twisted it. Ben, sitting astride the huge man, seized Shaka's arms and drove a knee into his rib cage. The powerful man hurled him off, breaking the amulet's cord, but enabling Ben to breathe again.

Shaka rose to his knees. Ben saw his right hand go to the small of his back and come out clutching a knife. Ben had regained his feet, but barely dodged Shaka's knife thrust. Shaka had missed, but Ben did not. His chop to Shaka's nose sent blood spewing. Ben seized Shaka's wrist.

They wrestled for control over the knife and again found themselves on the ground. Ben regained his position astride the shaman and pinned his knife hand, bending his wrist back, forcing him to drop the weapon.

Once more Ben's fists repeatedly struck Shaka's face, venting all the rage he'd amassed since childhood. He raged for his mother and father, for the clan he had lost, and for the way of life this shaman had destroyed by instilling fear in the hearts of his people.

And now the monster had tried to take Pop!

When Shaka's resistance weakened, Ben leaned over and seized the knife lying close by. He quickly raised it and prepared to drive the blade through Shaka's black heart. He had Shaka at his mercy now, semiconscious.

As Ben held the knife high above Shaka's heaving chest, he thought of the words Pop had spoken to him, that it was God who judged and meted out punishment. Shaka no longer posed a threat. Could he kill him out of his hatred? Scripture told him to love his enemies.

Could he live with himself after this?

Alice and her group sat quietly in the generator hut listening for any sounds from the attackers or from Ben, but they heard nothing.

Her husband remained unconscious. She had managed to remove the trapped air that had collapsed Clay's lung by using a syringe and chest tube. The lung slowly inflated. He was out of immediate danger, but the concussion presented another serious matter. He needed medical trauma attention soon. She had done all she could.

Fina and Anache heard the crunching gravel outside. Their eyes told Alice and Kimis someone approached. Kimis stepped around the generator where he had kept vigilant watch through a crack in the wall. He placed a finger on his lips and removed a twenty-four-inch pipe wrench from its hook on the wall. He had used wire to secure the door from the inside, but it would only hold so long. Alice lifted a small fire extinguisher from its clamps.

Outside the shed, Dima and Pata were wrapping up their search. They had found all the homes vacant when they spotted the small generator shed.

"We will check that building and then find Shaka," Dima said. "I think the Korsi here took the westerner and hid him in their village. We have been here too long. We need to leave."

Pata nodded in agreement. His eyes were still swollen. He wanted to get out of this place, the sooner the better. They approached the generator shack. The padlock was missing, yet when they tried the door, it would not open. Dima looked down. Blood spots dotted the bare ground in front of the entry. He pointed it out to Pata. Dima picked up a long steel rebar lying on the ground and used it to pry the door.

Pata readied his machete while Dima used all his strength to push, grinning at the thought of cowering westerners on the other side.

The door flew open.

The blast of a fire extinguisher met them. The smothering gases hit Dima full force, blinding him and robbing him of his oxygen. Alice turned the extinguisher toward Pata, aiming it squarely at his swollen eyes.

Both men had had enough. They ran from the shack toward the path, only to be met by Eli returning with eight Korsi villagers, armed with bows and arrows.

The half-blind men ran across the airstrip toward the mountainside jungle. Pata and Dima managed to stay ahead of the pursuing villagers in a race back to their boat.

Eli, wielding his borrowed machete, broke off from the group and ran straight to the generator shack. Alice stood in the doorway, still holding the empty fire extinguisher.

"No one hurt?" Eli peered inside the doorway looking for Anache.

Alice shook her head. "Everyone is all right."

"How is Pak Clay?" Eli tried to peer into the shack behind her.

"He is stable, but he needs more help than I can give him," Alice said.

The crack of two gunshots rang out. Alice and Eli froze.

"Ben!" Alice cried. "Everyone stay here—I have to find Ben!"

Fina rushed forward. "I'm going with you."

Eli already moved in the direction of the gunfire. The women took off at a dead run behind him.

"Please, Lord, protect my son." Tears stung Alice's eyes as she ran. They arrived just behind Eli to see Ben with his back to them—and astride Shaka. They saw the gleam of a large knife that Ben held poised over the defenseless Shaka.

Ben's rage had dissipated, and fatigue had set in. He staggered to his feet and dropped his hand, the knife dangling from it. Then he addressed the man on the ground.

"You deserve to die. And you will, but not at my hand. The courts will end your evil life, and God will judge you."

Shaka appeared to be unconscious. Stones crunched and Ben spun around, the knife at the ready.

Alice raised her hand. "Easy, Ben. It's us. The other two are on the run with the Korsis behind them."

The man on the ground moved. As Shaka regained his senses, he subtly turned his head to look around with his good eye. The M16 lay by the shallows of the lake. With utmost stealth, he moved his hand down to the cargo pocket and removed the extra magazine. The bleeding shaman edged closer to the weapon while the group focused on Ben. Then, with one swift motion, he summoned all his strength and leapt to his feet, seizing the M16. He slapped the fresh magazine into the receiver.

Ben's heart sank at the sound of the magazine being jammed into the weapon. Why had he taken his eyes off the man?

Shaka looked unsteady on his feet, but he managed to rack the first round into the chamber. He pointed the rifle at the group. He smiled, showing his bloody teeth. He still held Ben's amulet in his hand, its cord tangled around his wrist. He held the tooth up in one hand and trained the rifle on the group with the other.

346

"Ha! See, this brought me good fortune. But for all of you, not so good."

Shaka braced the M16 with the amulet hand and looked down the barrel.

In that split second, Ben made his move. With his left arm he swept his mother behind him as he spun to face Shaka once again and simultaneously brought up his right hand, still clutching the knife.

Benjad hurled the knife toward Shaka. Although the heavy knife was not designed as a throwing knife, the young combatant called up years of target practice with his father and compensated for its imbalance. The projectile flew high and a little off-center to plunge into Shaka's chest. The big man dropped the rifle.

Shaka staggered backward with a look of surprise on his face. He seized the handle of his own knife, the one that had taken the life of Benjad's parents. Disbelief etched across his features as the shaman pulled the knife from his body, groaning with pain. Shaka dropped the bloody knife to the ground using the hand entwined with the amulet. The wound was not mortal, but he was beaten—he could barely move.

Ben ran forward and seized the rifle lying on the ground as the shaman staggered backwards to the water's edge. Ben backed up with the rifle in his hands to put more distance between him and his assailant. No one spoke, but the shaman spewed hate and rage toward Ben with his one good eye. Ben, to his own surprise, felt pity for the man.

Something in the background broke into Ben's fixed gaze. Suddenly, in a surreal scene, the waters boiled behind the shaman and a huge dark form erupted with such speed he could hardly follow it.

Mati Raja's massive jaws seized both of Shaka's legs, yanking him face-down into the shallows. The giant croc lunged forward again, strengthening his grip on Shaka's body.

Shaka, in shock, at first made no sound. Then he screamed as the crushing jaws of the massive creature closed around him. Mati Raja backed into deeper waters, with Shaka frantically beating at the snout with his fists. Now the reptile had an unbreakable hold around Shaka's waist, and blood painted the waters around the croc's jaw.

The spectators stood in stunned silence as Mati Raja pulled the shrieking man into deeper waters and started his death roll. The massive body alternately pulled Shaka under the water and then returned his head to the surface, as the victim fought for air. After the fourth roll, terror and pain faded from his face.

The patch that covered Shaka's missing eye had been lost during the spinning battle. His dark empty socket matched Mati Raja's own sightless eye.

The people on the shore stood transfixed. When his prey ceased resisting, Mati Raja paused on the surface as if posing with his kill. One of Shaka's arms lay across the snout of the prehistoric reptile. His fingers still clutched the cord attached to Ben's amulet.

Mati Raja moved slowly backward and sank below the surface of the lake, taking his prize with him. A few slight ripples and then nothing.

Everyone fell silent. Fina ran forward and embraced Ben with gasping sobs. Ben kissed her on her head and said, "It is over. Evil has devoured evil."

# CHAPTER 32

The group hurried back to the generator shed, where Alice knelt and checked Clay's pupils. His eyelids fluttered open. "Alice ... Alice ..."

She touched his forehead softly. "Shhh. You rest. Don't talk."

"Is everyone safe?"

"Everyone is fine." Alice kissed him lightly on his cheek.

"Ben? Where's Ben?" Clay tried to rise.

Ben stepped up and knelt beside Clay. "I am here, Pop. I'm fine."

"Shaka ..."

"The men who attacked you, including Shaka, are no longer a threat." Ben paused and looked at his adopted father. "Shaka is dead. He will not hurt anyone now."

Clay swallowed. "Did you kill him?"

"No, Pop. I had the chance, but I didn't. I certainly damaged him, but that is all you need to know for now. He is dead. I can fill you in later." Ben patted Clay's arm.

Clay settled back, satisfied. "I'm so tired." He closed his eyes.

Eli had been to the radio shack. He returned and said, "They sabotaged the radio. It cannot be used."

"We have to get word out to evacuate Clay." Concern furrowed across Alice's forehead.

Ben brightened. "Wait a minute! Pop was delivering a new radio when he was shot."

"Yes, yes he was," Eli exclaimed.

Kimas, the lawn man, said, "I will look for it." He raced out the door and down the path.

While they prepared to move Clay to his home to await evacuation, they heard the distant sound of an aircraft ... not the usual Helio or Cessna, the type of aircraft that routinely came to Sago Lake, but a staccato sound. Eli and Ben went outside the shack and shaded their eyes to see the approaching aircraft—a military transport helicopter. The big craft lowered onto the runway with deafening thunder. Through the open cargo doors, Ben and Eli saw uniformed soldiers. The Huey squatted on the grass field, and four soldiers sprang from the doorways, armed and in a defensive posture. The beating blades slowed to a stop as the noise of the engine waned. The soldiers set up a perimeter around the helicopter.

Ben recognized the officer who emerged from the chopper. Colonel Imade walked briskly to Ben and Eli.

"Ben, what is going on? Is anyone hurt?"

"My father's been shot. But how did you know to come?"

"I will explain later. Are Shaka and his comrades here?"

"Two of his friends are being chased by some Korsi villagers. As for Shaka, he is dead."

Eli grinned. "He has become crocodile mud!"

The colonel knitted his brows. "You mean a crocodile killed him?"

"Yes, sir." Ben nodded. "Eli has his own way of telling the facts."

The colonel shook his head at this and tried to visualize the scene. "Ohh. That's ugly, even for a man like Shaka."

Ben touched the officer's arm. "Colonel, my father is alive, but badly hurt. We hid him in the generator shack. My mom is with him."

Colonel Imade waved to two other soldiers sitting in the doorway of the chopper waiting for orders. "Medics! Bring your kits!"

Two soldiers seized their packs and reported to the colonel.

He turned to Eli. "I will send four of my men to search for the others. Please go with them so they can join the villagers in the search. You can identify Shaka's men?"

Eli had been running more in the past hours than he had since his childhood. However, pride demanded that he fill this important role. "Yes, Bapak. I know them and will track the assassins."

The colonel issued rapid-fire orders to the four men, who quickly fell in behind Eli. Imade turned to Ben. "Take us to your father."

Alice met the soldiers at the door. "Colonel, I am so relieved to see you."

"Ibu, I am sorry this has happened." Imade sighed at the sight of his friend lying on the floor and motioned the medics forward.

Alice updated the medics on Clay's condition. They listened carefully to her report and checked his vitals, then unfolded a collapsible stretcher and gingerly placed Clay upon it.

While Alice and the medics tended to Clay, Ben repeated his question to the colonel.

"How did you know to come here?"

"We've been watching Shaka for some time," Imade said. "This morning, an assistant to Shaka named Sim showed up at Pak Satono's office and told him of the assassination plan. Pak Satono immediately brought him to my office. It took over an hour for Sim to reveal the whole story. He was terrified. Despite his involvement, Sim feared that if he participated, his own death would be assured at the hands of Shaka to keep him quiet."

Ben shook Imade's hand. "Colonel, your timing is perfect."

The medics were moving Clay. Colonel Imade addressed both Alice and Ben. "When things settle down, we need to have a full report. Right now, we need to get Pak Clay medical attention. Ibu, you are welcome to ride with us." Alice nodded and turned to Ben.

Ben urged her to go. "I will be fine. I will stay and watch over things. You go and take care of Pop."

They had just finished loading Clay into the Huey when Eli and the soldiers returned. A sergeant saluted Colonel Imade and conversed quietly for a few minutes. He gave a few orders to four men and then walked to the waiting helicopter and spoke to Alice and Ben.

"The two men did not get away. They tried to escape in a boat. Evidently, they were unfamiliar with boat motors and hit a submerged stump. The canoe flipped. Being from the mountains, they had poor swimming skills. They both drowned." He looked at Alice, belted into the seat near the door. "What do you Americans call it? Poetry justice?"

Alice shook her head. "Do you mean 'poetic justice'?"

"Yes, ma'am."

Four soldiers remained at Sago Lake for security purposes in case more of Shaka's gang still lurked. Alice left instructions to put the soldiers up at the guest house, and the Huey lifted off.

That evening, Ben walked Fina to her home to pick up some belongings. He waited in a swing on her front porch. Fina pushed the screen door open and exited the house. Ben rose from the swing and extended his hand in offer to carry her bag.

"My arm is not broken. I can carry my own bag."

Ever the independent woman. Ben shrugged, and they walked down the steps together.

"I don't know why I have to leave my home and stay with Anache and Eli tonight."

"Well, Mom left strict instructions that you stay with them. If I didn't make sure that happened, I would end up on the endangered species list." Ben chuckled.

Fina fell silent as Ben walked her home, taking a roundabout route. Ben left her immersed in her own thoughts. He had learned to give her space.

As Ben and Fina walked in silence, Fina stopped abruptly.

"I almost lost you today." Her voice quivered.

Ben stayed silent for a few seconds as he stared into her dark eyes.

"I guess all that happened today has not hit me yet. But, not to add to your distress, the truth is, all of us could have been killed. I know the Lord had his hand over us." Ben's words were measured and sincere.

Fina fell into his arms and cried, as if unleashing a day's worth of pent-up fear. Ben held her and whispered, "I love you."

"You know I have loved you forever," Fina said, lifting her tear-filled eyes to his.

Ben left Fina at Eli and Anache's home. He didn't want to leave.

One day they would not have to part like this.

# CHAPTER 33

Daryl returned from Jakarta, where he had taken his pilot's license recertification, a week after the events at the lake community. As soon as the commercial flight landed in Sentani, he and Betty immediately went to their friend's side. Clay had been moved into the guest house where Alice and two Indonesian nurses cared for him.

Alice was preparing a meal for Clay in the kitchen area when Daryl walked in. He dispensed with all formality. "Where's Clay?"

Alice turned. "I wasn't expecting you and Betty this soon, but I am glad you're back." She gave the pilot a quick hug. "Clay is in the room on your right down the hallway."

"How's he doing?"

"See for yourself. He's hurting, but able to give the doctor and me a hard time."

Daryl strode down the hallway and tapped on the door to Clay's room. Without waiting for a response from inside of the room, he pushed the door open.

Clay sat up in bed propped by pillows, drinking fruit juice through a straw. His head looked small beneath the white bandage wrapped around it, and gauze enveloped his lower chest.

Clay looked up and grinned. "Well, well. If I had known you were coming, I would have dressed for the occasion."

Daryl shook his head and took his friend's extended left hand in greeting. "Mate, I leave you alone for even a week and you get yourself in trouble. I heard you were shot in the head. That's probably what saved you."

The pilot couldn't hide his concern for long. He sat with a sigh. "You had us all going. I normally sleep on the long flight, but I traded in my sleep to pray for you."

Clay's expression matched his friend's concern. "Thanks. I'm not in the best shape, but the doctor expects me to fully recover."

Alice appeared at the door along with Betty carrying a tray of food. "He won't have a full recovery if he refuses to stay in bed and allow healing to take place. He convinced the doctor at the hospital that he needed his space and promised to take it easy at the guest house." She set the tray down on a little table near his bed. "Problem is, he lied. Now he's trying to arrange a flight with a mission aviation service to get back out to the lake."

"That so. Slippery, yer out of luck. I just have to say the word to my pilot comrades, and they will not accommodate you. Besides, I want to give you your first flight home, complete with barrel rolls and controlled spins."

Betty went to the bedside and grasped Clay's hand. "I would hug you, but I don't think you're huggable yet. You had us both worried."

Clay grinned. "I had me worried too." He sank back into his pillow, wincing.

Alice filled Daryl and Betty in on the details, as Clay still tired quickly. After a short time, Daryl saw Clay needed to rest and said his farewell.

"You just listen to nurse Alice if you want me to get you back home anytime soon. I promise you, as soon as you're cleared, I will take you."

Clay nodded. Then as Daryl and Betty left, Daryl looked back to see his friend had already fallen asleep.

Ben, Fina and Eli gathered around the newly rigged radio in the shack twice a day for news about Clay's status. Alice took a taxi to the airport every day to touch base with them.

A week after Daryl returned to Sentani, his Helio cleared inspection, enabling him to fly again. Daryl radioed Eli of his plan to return to the lake that afternoon, and Eli headed over to tell Ben.

Eli looked through the screen door and saw Ben filling the water filtering system. "Ben, I have some good news."

Ben finished filling the bucket and walked to the screen door. "Come on in. I would love to hear some good news."

Eli entered the house. "Pak Daryl will be returning this afternoon."

Ben let out a whoop. "Great! Hey, ask Ibu Anache if she would come and help me prepare dinner and I will invite him to come and eat with me. And ask her not to tell Daryl she helped me." Ben grinned.

Eli opened the screen door. "I will do that. I have to get back to the hanger and recruit some men to cut the grass."

"Okay. I need to get this house in shape. Thanks for the good news."

Ben scurried around tidying up the house for his guest, anxious to talk to Daryl about his impending departure. He worried that Clay would be unable to take care of things here as he recovered from his wounds.

Later that morning, while eating his lunch, Ben heard the familiar sound of the Helio as it circled the grass strip. He was early. Ben could picture Daryl scouring the ground to make sure it was clear.

It would be good to see him again.

Ben jumped up from his half-eaten meal, spilling his drink in the process, but cleanup could wait. He ran out the door and jumped the veranda railing, landing on the soft ground. The young man started off at a trot down the path to the airfield. He heard the sound of the engine gunning in its final approach and increased his trot to a run. He wanted to be there before the prop stopped spinning.

Eli had exited the radio room when he had completed all necessary radio traffic and stood in the front of the hanger, shielding his eyes from the sun with his hand as he watched the pilot settle his plane on the inclined strip.

Breathing heavily, Ben halted beside Eli. "I did not expect him until this afternoon. Maybe he can update us on Pop. I know he would have checked up on him before returning."

As the aircraft bounced on the runway nearing them Eli squinted. "Looks like he has passengers, but he did not let me know. Ben, your eyes are better than mine, what do you see?"

The aircraft swung around and came to a complete stop. Only then did Ben recognize the passengers. "It's Pop and Mom!"

Ben raced to the plane before the prop stopped turning and positioned himself at the door. Daryl leaned across Clay to unlock it. Clay slipped out of the copilot seat gingerly as Ben opened the door wide.

"Pop, Pop, I was not expecting you!"

Clay, although noticeably thinner and wearing bandages on both his head and forearm, still wore that same old wide grin.

"You think I was going to leave you in charge of this place for any length of time?"

Clay grabbed Ben's shoulders and crushed him in an enthusiastic bear hug, but quickly released him with a grimace.

"You all right, Pop?"

"I feel great. That little twinge will go away." Clay's eyes shone.

Alice climbed out of the tight quarters of the back seat of the aircraft. Ben ran to greet her. "Mom, I did not expect you this soon!"

Alice hugged him and kissed his cheek. "Well, you know your Pop. He refused to stay in bed at the clinic. As soon as his x-rays came back clear, he wanted to get out of there. Then he reached a compromise with the medical team to let him stay in the guest house. I think the doctors and nurses were glad to see him go." Alice winked.

Daryl sauntered over to the three and addressed Ben. "Well, I thought I wouldn't surprise you with only the illustrious me, so I brought your Pop along. By the way, time is getting short. You ready for school? You know I want you to make me proud."

"Thanks Uncle Daryl. I will do my best," Ben assured him.

That evening, the family ate an early meal. Daryl joined them, as Betty had stayed in Sentani to get supplies and planned to return in the morning. Fina and her parents, who had returned from the village, also joined the celebration. Ben couldn't remember a better dinner—not because of the food, which he enjoyed—but because of the twining of spirits as each person at the table offered thanks for safety, the meal, the recovery of Clay, the ultimate blessings of God and the banishment of evil.

After dinner, Daryl and Fina's parents went to their respective homes. Fina helped Alice clear the table while Clay and Ben stepped out onto the porch sipping their teas. They watched the sun slip lower in the sky. Neither spoke for a few minutes.

Clay broke the silence. "You saved my life, and probably Mom's too."

Ben turned and looked straight into his face. "Pop, you not only saved my life many years ago, but you and Mom gave me a life. What I did can never match what you both did for me."

Clay nodded. "I have to sit down." He sat, and Ben followed suit. Quiet reigned again. Then Clay spoke to his son, "I notice you are not wearing your croc tooth." It was more of a question than a comment.

"Shaka ripped it from my neck during our wrestling match. In fact, he had it in his hand when the croc attacked him." Ben stopped to think about that scene. "Apparently, the talisman did not work for him."

Clay nodded. "For sure."

"I found out one thing for certain." Ben leaned forward.

"What's that?"

"My protection does not come from a tooth either. It comes from the Lord."

"Well said, my son." Clay's tone took on a weighty seriousness. "One more question, and I will never ask again."

"Go ahead."

"What made you change your mind about killing Shaka?" Clay searched the boy's face. "You felt you had justification, you had the opportunity, and the determination."

"It was because of you, Mom, and of course, the Lord. I realized that, as a believer, my heart could not hold a place for the hate, and there could be no place for the guilt I would have felt in the future. I often thought you did not understand the Papuan old ways. But I realize now, the ways you understand are older than the creation of the world." Ben looked down, thinking. "Besides, after I gave him the chance to live, I did try to take it again by throwing the knife. But it was different the second time. Pure survival for all of us. No anger or hatred, I just wanted to save our lives."

Clay pondered Ben's words. "I guess it goes to what is in the heart. As long as we live in a world of evil, difficult decisions have to be made. I am proud of you, Ben."

Clay took a sip of tea to hide his emotions. Ben did too. They sat quietly for a few minutes, then Alice and Fina came onto the veranda.

"What are you guys talking about?" Alice set some fruit on the table.

Clay turned to Ben. "I think baseball. For sure the game of life."

Ben grinned. "Something like that."

For a few minutes, the harrowing events of the past were forgotten as they enjoyed the approaching evening. Then Fina said, "I need to get home before dark."

"You have at least forty-five minutes," Ben said. "Come and take a walk with me."

Fina said goodnight to Alice and Clay, descended the stairs and walked down the trail with Ben.

Clay called after them, "Stay on the path!" Ben waved without turning his head.

Ben and Fina walked to the top of the ridge over the airstrip, where Ben used to race up to the mountainside. They stopped about halfway and viewed the quiet, cool evening from the vantage point.

Fina said, "I see why you always liked coming here and looking out over the lake and the hangar."

Ben nodded. "I could dream here, I could think here, and I could imagine my life here as a pilot. You want to know part of my dream?"

Fina looked into his eyes. "I'm afraid to ask."

"I'm being serious." Ben emphasized the word. "Since the time I knocked you down when we played our first game of soccer, I knew I wanted to be with you."

She stared at him, as if looking for a coming joke.

"I felt the same way, too, even if you were a birdbrain." Fina smiled.

"Will you agree to not see anyone at your school in Houston?"

"Will you agree to not see anyone at your school in Longview?"

Ben nodded. They kissed. He looked into her eyes and said, "I don't know what the future holds. It can have a lot of twists and turns, like a river. You cannot grasp it.

However, I do know now the river is the living waters of the Lord. You do not need to grasp it, only go with the flow."

They stood, arms around each other, as a flock of egrets descended on the lake, and Ben murmured, "Yes, I am blessed."

# ABOUT THE AUTHOR

Dr. Brent Brantley lived and worked in the South Pacific as a Community Development Specialist with emerging minority language groups and taught internationally. Brent also served in missions for twenty-eight years, after a ten-year career in law enforcement. He has authored a textbook on 'critical thinking' for Papuans, published numerous academic articles and papers on Worldview, Development, and Cross-Cultural Insights. After traveling and training globally, Brent and his wife, Jeanette, make their home south of Dallas, TX. He is now devoting his full time to writing. His intentions are to educate and entertain by using stories that are suspense/thrillers with plausible plots and unexpected endings.

Made in the USA
Middletown, DE
24 April 2021